summer *by* the tides

ALSO BY DENISE HUNTER

BLUE RIDGE NOVELS
Blue Ridge Sunrise
Honeysuckle Dreams
On Magnolia Lane

SUMMER HARBOR NOVELS
Falling Like Snowflakes
The Goodbye Bride
Just a Kiss

THE CHAPEL SPRINGS ROMANCE SERIES
Barefoot Summer
A December Bride (novella)
Dancing with Fireflies
The Wishing Season
Married 'til Monday

THE BIG SKY ROMANCE SERIES
A Cowboy's Touch
The Accidental Bride
The Trouble with Cowboys

NANTUCKET
LOVE STORIES
Surrender Bay
The Convenient Groom
Seaside Letters
Driftwood Lane

Sweetbriar Cottage
Sweetwater Gap

Novellas included in Smitten,
Secretly Smitten, and
Smitten Book Club

summer *by* the tides

DENISE HUNTER

THOMAS NELSON
Since 1798

Doubleday Large Print Home Library Edition

SUMMER BY THE TIDES

© 2019 by Denise Hunter

Published in Nashville, Tennessee, by Thomas Nelson. Thomas Nelson is a registered trademark of HarperCollins Christian Publishing, Inc.

Printed in the United States of America

ISBN 978-1-64385-333-8

**This Large Print Book carries the
Seal of Approval of N.A.V.H**

summer *by* the tides

CHAPTER 1

Maddy Monroe was cowering behind a ficus tree near the hostess station when her cell phone rang. Her hands shook as she silenced the phone before it drew the attention of the staff.

She jabbed the elevator button for the third time. "Come on, come on." A star could be born in interstellar space, a polar valley carved by a glacier in the time it took the elevator to reach this floor. Stairs were not an option, as she was on the twentieth floor of the Waterford building and sporting heels.

She sniffled. Drat. She seemed to be crying. She swiped a hand under her eyes, heedless of her makeup.

She heard voices, Nick's boisterous laugh. Maddy shrank deeper into the ficus and finally, finally, the elevator dinged its arrival.

"Maddy?" Noelle's concerned voice tunneled down the hall. "Maddy, wait."

"Oh, come on," she muttered, tapping her fingers against her leg until the gold doors crept open. As soon as she could fit, she squeezed inside and punched the ground-floor button.

She didn't draw a breath until the doors sealed and the elevator began to drop. She placed a palm over a heart that was threatening to beat its way out of her chest. Her white blouse clung to her back, and her skin prickled beneath her arms.

She closed her eyes, the scene that had just transpired playing out in fast-forward in her mind. And then, as if that montage weren't painful enough, the image of Nick's face appeared. The look on his face just before he'd kissed her good-bye last night.

Nick. She clamped her teeth together until her jaw ached.

There had been signs. Many of them, really, she was realizing now. They ranged from whisper-subtle to neon-sign obvious. But like so many other walking clichés before her, she was only seeing them in retrospect.

Maddy opened her eyes to the buttery sunlight streaming through her blinds. She scrambled for her iPhone to check the time. But as she did so, the events of yesterday washed over her like a tsunami. She didn't have to get up at all, because she didn't have a job anymore.

Her cell buzzed with an incoming call, and she squinted bleary-eyed at the unfamiliar number on the screen before declining it.

She drooped against her pillow, only now aware of how fat and swollen her eyes felt. Of the persistent achy lump pushing at the back of her throat. Her heartbeat made the bed quake. Her eyes burned with tears. Yesterday's anger had faded, and something worse had filled its spot.

Yesterday she'd come home, changed into yoga pants, and worked in her little garden until she was too exhausted to do anything but flop on the sofa. She hadn't fallen asleep until after three o'clock in the morning.

She didn't want to talk to anyone, didn't want to see anyone. She didn't even want to be awake today. She pulled the covers over her head and prayed for oblivion.

A steady pounding pulled Maddy awake. She turned her face into the pillow. Sleep. She just wanted to sleep. But the noise was relentless. Someone was pounding at her apartment door.

"Go away," she mumbled.

She wondered if it was Nick, coming with some lame apology. As if "sorry" could make up for what he'd done.

Her phone buzzed an incoming call on her nightstand. Why couldn't everyone just let her be? When the buzzing stopped the pounding resumed.

"Argh!" She tossed back the covers and checked her phone as a text buzzed in.

Her best friend, Holly: **Open the door.**

Before she could put down the phone it buzzed again. **I know you're in there.**

Maddy let loose a sigh that had been building awhile. She pushed off the mattress, realizing she'd fallen into bed in the same yoga pants and T-shirt she'd gardened in. **Gardened** was such a tame word to describe her treatment of those poor weeds. She hated to think of the sight she must've made, tearing through her zinnias like a crazy woman.

A glance at the hall mirror also told a sad tale. A bedraggled ponytail captured only half of her hair, and dark smudges underlined puffy eyes.

She walked to the door and pulled it open, interrupting the loud banging. "All right already. Jeez."

Holly's brown eyes widened in surprise, whether at Maddy's sudden materialization or her disheveled appearance, she didn't know.

Leaving the door open, Maddy retreated into her living room, seeking the comforting embrace of her overstuffed sofa. She grabbed a fluffy yellow pillow and pulled it into her stomach.

Holly dropped beside her, the smell of fresh soil and flowers emanating off her. They'd met three years ago at the nursery where Holly worked, bonding over their love of all things green and growing.

"What happened yesterday?" Holly asked. "Noelle said there was some squabble at the restaurant and you tore off."

Yesterday's scene at Pirouette played out yet again in Maddy's mind, making her eyes sting.

Holly set her hand over Maddy's. "Honey, what's going on? Did you lose the promotion? It's not the end of the world. You're still assistant manager of Charlotte's most prestigious restaurant. There'll be other opportunities for—"

"I caught Nick and Evangeline together."

Holly blinked. "Evangeline, the owner? What do you mean, 'together'?"

"I mean exactly what you think I mean. They were all over each other." The image of it made her heart crumple up like a wad of trash.

Holly's eyes narrowed and her nostrils flared. "That jerk."

"But it's worse than that. I heard him accepting the promotion."

"What?" The indignation on Holly's face was like salve on a raw wound.

But his words still haunted her. **You made the right decision... Maddy's a terrific girl, but she gets frazzled... Wouldn't be able to handle more responsibility...**

Was there a nugget of truth in what he'd said? Had she been deluding herself all along?

"Did they see you?"

Maddy gave a harsh laugh. "Oh yes, they saw me. I stood there like a guppy, my mouth just working."

"Who could blame you? You were blindsided, you poor thing." Holly's eyes pierced hers. "How long do you think it's been going on?"

"I don't know, but when I saw them together...I ran. I just ran away. Oh, Holly, he planned this, didn't he? He played me like a fiddle." Tears seeped out the corners of her eyes.

"I could just throttle him."

It almost brought a smile to her face, trying to envision petite, pacifist Holly doing any such thing. She'd never cared for Nick, not that she'd said as much, but Maddy could tell. She should've trusted her friend's instincts since, apparently, she couldn't trust her own.

"I thought I was a shoo-in for that job." Pirouette's general manager was retiring and, as assistant manager, Maddy was next in line. "I feel so stupid."

Nick, the restaurant's beverage manager, had pursued her for months before Maddy finally went out with him. Holly had been encouraging her to put herself out there, and six months ago Maddy decided to give Nick a chance.

One date led to another. He was easy to talk to, he shared her faith, and since they were both passionate about the restaurant industry they found plenty to talk about.

"Let's keep it professional at work,"

he'd said as their relationship progressed beyond casual. It had seemed like a wise idea. But now she realized she may have played right into his plans.

Holly squeezed her hand. "I'm so sorry, Maddy. You don't deserve this."

"I'm not gonna lie, losing the promotion is bad, and losing my job is even worse. But having Nick betray me like this...You know how hard it was for me to take a leap of faith like that."

"Aw, honey." She drew Maddy into an embrace. "I just hate this. It won't always be this way, Mads. Someday you'll find the right man to love, and it'll all be worth it. I promise."

"Was this his plan all along? To keep me out of the way while he sucked up to Evangeline? Did he ever care for me? I thought he did, but what do I know?" Maddy's throat constricted around her words.

Holly rubbed her back. "Would it help if I told you he's not worth the lint on this old, smelly T-shirt you're wearing?"

"I feel like such an idiot. I keep

remembering little things he said and did. I must've had blinders on."

"Hey." Holly pulled back and gave Maddy one of her stern looks. "Don't you be putting this on yourself. You trusted him. You gave him the benefit of the doubt. Nick's the idiot. Anyone who tosses you over like that needs his head examined."

Maddy absorbed the warmth from Holly's eyes. "I don't know what I should do now."

"You should tell Evangeline, that's what you should do. Tell her you and Nick have been dating for six months and he was cheating on the both of you."

"I'd love nothing more, believe you me." She gave Holly a guilty look. "But I told Nick about my résumé."

The air escaped Holly, deflating her posture. "Oh, Maddy."

Four years ago when Maddy applied for the assistant manager job, she'd falsified her experience. It was only one job. She'd been at a low point and overly ambitious—not that that was an excuse.

She wasn't proud of it. She'd never done anything like that before or since, and she'd nearly come clean to Evangeline a dozen times over the years. She wished now that she had.

"Even if I go to Evangeline I won't get my job back. And that's on me. I knew what I was doing was wrong, and I did it anyway. That is my fault."

Holly studied her thoughtfully. "What are you going to do, honey?"

"Eat an entire package of Oreos."

Holly gave her a look. "After that."

"Look for another job, I guess. At least I've got money in the bank. I'm not flat broke or anything. I just feel so...ruined."

"You are not ruined."

Maddy's phone buzzed against her palm, and Holly uncurled her fingers and took it. "It's Noelle. She's worried about you. I'll let her know I'm here and you're okay."

"Nice of her to check up on me," Maddy mumbled, feeling numb after letting out her feelings.

She thought of all the people she was

leaving behind at Pirouette. They weren't friends exactly. She was their boss—used to be their boss. She thought of everything she'd put into her job. All the overtime, all the energy. She'd lived and breathed that place. It was the reason she'd gotten to the ripe old age of thirty-one without a ring on her finger. Well, part of the reason.

She'd loved everything about her job, from the staff to the patrons to the amazing aerial view of Charlotte. It was like throwing a party every day. She'd made the restaurant the most important thing in her life, had made Nick runner-up, and now they were both gone.

"Honey, you've got, like, twenty unopened texts on here. And a bunch of missed calls."

Maddy shook away the cobwebs. "What time is it anyway? And why aren't you at work?"

"It's after three, honey. I just got off. Have you been in bed all day?"

"Maybe."

She was going to have to put out her

résumé again—undoctored this time. She could do this. Maybe she'd wind up at an even better restaurant. But they didn't come much better than Pirouette. Was she willing to move away from Charlotte? She didn't even want to think about that.

Holly held up the phone. "Who's this from a 910 area code?"

"Telemarketer probably."

"They've called five times. Look."

"I don't recognize the number."

"They left a bunch of voicemails."

Maddy took the phone, put it on speaker, and tapped the arrow beside the oldest one, which had been sent yesterday at 3:12—just about the time everything had gone down at Pirouette.

"Um, hi, my name is Connor Sullivan. I'm a friend of your grandmother's over in Seahaven. I was hoping you could give me a call as soon as possible if you would."

Maddy frowned at the cryptic message. Her grandma lived alone at the beach. The same cottage where her family had once spent many an idyllic summer.

"I hope everything's okay," Holly said.

"Me too."

She played the second message, sent a couple hours after the first. "This is Connor Sullivan again. Um, I really need to reach someone in the family, so please call as soon as you get this."

Maddy's heart sank at his urgent tone. What if something bad had happened to Gram? "This doesn't sound good."

"Call him."

Before she did, Maddy played his most recent message, sent early this morning. Her heart squeezed in dread.

"This is Connor again." Impatience edged his tone this time. "Look, I didn't want to leave this on your voicemail, but I'm very worried about your grandma. She seems to have gone missing. There are signs she's been gone a few days, but her car's still here. It's really not like her to take off like this. Please call me."

Her fingers shaking, she hit Reply and held the phone to her ear.

"Maybe she turned up," Holly whispered. "Maybe that's why he hasn't called since this morning."

Maddy held tight to that hope. But what if her grandma had fallen and broken her hip or something? She'd always been pretty spry for her age, but these things happened. What if she'd been lying on the floor in pain for all these hours while Maddy had been hiding from the world like a sulking toddler?

"Hello?" A low, lazy voice drawled in her ear.

"Mr. Sullivan, this is Maddy Monroe. You called about my grandmother."

There was a brief pause. "Yes, I did. Thank you for returning my call."

She detected a hint of sarcasm in his tone. "Has she turned up yet?"

"I'm afraid not."

"Can you tell me what you know? How do you know she hasn't simply gone on a trip? She takes the ferry to Bald Head Island sometimes."

"For day-trips. I've never known her to spend the night there."

He seemed familiar with her grandmother's habits but sounded too young to be a significant other. Red flags were waving. Connor... She couldn't remember Gram ever mentioning the name.

Her grandma was a wealthy woman. Had this guy ingratiated himself to her for selfish purposes? What if he was even responsible for her disappearance?

"I went over to do some work on her house yesterday and found three newspapers on her porch. That's not like her. She reads the paper over coffee every morning. And there was no answer at the door, though her car was in the drive."

"She could just be ill or something."

"That's what I thought, so I let myself in. But she was nowhere to be found. I didn't see a purse, and of course she doesn't carry a phone, so I found your name in her address book and called you."

He had a key to her place? In the background she heard the piercing cry of sea gulls and the distant hum of a boat's engine. She imagined the guy bobbing around in the sunny bay while her grandmother was who-knew-where.

"You seem to know her quite well." She

hadn't meant to sound so suspicious.

"We look out for each other around here, Miss Monroe."

"Have you filed a missing persons report?"

"I didn't feel that was my place. I tried you first, since you're within driving distance, and when I couldn't reach you, I got hold of your sister. Emma's flying in now, so I'm sure she can handle things just fine."

Guilt pinched hard. Seahaven was only a four-hour drive for Maddy, but it was a far piece from Denver.

"I'll be on my way just as soon as I can pack a bag."

"All right. Listen, I have to go now. You have my number if you need anything."

She said good-bye and turned off the phone, looking at Holly as adrenaline flooded her system. Dread built with each surge of her blood. "I guess I'm going to Seahaven."

CHAPTER 2

Connor dipped his brush into the white paint and guided it steadily over the weathered siding of the beach cottage. The ladder wobbled slightly with the motion. He was losing daylight, but Louise's granddaughters would be here soon anyway. He wanted to be on hand in case the sheriff wanted a word with him.

He'd been trying to keep busy. He sure hoped Louise was all right. He'd taken half a day off work yesterday to ask around, but none of her friends knew anything about a trip. He hadn't known what else to do but call the family.

He thought of the youngest sister, Maddy. Louise spoke so highly of her, but the woman's lack of response to his calls and her suspicious tone had put him off.

At least Emma had answered her phone and been quick to say she'd come right away. She'd even thanked him profusely for his efforts. He knew the sisters weren't close and sensed there was a long story there. Louise had never gone into details, but he knew it grieved her. She seemed lonely, which was one of the reasons he checked on her regularly.

When the brush ran dry, Connor descended the ladder. The sun was setting, and besides, he was worried about Louise. Maybe he'd overlooked something in the house.

His shirt clung to his back and sweat trickled down his neck as he rounded the corner of Louise's two-story cottage. It sat about fifty yards from his own house atop a small rise. The yards on this stretch of beach undulated with sandy dunes. The tall, sparse grass waved as a salty breeze swept over the landscape, cooling his skin.

He took the wooden porch steps, his eyes catching on the mailbox beside the front door. Maybe there was some clue in the mail. The lid opened with a squawk, and he pulled out the thick stack and began sorting through it.

A utility bill, circulars, a notice from the post office, a credit card statement, fliers from local businesses. He wasn't sure what he'd hoped to find, but it wasn't here.

The sound of a car engine caught his attention. A black Volvo was pulling into the shelled driveway beside the house. One of the sisters had arrived. He caught a glimpse of dark hair and recognized Maddy from the photos on Louise's wall.

She emerged, her eyes pinning him in place before she even closed her car door. She was taller than he'd expected, her trendy clothes only hinting at curves. The golden light glinted off long brown hair that fell straight like a dark curtain. She wore little or no makeup, he saw as she neared, and her eyes appeared swollen, a little bloodshot. His earlier impression of her softened at the hint of distress.

As she came up the porch steps her gaze swept over him, making him mindful of his stained jeans and T-shirt.

"Can I help you?" she asked.

"I'm Connor Sullivan—the one who called you."

She reached out and took the mail from him, her eyes darting to the open mailbox, then back to him. The desire to defend himself rose up inside him, but he resisted the urge.

"I'm Maddy."

"I know."

She riffled through the mail. "She hasn't turned up yet then?"

"Afraid not." He nodded toward the mail. "I thought I'd check and see if I could find any clues about where she might've gone." It irritated him that he felt the need to explain himself to a woman who never even saw fit to visit her grandma.

As she breezed past him, a soft, feminine scent pulled at him. "I couldn't reach Emma. She must still be in the air."

"I left it unlocked," he said, but she'd already twisted the knob and slipped inside.

Maddy stopped just inside the house. She'd forgotten the smell—a blend of salt air, lemon cleaner, and a hint of mustiness. A hundred memories rushed over her, good ones she'd forgotten, filled with laughter and childish glee. Bad ones, from that last summer, that stole her breath and tightened a vise around her heart.

The sound of feet shuffling behind her snapped her attention back to the present. She moved toward the kitchen. Warm evening light filtered through the gauzy curtains, giving the room a pale golden glow. Nothing had changed in recent years except the tablecloth and refrigerator.

"I didn't move anything except her address book," Connor said. "She left the cereal bowl and coffee mug on the table just as they are."

Maddy eyed the ceramic dishes. There was a bit of discolored milk in the bottom of the bowl, concealing the bottom of the spoon. A folded-up newspaper sat nearby with a pair of readers. Did Gram have more than one pair? Her eyes drifted around the room, catching on the knitting bag slouched on a kitchen stool.

"She wouldn't have left her knitting if she'd gone on a trip. She wouldn't have left her dishes out either. I don't like the looks of this."

She turned to Connor and realized he towered over her. She put some space between them. "Are you sure she didn't mention a trip?"

"Not to me, she didn't. Or to any of her friends I spoke with."

He had long golden hair, and his jaw was covered with at least a week's worth of scruff. A wayward lock flopped over his forehead—just like Nick's. What was it with guys and that stupid flop of hair? His eyes were gray, but maybe it was only the lighting that made them appear void of color.

"And that's unusual?" she asked.

"She normally asks me to keep an eye on the place. I live right next door." He jerked his head to the south. "And she usually sets the thermostat to conserve energy."

Maddy walked over to the wall. The air was set to seventy, and it was running even now. She didn't even know Gram had gotten central air.

Chills popped up on her arms that had nothing to do with temperature. She crossed them, brushing away the goose-flesh. She went up the stairs, relieved when Connor remained on the main floor. Maybe he sensed her distrust.

The steps squeaked in familiar places, and the collage of photographs on the wall made memories bubble up. Collecting shells on the seashore. Kayaking with Emma. Fishing with her dad. She popped each one of them with an imaginary pin.

All the lights upstairs were off. Her grandma's bed was made, the quilt tucked neatly under the pillows, a faint hint of Chantilly still lingering in the air. In the bathroom Gram's Estée Lauder lotions were arranged on the counter, and a fluffy blue towel hung from the towel

bar. A white robe hung from a hook on the back of the door.

When she came back downstairs, Connor seemed to be waiting for her assessment, hands tucked in his front pockets.

"Nothing seems to be missing," Maddy said. "It's as if she just disappeared into thin air."

She grabbed onto the box newel at the bottom of the stairs, worry clawing at her. If Gram hadn't gone on a trip, and the house hadn't been broken into, what else was there? Could she have been kidnapped? She had the means and was an easy target, but that seemed far-fetched. And there'd been no ransom call.

"There was no sign of forced entry," Connor said. "But she kept a key under the plant on the porch."

Maddy imagined someone slipping into her grandma's house in the middle of the night and taking her from her bed. But no, her bed was made. It appeared she'd gone missing right after breakfast. Surely someone hadn't taken her in broad

daylight.

She closed her eyes against the image and told herself there would be signs of a struggle. Her grandma was slight, but she was no pushover. She wouldn't go easily.

Her eyes drifted blindly around the living room as her mind spun with other possibilities. "Is it possible—have you noticed any forgetfulness? Any signs of dementia? Could she have just wandered off?"

"None at all. She might be eighty-three, but she's still sharp as a tack."

She gave Connor a sideways look while he checked the windows. What did she really know about this man? He could be lying about all of this. But to what end?

She needed to file a missing persons report, the sooner the better. She'd let the police get to the bottom of this.

At the crunch of tires on the shell driveway she moved past Connor to the front door. "That must be Emma."

But as Maddy stepped out onto the porch, her eyes honed in on the silver

Mercedes—on the Massachusetts license plate—and on the woman behind the wheel. It was not Emma.

Her heart beat up into her throat as dread prickled her skin. She turned a dark look on Connor. "You called **Nora**?"

He blinked, confusion on his face a moment before his lips thinned and his eyes flashed. "You didn't return my call, so I called both of your sisters."

Their gazes clashed. Surely he'd known that was a mistake. He, who knew her grandma's daily newspaper habits and the location of her hide-a-key, had to know of the tension between her grand-daughters.

At the sudden hush of the engine Maddy turned and watched helplessly as her oldest sister unfolded from the luxury car, looking every bit the high society woman she was.

And then she thought of Emma, due to arrive any moment. This wasn't good. This wasn't good at all.

CHAPTER 3

"Nora." Maddy stepped closer to her oldest sister and received a stiff hug. Nora was about Maddy's height and just as slender as she'd always been. "I didn't know you were coming."

Nora withdrew. "I didn't know you were coming either."

Her sunglasses were perched on the top of her head, holding back her shoulder-length auburn hair. She was carefully made up, her sea-blue eyes stealing the show. But at forty-three her age was beginning to show in the lines at the corners of her eyes and the slight droop of her perfectly arched eyebrows.

"I'm Connor Sullivan." He extended his

hand. "I'm the one who left the voice-mail."

Nora shook his hand. "Of course. Thank you for contacting me. Gram hasn't turned up yet?"

"No," Maddy said, the full weight of that thought hitting her fresh, making her throat close up.

"There are no indications that she left for a trip," Connor said. "There's a suit-case in her closet, but she may have another one. Used dishes were left on the table, and as I said in my message, there were three newspapers on the porch."

"I think we should file a missing persons report." Maddy's eyes connected with Nora's, and a moment of gravity passed between them. She wondered if her elder sister shared the same naggings of guilt and regret.

Maddy was exhausted by the time Sheriff Warren left the house. He'd had dozens of questions, many of which they had no an-swers for. Important ones, like what was Louise wearing when she disappeared and what were her daily habits? He looked around the house and inspected the points of entry.

Nora let Maddy take the lead, probably since Maddy had remained in closer contact with their grandmother. But Maddy was reeling with the additional stress of the past two days and a lack of quality sleep.

"Surely they'll find her," Nora said as she closed the door behind Connor and the sheriff. She and Maddy had been worried about the waiting period, but as it turned out that was only a TV thing. The sheriff had filed the report immediately.

"I surely hope so," Maddy said. "I can't help but think she'll come walking through the door any minute."

"Me too."

"She's been after me to come for a visit. She wanted help cleaning out the house, but I've been so busy with work..."

"If it's any consolation, I've put her off too. I haven't been here in years. The last time was when Chloe was in middle school. She was bored silly with no other children around—and she never was a good traveler. She always gets motion sickness."

"I'm sorry you came all this way," Maddy said. "I should've answered my calls and saved you the trip."

"I couldn't sit at home with Gram missing. Besides, with Chloe away at school, there's nothing keeping me home anymore."

Nora had been a devoted stay-at-home mom, but these days she kept busy chairing committees and serving on charity boards.

"It's hard to believe she's old enough to be in college. How's Jonathan? His business still doing well?"

Nora straightened the afghan on the armchair. "Oh, he's just fine. The booming economy has been very kind to businesses. Would you like some tea? I'm sure Gram still keeps an assortment."

"No, thanks." She could really do with some Oreos, though.

Maddy watched Nora slip into the kitchen. She envied the ease with which her sister had settled into a family and found her place in the world.

Years ago Jonathan and his best friend had opened a mortgage company together. It had been profitable enough to boost them into the upper echelons of Boston's high society. They'd sent Chloe to the best private schools and posted pictures of their European vacations on Facebook. They were the perfect all-American family.

Whereas Emma…It just didn't seem fair.

Maddy pulled out her phone. Emma had texted her when she'd landed, but Maddy had been in the middle of the sheriff's questions at the time. It's too bad her sisters had come all this way. Maddy could've handled this on her own. With her sisters came unnecessary tension, and it was already a stressful situation.

Nora returned to the living room a few minutes later, cupping a mug of steaming tea. She sat in the armchair in the corner and dunked her tea bag in a careful, repetitive motion.

"I feel like there's something we should

be doing," she said. "Gram's out there somewhere, and here we sit."

"It's late. We'll get a fresh start in the morning." Night had descended and with it a vague feeling of unrest and hopelessness. They still had a major battle ahead this evening, and Maddy was running out of time.

"Nora...," she started, dread wedging up next to her heart. "There's something I have to tell you."

Her sister's hand stilled, and she gave an awkward chuckle. "That sounds rather ominous."

"It's Emma—she's on her way."

Nora's shoulders stiffened. "Here? Now?"

"Connor called her too. Her plane landed thirty minutes ago."

Nora set her tea aside, the teacup clattering on the saucer. "You should have told me, Maddy."

"I didn't know you were coming. I was expecting Emma, but Connor didn't mention—"

"I never called him back. When I got his

message I just got in my car and…Maybe
I should go."

"You just got here." Maybe she could
bring herself to play peacekeeper one
more time. "Nora…maybe it's finally
time the two of you put aside your
differences."

The ticking of the grandfather clock
filled the long silent gap.

Nora folded her perfectly manicured
hands in her lap, only a slight tremble
giving away her nerves. "Does Emma
know I'm here?"

"Not yet." Her reaction would be worse
than Nora's. Maddy drew in a deep breath,
trying to brace herself for the coming
altercation.

Nora suddenly stood and paced across
the room. "This is a terrible idea. I should
just go. She's not going to want to find me
here."

"It's been twenty years, Nora. You're
both happily married now. Don't you
think it's time we put this behind us once
and for all? Tried to put our family back
together again?"

The hum of an approaching engine halted the conversation. Headlights swept across the living room walls.

Nora crossed her slender arms. "Wonderful. Just wonderful."

A new tension had filled the space between them, as if some great force had sucked the oxygen from the room. The clock ticked, and the muted sound of the waves crashing the shoreline carried through the walls.

Nora turned to face the fireplace, her posture rigid, her arms crossed.

The doorknob twisted with a squeak, and the door swung open. "Maddy?"

Emma's eyes lighted on Maddy, a somber smile breaking out. But before it fully emerged she caught sight of Nora. The corners of Emma's brown eyes tightened, and her rosy lips pressed into a hard line.

She raked Nora over from head to toe. "What are you doing here?"

Nora turned, her chin lifting a notch. "Hello to you too."

A small white curly-haired dog squirmed

in Emma's arms. She let the dog down, dropped her bag, and approached Maddy, drawing her into a hug.

Maddy had to stoop a bit to account for Emma's shorter stature, but her embrace was warm and soft. She hadn't changed much in the months since Maddy had seen her. Her dark-blond hair was in a low messy bun, and she wore little make-up on her pretty features. She had the curvy figure you might expect from a woman who managed a bakery.

"What's going on?" Emma asked as she pulled away. "Has Gram turned up yet?"

"I'm afraid not," Maddy said. "We just filed a missing persons report with the sheriff."

Emma's face fell. "That sounds dire."

"He was hopeful she'd turn up." Maddy tugged her sister down on the sofa and filled in all the details while Nora stood in the corner as still and silent as a potted plant.

Emma lifted the dog onto her lap, calming both herself and the animal with distracted strokes.

"This must be Pippy." Maddy reached out, letting the trembling dog sniff her hand. Emma had often mentioned the poodle mix she'd rescued from a shelter a few years ago.

"She's a little traumatized from the flight, aren't you, girl?" Emma smoothed Pippy's fur back from her face. The dog looked up at her with adoring eyes. "So," she continued. "What's next? What can we do? Should we start looking for her?"

"There's not much we can do until morning. Everything around here is closed. Connor, the next-door neighbor who contacted all of us, has already called some of her friends, but we can go through her directory ourselves. Someone has to know something."

Emma's brown eyes teared up. "I just talked to her a couple of weeks ago. She didn't say anything about an upcoming trip."

"We'll get to the bottom of this," Maddy said. "I'm sure she's fine. Gram can be a little eccentric sometimes, but she's savvy and strong. There has to be a logical explanation."

Emma shook her head. "I just can't imagine her disappearing like this, without a word."

"Like grandmother, like granddaughter." Nora finally spoke up.

Emma's spine stiffened, and her eyes snapped with fire. "At least I don't take what's not mine. You have some nerve showing up here, Nora."

"If I'd known you were coming I wouldn't have."

"And neither would I."

"Okay, okay, that's enough." Maddy stood to her feet. "It's been a long day for all of us. Why don't we just head upstairs, get settled, and get a fresh start in the morning."

A fresh start, she thought as her two sisters reluctantly complied. That was asking for the impossible.

CHAPTER 4

The sun was almost overhead by the time Connor had a moment to breathe. He drew in a lungful of salt-laden air—never grew old—and straightened from tying the boat off to a cleat. He tried not to take his work for granted. He was blessed to do something he loved. Owning a marina allowed him to be outdoors, work with boats, and be surrounded by beauty, day in and day out. What could be better?

The docks jutted out into a bay that was blue and serene. White masts of varying heights pointed skyward, and the gentle breeze blowing in made the metal hardware ping against them.

Two sea gulls swooped overhead, their

piercing cries making him feel lonely somehow. He thought of Louise and breathed a prayer for her safety. He wondered how the three granddaughters were faring back at the cottage and if they'd heard any news.

The house had still been dark when he left this morning. Although his dockhands didn't arrive until the marina opened at eight, he'd arrived before dawn to catch up on the paperwork he'd put off yesterday.

Saturdays were their busiest day, and this morning it had been all hands on deck—literally. He'd worked alongside the men to launch and gas up boats as fishermen set out for a day of leisure. He loved talking to his customers on the front end of their day when they were full of hope and anticipation. He gave out the occasional tip on the hottest fishing spots and was always prepared with the weather forecast. It was all part of the service at Sullivan's Marina.

He took out his phone and texted his youngest sister, Lexie, reminding her to get her oil changed. He'd noticed her overdue sticker the last time he'd ridden with her. While he had his phone out, he texted his other sister, Tara, to ask what his nephew wanted for his upcoming birthday. She frequently accused him of spoiling her kids rotten, but hey, that was his job.

As he returned his phone to his pocket, the dock quaked under his feet. He turned to see Cheryl Watts coming his way. Her gray-streaked hair was pulled neatly back from her face, making her red-framed glasses stand out. Her quick stride and serious expression told him something was up. Plus, it was lunch hour at Sullivan's Landing, and Cheryl wouldn't leave the restaurant unless it was important.

He immediately thought of Louise and met Cheryl halfway up the dock, worry churning in his gut.

"You have a minute, boss?" she asked as she approached.

"Of course. What's up? Have you heard from Louise?"

"What? Oh, no, I'm sorry." She set her

hand on his arm. "I didn't mean to put the fear of God into you. No word yet?"

"Afraid not. Her granddaughters are in town now, though, and the sheriff's on it."

"Good. That's good. I hope you hear something soon."

Well, something was bothering the woman. Her cheerful countenance and can-do spirit were noticeably absent. "What's going on, Cheryl? Problems at the restaurant?"

"No, no, everything's running like clock-work. It's my dad. My brother called this morning and—" Her eyes went shiny behind her glasses. She blinked and swallowed.

"What is it?"

"My dad had a stroke last night. They didn't realize that's what was happening so they didn't take him to the hospital until this morning. He's not doing very well. They don't know if he'll recover, but he'll need a lot of therapy, and of course my mom is gone, and my brother is my only sibling, and he's busy running his business—"

"Cheryl." Connor set his hand on her arm. "You have to go take care of your dad."

"But the restaurant—"

"Will be here when you get back."

"But there's no one to take my place."

He gave her a rueful grin. "What am I? Chopped liver?"

"You have the marina to run."

"And a full staff of dockhands to keep it all going. We'll be fine. Don't you worry about us; just go take care of your dad."

She blinked back more tears. "Are you sure? I feel just awful leaving you in the lurch like this."

"Family first, no matter what. Go ahead and get on the road. I'll be up to check on the restaurant in a few."

Before Cheryl even made it back to the boardwalk, Connor heard a splash and a man's voice saying, "Oh dear."

Dave and Dot Lewis had just tied off their runabout on the next pier and stood peering down at the water.

"Dave?" Connor called as he made his way over to the older couple. "Everything all right?"

Dave waited until Connor was nearby before answering. "I'm afraid I lost my keys in the water."

Connor looked down through the glimmering water, and sure enough, there was a speck of red at the bottom.

"I told you to put them in your pocket," Dot said. "You never listen to me."

"I did put them in my pocket. But there's a hole in my pocket that you haven't gotten around to sewing yet."

"Well, maybe I would've done that this morning if you hadn't insisted on dragging me out here to waste hours on the water."

"I'm sorry you consider time spent with me a waste."

"Not to worry." Connor broke in before the argument could go any further. "Happens all the time." He stripped off his shirt. "And I was just thinking it was a great day for a swim."

CHAPTER 5

Maddy rubbed her temples where the beginnings of a headache throbbed as Nora pulled her Mercedes into the cottage's drive.

After trying to reach Gram's friends they'd decided to visit some of her favorite places to see if there was any trace of her. They'd stopped at the sheriff's office for an update, but there was nothing to report yet.

Nora had insisted on driving, so Maddy took the passenger seat. Emma sat behind her, as far away from Nora as she could get, Pippy curled on her lap. It had been a tense morning, laden with passive-aggressive comments between the two of them. Maddy found herself once again in the position of mediator, a role she did not embrace. She'd rather avoid conflict altogether, but her sisters didn't seem to be of the same mind.

Nora shut off the engine, and the sisters quietly exited the vehicle, Pippy trailing on a leash. They'd agreed to stop back home for a quick lunch and to check Gram's voicemail. After lunch they'd make up fliers to post around town, then take the ferry to Bald Head Island. It was possible Gram had gone there and been unable to return for some reason.

Maddy was going to suggest they split up and conquer both jobs at once. They'd get through the tasks more efficiently, and besides, it was exhausting having Nora and Emma together.

Emma took Pippy to do her business while Maddy and Nora checked the phone—no messages. Maddy fought the tide of hopelessness that threatened to swallow her. What in the world had happened to their grandmother? It was as if she'd simply dropped off the planet.

Despair rolled in like fog off the harbor.

She walked over to the bank of windows at the back of the house, where bright sunlight streamed into the kitchen. Beyond the deck the rolling dunes stretched out, leveling to a wide strip of sandy beach. Waves frothed at the shoreline, and beyond it the water grew darker as it extended toward the horizon, a sharp line against the pale blue sky. On many days she'd stood and appreciated this very view, but today even such beauty failed to lift her spirits.

She thought of Nick back home and wondered what he was doing. He hadn't so much as called since she walked out of Pirouette. That said it all, she supposed. An ache opened up in her middle. Hard to believe it had only been two days. She hoped time and geographical distance would bring perspective.

Clearly she hadn't known Nick the way she thought she had. The betrayal had only reinforced her distrust in love and her distaste for secrets. She wanted to stay as far away from both as possible.

She determined to push all thoughts of Nick from her mind. There were enough worries here.

She turned to find Nora rooting through the pantry. Even when her sister was out of her element she appeared put together, with her styled hair and flawless makeup. Her ivory pants and sleeveless blouse were more suited to lunch at the club than a search-and-rescue party.

"Why don't you let me do that?" Maddy said.

"I need to stay busy. You know, as long as we're here we may as well start sorting through things upstairs. Gram's been after us to clean this place out forever."

Guilt pinched Maddy hard. Their grandmother had been wanting to put the house on the market for a couple years. The upkeep was getting to be too much for her—as was obvious by the weathered shingles and overgrown flower beds. But Maddy had been too busy to take the time. They'd all been too busy for Gram.

"We should definitely do that," Maddy said. It would help pass the long evening hours, and doing something nice for Gram might assuage her guilt.

"Actually…" Nora finished opening a can of soup and began scraping it into a pan. "There's really no reason for all of us to stay. I can handle things here with Gram and keep in touch with the two of you."

Maddy turned. "Don't be silly. I'd only be worried senseless."

"I know your job's important to you. You've worked very hard to get where you are. There's no reason to jeopardize your position."

Maddy bit her lip as she pulled bowls from the old white cabinets. She should tell her sister the truth, but the words got caught in her throat. She didn't **want** to rush home, she realized. What was waiting for her? An empty apartment? The unemployment line? Disappointments and heartache?

She set the bowls beside the stove and went for napkins and spoons. "There's nothing more important than Gram. Besides, as you said, this would be a great time to clean out the house."

"I can handle all that. I'll box up your things and send them on to you and Emma."

"You shouldn't have to do it alone. There's a lot that needs done around here. Gram obviously hasn't been able to keep up the place. There's at least a month's worth of work, even if we all pitch in. Besides, going through all the stuff stored here might not be very...easy."

Emma appeared on the kitchen threshold, cradling Pippy, her brown eyes toggling between Maddy and Nora. "What won't be easy?"

"Nora and I were thinking we should start cleaning out the house tonight, since we're here anyway. The house needs some work too."

"Actually..." Nora turned from the stove top. "I suggested that the two of you go on back home and leave me here to handle things. Once Gram turns up, I can stick around and help her with the house."

Emma smirked. "Good ol' Nora. Always

taking control of the situation."

Nora straightened. "I was merely think-ing you might like to get back to your jobs," she said in a measured tone.

"And you should stay, since you don't have to worry about plebian things like weekly paychecks?"

Nora's left eye twitched. "Why must you always read so much into everything I say? Might you consider the possibility I was trying to be helpful?"

"How generous of you." Emma crossed her arms. "I think I'll stay and help with the house too. I have some vacation time coming."

"It's a plan then. We'll all stay." Maddy was eager for some time away from Charlotte. "Let's just get lunch on the table. Maybe we can split up this after-noon and cover more ground. We have to focus on finding Gram. And that would be a lot easier if you two put your differences on hold for now."

"Differences?" Emma scoffed.

A knock sounded on the door. Their eyes collided for a long moment before

Maddy took off toward the living room.

Please, Lord, let it be good news about Gram.

She caught sight of Connor through the screen door. "Any news?" she asked hopefully.

His face fell. "I was about to ask you the same thing."

Her spirits flagging, Maddy pushed open the door, letting him in.

"I had to stop at the house and thought I'd check in and see if you'd heard anything."

The light from the windows illuminated his face. His eyes were definitely gray. He hadn't shaved this morning—or for several mornings for that matter. His golden-brown hair tumbled over his forehead, and he wore a fitted blue T-shirt, worn jeans, and sandals.

He had the careless look of a beach bum. She wondered what he did for a living that allowed him to come home in the middle of the day—or take the previous day off entirely—never mind that he'd been searching for her grandmother.

He lifted a brow, and Maddy realized the pause had grown uncomfortably long.

She grabbed an empty coffee mug from the end table. "There's nothing to report, I'm afraid. We spent the morning looking and stopped by the sheriff's office."

"I'm sorry to hear that. I'd hoped…"

When his words petered out, she turned toward the kitchen. "We're putting up fliers this afternoon and running over to Bald Head Island."

"Good ideas." Connor followed her into the kitchen and greeted her sisters as he stooped to pet a curious Pippy. Nora was stirring the soup, and Emma had finished setting the table.

The phone rang, and since Maddy was the closest, she grabbed for it. Maybe the sheriff had news.

"Hello?"

"Maddy! Oh, good, you're there."

The sound of her grandma's voice nearly made her knees buckle. She grabbed for a chair back. "Gram!"

Three heads spun her direction.

"Where are you?"

"I'm in Boise, dear. For my high school reunion—our sixty-fifth! I can hardly believe it's been that many years. Why, I still feel as young as a spring chicken."

"Gram, what—We've been so worried! No one knew you had a trip planned! Your neighbor Connor called us all worried and—"

"Oh, that Connor...He's such a dear boy, so helpful. I don't know what I'd do without him. It was sweet of him to be concerned."

"Where is she?" Nora whispered.

Maddy covered the mouthpiece. "She's fine. She's in Idaho."

Emma frowned. "Idaho?"

Nora's shoulders sank. "Thank God."

"Gram..." Maddy struggled to keep a respectful tone. "We've been so worried about you. We were going to put up fliers with your picture in town this afternoon, for heaven's sake."

"We? Who's we?"

"Nora, Emma, and I. We all arrived yesterday, and we've been worried sick. We filed a missing persons report with the sheriff's office!"

"Oh dear. You might want to cancel that. I'm just fine and dandy."

"Why didn't you tell anyone you were leaving? You left dishes on the table—and newspapers have been gathering on your porch."

"I'm sorry to have worried you all, honey. I must've forgotten to cancel my paper. But I'm just fine. I'm having a grand time, in fact. I've decided to make a real vacation of it. My return flight is open-ended."

Maddy palmed her palpitating heart, trying for patience. Trying to let the relief that had engulfed her when she'd heard Gram's voice take precedence.

Wait a minute. Why had Gram called her home phone if no one was even supposed to be here? Her eyes drifted to Connor, sharpening on his face.

He's a dear boy, so helpful...I don't know what I'd do without him.

Her fingers tightened on the chair, and heat rose up the back of her neck. "Gram..."

"You know what, dearie? Since the three of you are already there, you may as well take a little time away from your busy lives and enjoy each other's company. You have a lot of catching up to do."

With those words, Maddy's sneaking suspicion became a full-on certainty. Her grandmother had done this on purpose.

Her eyes fell shut. For years Gram had been trying futilely to reunite the sisters. She'd put out invitations, she'd begged, and now she'd resorted to luring them to Seahaven under false pretenses. Never mind that they'd had her lying in a gutter somewhere.

"What?" Emma whispered from nearby. "Is she okay?"

Maddy opened her eyes to find the others staring at her. She waved their worry away.

Her grandmother was still talking about reconciliation and the importance of forgiveness and family ties. She reiterated for the dozenth time that their father would be heartbroken to see what had become of their family. There was plenty Maddy wanted to say, but with the self-discipline of a saint she bit her tongue and let her grandmother finish.

Meanwhile she watched Connor wander over to the back door, take his phone from his pocket, and thumb out a text. Just where did he fit into this scheme? Was he really the concerned neighbor— or had he actually been her grandmother's willing pawn?

When Gram finally ran out of steam, Maddy assured her she'd talk to her sisters about reconciliation and wound up the conversation.

"What'd she say?" Nora demanded as soon as Maddy hung up the phone. "She's all right?"

"She's perfectly fine. She's in Boise for her sixty-fifth high school reunion, and she apologizes for worrying us."

"But that doesn't make any sense," Emma said. "Why'd she leave her dirty dishes out? Why didn't she tell anyone where she was going—even her neighbor who looks in on her?"

Maddy turned toward Connor.

When he looked up from his phone, she gave him a piercing look and crossed her arms. "That's a very good question, Emma. What do you think, Connor? Why would our grandmother simply disappear without a trace? Why would she neglect to tell a soul? Why do you think she might scare her own granddaughters half to death?"

His eyes flitted between the three sisters, finally landing back on Maddy. "I feel like I'm supposed to have the answers to all these questions."

Maddy quirked a brow. "Don't you?"

He regarded her with a tight smile. "Why don't you just spell it out for me, Maddy."

"If you want to be obtuse…fine." She narrowed her eyes on him. "It seems Gram has been awfully eager for the three of us to come together and reconcile. It seems she left our numbers awfully handy, and her helpful neighbor reached out to not just one of us, not just two of us, but all three of us."

"What?" Nora said.

"You think Gram lured us here?" Emma said. "That she worried us sick like that on purpose?"

"I have to admit," Nora said, "it sounds just like the kind of harebrained thing she might do. Remember how she set up Mama and Daddy when they were dating and had broken up?"

Emma crossed her arms. "Let's not forget the time she went behind their backs and enrolled us in that music camp she was so excited about. They were furious."

Connor still held Maddy's gaze—somewhat stubbornly, it seemed to her.

"She didn't own up to anything," Maddy said. "But she may as well have. I can put two and two together easily enough."

"Your math's a little off. I can't account for your grandmother's actions, but I can tell you that I only called you out of concern for her."

Connor pocketed his phone, giving the sisters a wan smile. "I have to go. But I'm glad your grandma's all right. If you need anything, just let me know."

A few seconds later the front screen door slapped quietly behind him, and the muted sound of his footsteps receded.

Emma turned a look on Maddy. "You're being a little hasty, don't you think?"

"Why else would he have called all three of us when one of us could've easily handled the situation?"

"Exactly what I've been trying to tell you," Nora said.

Maddy thought over the whole situation. Maybe she had jumped to conclusions. But it all seemed a little fishy. Besides, she just didn't like the looks of Connor. To be fair, she didn't like the looks of any man at the moment.

"Well, whether he knew or not is beside the point," Emma said. "What's important is that Gram is all right."

"Exactly," Nora said. It was the first thing the two had agreed on since their arrival. Nora pulled out a chair. "Come on. Let's eat while it's still hot."

They sat down to large steaming bowls of vegetable soup. They ate in silence, each seemingly lost in her own thoughts, nobody wanting to talk about why Gram might have lured them here.

The soup was tasty for canned fare, but Maddy had lost her appetite. She was equal parts relieved and annoyed. With Gram, and yes, with Connor. Had this situation with Nick completely ruined her opinion on half of humanity?

"I'll stay and get the house cleaned up for Gram," Nora said when they'd finished the soup. "I don't have anything pressing back home. Did she say when she was coming home?"

"She said her return flight is open-ended. I got the feeling she might stay put awhile. And believe it or not, she didn't even mention cleaning out the house." She'd been far too focused on the sisters' relationship.

"Do you really think it was all a scheme?" Emma said.

"That's exactly what I think," Maddy said. "Why would she have called her home phone if no one was supposed to be here? And as soon as I confirmed we were all here she started on the whole family reconciliation theme."

"I'm familiar," Emma deadpanned.

"We're all familiar." Nora's gaze flickered off Emma. "But some of us are too stubborn to listen to reason."

"As if you're so much better. I haven't heard from you since the Christmas card you sent last December. Nice photo, by the way. Paris looks so wonderful on all of you."

"At least I **sent** a Christmas card."

"See, this is just what Gram's talking about," Maddy said. "If she went to such great lengths to get us here, can't we at least try? We used to be close. We've all moved on with our lives. It's been twenty years, for heaven's sake. Isn't it time to put all this behind us?"

Emma shot to her feet. She took her water glass and bowl from the table. "I'll stay long enough to get the house in order. But I'm not interested in pretending the past never happened." She set her dishes in the sink, picked up Pippy, and went through the kitchen door and onto the deck.

Without a word Nora got up, placed her bowl in the dishwasher, and retreated to the living room.

Maddy dropped her aching head to the back of the chair. If they were all staying in Seahaven, it was going to be a long few weeks.

CHAPTER 6

June 4, twenty years ago

The sun felt divine against Maddy's skin. **Divine** was her favorite new word, and it fit perfectly. She rolled over onto her stomach and sifted the sand through her fingers, losing herself in the familiar sound of the surf hitting the shore.

A light wind was brewing, carrying the briny scent of the sea and rustling the sea oats. Beyond the rolling dunes, the beach cottage squatted on a rise, the white paint blinding under the noon sun.

Mama and Daddy were still inside, lingering over their lunch, and Nora was probably somewhere with her nose stuck in a book. She came outside only under the cover of a beach umbrella, as her porcelain skin burned easily.

Maddy couldn't wait for Emma to arrive. Though there were ten years between them, they were still close. Ever since Emma had gone off to college three years ago, Maddy cried every August when summer at the cottage was over and she had to say good-bye. Good-bye to Gram, good-bye to the ocean, good-bye to Emma.

Maddy wasn't as close to her other sister, Nora, who sometimes seemed irritated by Maddy's immaturity. But Nora could be helpful too. She was sensible, wise, and discreet, making her the best person to ask for advice. Daddy said Nora was twenty-three going on fifty.

She even looked older than her years with her hair back in a bun most days and her librarian glasses perched on her nose. If Maddy had Nora's long auburn hair she'd wear it down around her shoulders. But brainy Nora cared little about her looks.

Nora and Emma, only two years apart, were the closest of the sisters, which drove Maddy crazy. Was it her fault she'd been born so far behind them? Sometimes the two of them would go on excursions that Maddy wasn't deemed old enough to participate in.

But Emma always made it up to her by treating her to an ice-cream run or looking for shells with her or taking her kayaking around Pelican Point. Still she'd wished many times that there wasn't such a large age gap between them.

This summer was sure to be different from others, though. Emma was bringing her fiancé, Jonathan, home from college. He'd already met the family—minus Nora, who'd been away at college when they'd visited the family in Charlotte. Maddy hoped he didn't hog all of Emma's time.

Maddy didn't see Nora until her sister lowered herself gracefully onto a beach towel. She had on a floppy straw hat, and her hair was down for once. She wore a grass-green one-piece that made Maddy wish God would hurry up and give her some curves.

"You're gonna get burnt," Maddy said. "What's the big occasion?"

Nora gave her a wan smile. "Impertinent child. Mama and Daddy were having one of their quiet conversations, so I wanted to get out of the way. Besides, you'd better get used to hanging out with me. Emma will be otherwise occupied for the next three months."

Maddy scowled. "She'll make time for us. We've known her a lot longer than Jonathan has."

Nora gave a wry chuckle, leaning back on her pale straight arms. "She's in love, Baby Boo. That changes everything."

"Not everything."

"You'll see," Nora said in that annoying big-sister way.

Maddy heard a squeal behind her and turned to see Emma running awkwardly through the thick sand, barefoot, arms outstretched.

"We're here!" Emma called.

"Emmie!" Maddy jumped up and ran

toward her sister, and a moment later found herself swallowed in a big hug. "I thought you'd never get here! We've been here two whole days!"

"We had to stop and see Jonathan's family in Boston." Emma gave her a big squeeze. "They're not too happy we've stolen him for the summer."

Maddy was nearly as tall as Emma now, she realized. She'd grown a full two inches over the last year, making her five foot four.

"You got taller," Emma said, as if reading her mind. She drew away to embrace Nora.

Whereas Nora was long and lean with subtle curves, Emma was built more like their mother, all soft and curvy. She was also the prettiest one, in Maddy's opinion.

"What?" Emma asked over Nora's shoulder. "You're out in the sun in the peak heat of the day? I can't believe it."

"Why is everyone so concerned about my skin health?" Nora said, laughing.

Good feelings bubbled up inside Maddy, widening her smile. She loved her family so much, and they had the whole wonderful summer ahead of them. Life couldn't be better.

Her eyes drifted behind Emma to where Jonathan stood, straight and tall. His short black hair was covered by a Red Sox cap, and his blue eyes squinted against the sunlight. He was very handsome, if a little overdressed in khakis and a short-sleeved button-down.

He was almost thirty—ancient!—and he came from old money, whatever that meant. Even though he was a Yankee, her parents liked him. Daddy thought he was smart and ambitious. He was a mortgage broker (something to do with selling houses), and he worked from home. This summer he'd be working from the cottage, which surely meant Emma would be free to spend time with them.

"Let's see the ring," Nora said in as close to a squeal as she'd ever get.

Emma held out her hand, fluttering her fingers proudly.

Nora and Maddy leaned dutifully over her hand.

"It's so big!" Maddy said. "And sparkly!"

"Well done, Romeo," Nora said, eyeing Jonathan from beneath long lashes.

"Oh, I haven't even introduced you." Emma grabbed Jonathan's hand, tugging him forward. "Jonathan, this is my older sister, Nora. Nora, this is the man I've been going on and on about on the phone." She snuggled proudly into his side.

Jonathan extended a hand to Nora, giving her a warm smile. "It's a pleasure. I've heard so much about you."

"You too. I'm glad you could join us for the summer."

"Well, I could hardly turn down a summer by the sea with my girl."

"We have wedding plans to make," Emma said. "And it'll be ever so much easier if we're together. You can help us, Baby Boo!"

"Sure!" Maddy's face went warm at the silly childhood nickname. It had never bothered her before, but she was nearly twelve now, and the name suddenly seemed terribly juvenile.

"I'll help too," Nora said. "I can keep everything organized."

"Nora is an absolute wonder." Emma looked up at Jonathan, popping a stick of chewing gum into her mouth. "You'll see."

"I'll just bet she is."

"Gum anyone?" Emma asked.

"Still chewing that stuff?" Nora asked when everyone turned down the offer.

"It's an appetite suppressant," Emma said.

"She thinks she needs to watch her figure." Jonathan, clearly disagreeing with the statement, gave Emma an affectionate squeeze.

"I have a wedding dress to fit into. Let's go find Mama and Daddy!" Emma dragged Jonathan away, leaving Nora and Maddy to tag along behind.

Maddy tucked her windblown hair behind her ears. "He's very handsome, don't you think?"

"He's all right."

Maddy laughed outright. "Oh, come on! He's totally hot and you know it."

"He's almost old enough to be your father," Nora said in that chiding tone.

"Those blue eyes and that coal-black hair." Maddy sighed dreamily and continued, mainly just to annoy Nora. "Not to mention those broad shoulders. I'll bet he works out in a gym."

Nora's chin notched up just a bit. "I can't say as I noticed."

But later Maddy would realize that Nora's words, like so many other things in her life, were just a big fat lie.

CHAPTER 7

Present day

Connor locked the marina office and headed up the boardwalk, making the turn and continuing on to the restaurant. Sullivan's Landing was a glorified crab shack located on the harbor adjacent to his marina. It wasn't much to look at, with its fading red roof and wavy metal siding. The inside was also rustic and casual, but with a large covered deck, the real draw was the waterfront dining.

The restaurant was crowded with locals every night of the week in the summer and bursting at the seams on the week-ends. Sunset hour was especially popular, drawing tourists who were willing to overlook the primitive vibe in favor of the magical view.

During the summer season they brought in local bands on weekend nights, and that kept a steady clientele until the joint closed at midnight. Under Cheryl's management it had become the most popular hangout in town.

Connor had never dreamed of being in the restaurant business, but when this one became available two years ago, his sister Lexie had talked him into it. She would manage the restaurant, she exclaimed passionately. She'd do all the work. He wouldn't have to so much as lift his finger.

She'd been twenty-one at the time, waitressing full-time at Patty's Diner and managing the night shift. Connor had lost his wife the year before and didn't have enough to keep him busy. Not busy enough to keep his grief at bay anyway, and he'd buckled under Lexie's pressure. The baby of the family, she was a little spoiled and adept at getting what she wanted. Especially from him. Actually, both of his sisters knew how to wrangle their way with him.

But he had to hand it to Lexie—she'd done a great job managing Sullivan's Landing. She hired a terrific chef who'd fine-tuned the menu, keeping the local favorites and adding popular new items. She'd put up twinkle lights inside and out and added other touches that made it seem as if the rustic atmosphere was by design. New ceiling fans now hung over the deck, making summer meals much more tolerable.

And then, barely a year into it, she up and decided she wanted to pursue an interior design degree. Well, what was he supposed to say?

He'd lucked out by finding Cheryl to replace her right away, and ever since the restaurant had been a steady stream of income and little worry to him.

Until now.

He walked into the already busy restaurant and was immediately confronted with chaos. Two servers had called in sick, and the young girl hostessing was over-whelmed and looked ready to quit on the spot.

Connor sent her for a break and took over her position. He could seat people. Anyone could do that, right? But thirty minutes later he'd given away tables that had been reserved by regulars and had to mollify them with free meals and promises of the very next available spot.

He was relieved when the hostess returned from break looking ready to resume her job.

He went into the kitchen next. They had a new cook in training, and the food was slow coming out, resulting in disgruntled customers. Two tables left before their food even arrived, one of them complain-ing loudly to him, "the manager," as the other patrons listened in.

By the time he'd finished swabbing the deck it was after one o'clock in the morn-ing. He'd have about four hours to sleep before he'd have to get up to meet a six o'clock fishing charter and do it all over again.

• • •

Maddy snuggled up on the couch, her phone pressed to her ear. Holly had called well after midnight when she'd gotten home from her date with her boyfriend. Nora and Emma had turned in long ago.

After the tense day, it was a relief to let off steam with her best friend.

"So how long do you think you'll stay?" Holly asked.

"As long as it takes to get our stuff cleaned out and fix up this place. A month. Maybe a little more."

"Maybe the time away will do you good. You've been working way too hard. I can check on your apartment and water your garden."

"That'd be great, thanks. I'll have my mail forwarded and suspend the paper." She didn't have many obligations back home at this point, but her sisters were a different story. "I find it hard to believe Nora and Emma can take that much time away from their lives. I especially can't imagine Jonathan agreeing to Nora's extended absence."

"Doesn't Emma own a bakery?"

"She manages it. Still, I don't know how she can be away that long either. But neither of them seems too worried about it. I honestly think sheer stubbornness is all that's keeping them here."

"I don't envy you, being caught in the middle."

"It's no fun, I can tell you that."

"So, do you really think your grandma schemed to get you all there? That seems a little crazy."

"Oh, I know she did. In retrospect, I should've figured it out before she called. It's just the kind of thing she'd do. Mind you, she only has our best interests at heart. But she clearly doesn't realize how stubborn Emma and Nora are. I wouldn't be surprised if, by the end of this, they aren't speaking at all."

"That's a real shame. I can't imagine anything coming between Noelle and me for so many years, even a man." It was true. Noelle had worked for Maddy at Pirouette, and the sisters were very close.

"I think Nora still has a lot of guilt over stealing Jonathan, but she's done trying to apologize. And you'd think Emma could forgive and forget after all these years, but she's been steeping like a tea bag in the anger and bitterness."

"Maybe Emma is jealous of Nora's life— it was the life she was supposed to have had. From what you've told me, Nora and Jonathan are living the good life, all the traveling and schmoozing and whatnot."

"I don't know. It's never really been about money or prestige for Emma. She's more about fulfilling her passions, and she's done that. She's got a great husband and a satisfying job. Clearly all is turning out as it should've, so why won't these two just put the past behind them?"

Maddy's heart gave a squeeze at the thought. Emma and Nora weren't the only sisters who hadn't put the past behind them, but Holly was the only one who knew it.

"It's not always that easy, though, is it?" she said.

That last summer here had left Maddy

completely untrusting of love. She'd been guarded at best in the relationships she'd had leading up to Nick. And that particular relationship hadn't exactly helped matters.

Maddy sighed. "I guess not. I finally got the courage to put my heart on the line with Nick, and look what happened. I'm feeling more guarded than ever. One step forward, ten steps back."

"How are you feeling about all that? I know it's only been a few days."

"Honestly—I'm beating myself up for not seeing it sooner. There were signs. The way he guarded his phone, the times he just kind of disappeared, the way his eyes strayed. How could I have been so blind?"

A long pause ensued.

Maddy shifted the phone. "Are you there?"

"Yeah...Listen, Maddy, can I be completely honest with you?"

"Well, nothing good ever comes after that question."

"It's just...I've noticed you can kind of bury your head in the sand sometimes.

Maybe you did that with Nick. Maybe deep down you knew something was wrong, but you ignored it to protect yourself."

Maddy bristled a little.

"I mean, I understand why you'd do that," Holly continued. "You've been hurt in the past, and it's only natural you want to avoid pain."

What she said had a ring of truth, Maddy had to admit. She'd sure ignored all the signs where Nick was concerned.

"Fair enough," she said. She knew Holly only wanted what was best for her.

"I know this thing with Nick hit you hard, but you can't give up on love, Maddy. With the right person, it's truly a wonderful thing."

Maddy laid her head against the sofa back. "I don't know if I believe that. I was already skeptical, and this thing with Nick just put me over the edge."

"I know, honey. But give yourself a little time to heal, and keep an open mind. God has someone special for you, I just know it."

Maddy gave a wan smile. Holly was the

ultimate romantic. She lived on romance novels and the Hallmark Channel. "We can't all have a Jacob in our lives."

Holly gave a breathy sigh. "He is pretty wonderful, isn't he? But he's not an anomaly, Maddy. There are other terrific men out there if you just let yourself open up a little bit."

"So you say." The muted sound of a car's engine filtered through the window as it passed the house. It seemed to be slowing nearby.

Maddy twisted on the sofa and pulled back the gauzy curtain. Whatever Holly was saying was lost on Maddy as she watched a car swing into Connor's driveway. A minute later the headlights went out. Even under the darkness of night she recognized his lazy gait as he approached his house. Someone was keeping late hours.

"Maddy, did you hear me?"

"What?"

Holly chuckled. "Where'd you go? I just gave some of the wisest advice of my life."

"Sorry. Gram's neighbor just got home.

Connor—the man who helped lure me here."

"**Lure?** That's putting a harsh spin on things."

"I just don't trust the guy." She watched as he mounted the porch steps and disappeared into his house.

"That doesn't exactly distinguish him from any other male you've met." There was humor in her tone. "Could it be you're just a little jaded, my dear?"

"It's not men I don't trust. It's love." But in the aftermath of her experience with Nick, she wondered if that first part was true.

She watched the house next door, for what she wasn't sure. "I just know he was in on Gram's scheme."

"So what if he was? Maybe he saw a little old lady trying to put her family back together and decided to give her a hand. Is that so awful?"

"Yes." A light came on upstairs in Connor's house, and Maddy let the curtain fall back into place.

"Either way, this was your grandma's

doing. I'm no expert, but you might be shifting some of your frustration from her to this guy. Sometimes it's easier to blame a stranger than someone you love."

Ouch. "All right, you might have a valid point. But I still don't trust him."

"You don't have to trust him. He's just a neighbor, and now that your grandma's turned up safe and sound—thank the good Lord—you can finish your business there and come back home."

"You're right." Maddy settled back into the couch. "I don't have to associate with him. I have enough on my hands with this house and my sisters."

"Just focus on that."

"I will. I absolutely will."

But an hour later, as she tossed and turned in the bed, it was thoughts of Connor that persisted. Thoughts of those enigmatic gray eyes. Thoughts of his calm response to her accusation yesterday. He was like sand on her skin after a day at the beach. No matter how hard she tried to get rid of it, it just kept turning up in unexpected places.

CHAPTER 8

Two days later Maddy was focused on the tasks at hand. After enjoying coffee and dawn on the deck, the sisters headed upstairs. They'd spent the last two days cleaning out their rooms, but the task of cleaning the attic still loomed.

Maddy opened the diminutive door at the end of the hall, flipped the light switch, and headed up the narrow staircase. She'd played up here as a girl on rainy days. Sometimes Emma and Nora would humor her with a tea party, or they'd dress up in some of Gram's old hats and coats, laughing at the old-fashioned styles.

Over the years there'd been a lot of talk about renovating the attic. The house was crowded when all six of them were there. But big talk in the summer faded away once it was August and they were all back in Charlotte, back to their normal lives.

Maddy reached the top of the stairs and stopped at the sight. "Oh my gosh."

Ever impatient, Nora edged around her. "What in the world?"

"What is it?" Emma edged in for a view. She gasped.

There were piles and piles of...stuff. Boxes, small pieces of furniture, mystery objects draped in white sheets like ghostly relics. A beam of light flooded in through the small window at the end of the room. Pippy took off, tail wagging as she rooted about. Dust motes danced wildly around her.

Emma halted her gum chewing long enough to sneeze.

"When in the world did all this happen?" Maddy asked. "There used to be just a few boxes and that old rocking chair."

"Well, that was a long time ago." Nora took a few steps into the room, making the floor squeak. "I'll bet Mama sent

Daddy's stuff here after..."

The sentence hung out there like a live wire, no one willing to grasp it.

"This is going to take forever to go through," Emma said.

"Maybe we don't need to actually go through the boxes," Maddy said. How much easier would it be to just haul the boxes to the dump unopened? Most of the furniture could go as well.

"We can't do that," Emma said. "There's probably memorabilia here that Gram wouldn't want to part with. Letters from Grandpa, things from Daddy's childhood."

"Well, maybe she shouldn't have left it all to us then," Nora said.

"That's cruel—even for you." Emma gave Nora a dark look. "These are Gram's memories; we can't just trash them."

"Emma's right," Maddy said. "She'd be heartbroken."

Nora crossed her arms. "Well, she's not going to have room for a bunch of boxes if she moves into a little apartment."

"Which is why we have to sort through

them," Emma said firmly.

"I see you've finally learned to speak up for yourself," Nora said.

"I learned that when I don't, **some** people will just take whatever they want from me."

Nora opened her mouth to retort.

"Stop." Maddy held up a hand. "Please, can we just call a truce or something? You don't want to kiss and make up—fine. But I refuse to hang out in this minefield between the two of you for days on end."

There was a long, awkward pause while Nora looked everywhere but at her sisters.

Emma gave a self-righteous sniff.

"Fine by me," Nora said finally.

"Of course it's fine by you. You're not the one who—"

"Emma," Maddy said sternly. "You can go back to hating each other when we're finished. For now, let's just handle business, all right? For Gram." And for her own sanity, though she didn't say that.

Emma pursed her lips. "Fine."

The doorbell rang, and Maddy knew a

convenient escape when she heard it. "I'll get that. Why don't you two make a plan on how to tackle all this, and I'll bring garbage bags back with me—we're going to need plenty of them."

She took the attic stairs, feeling a little cowardly. Oh well. Let the two of them sort this out. Hopefully by the time she got back there'd be a nice frosty silence, and they could work in peace. Maybe they'd have a super-productive morning. And maybe Maddy could keep an analytical frame of mind as she sorted through her parents' things and not be pulled into the emotional riptide of the past.

When she opened the front door, there was no one there. A small brown box sat on the porch. She went out into the already sultry morning and picked it up. It wasn't Gram's name on the address label, but Connor Sullivan's.

She looked toward his cottage. The morning sun cast a long shadow over the front of his house. She couldn't tell if he was home, as his driveway was on the other side.

Given the hour he'd been rolling in the last few nights, though, he was likely still in bed. She'd walk the package over and leave it on his porch. He'd never even know it had been left here by mistake.

Maddy went back inside, slipped on her sandals, then grabbed the box. The package was light, and the contents didn't bump around inside as she took the porch steps. The sender—a Tara Duval from Whiteville, North Carolina—had drawn two red hearts beside Connor's name.

Maddy rolled her eyes. Maybe it was his girlfriend, and the long trip back and forth is what kept him out so late.

The ground between the cottages was sandy and unlevel, hospitable only to clumps of tall grass, sea oats, and the scrubby blanket of red firewheel. A fresh breeze of salty air filled her nostrils and tugged on her long hair.

She had to admit the warmth of the sun felt good on her skin. When she'd been a young girl she'd played on the beach for hours a day, her skin turning deep golden brown, her nose freckling in a way she'd hated.

She'd been envious of the way the sun had browned Emma's freckle-free skin. And Nora, always cowering in the shade, had been jealous of them both.

Connor's house was quiet as she approached. She walked silently up the porch steps and set the package on his welcome mat, avoiding the large picture window on the far side of the door.

But as she straightened, a movement caught her eye. The deep shade of the porch made it easy to see inside, and she spied someone. Maddy's gaze sharpened on a woman who seemed to be kneeling in prayer, her full torso lowered to the floor, arms extended forward. But then she changed positions, easing her rear end skyward into what Maddy realized was a downward dog position.

As the woman came upright, eyes closed, Maddy had a silhouette view. She quickly took in a lithe figure, ponytailed blond hair, and a fresh, young face that put her in her early twenties.

Maddy edged away from the window

and down the steps before the woman—
or worse, Connor—could spot her peering through the window. How embarrass-
ing would that be?

She treaded carefully across the sandy
terrain. The woman must've come home
with Connor the night before. Maddy had
heard his car pull in well after midnight
while she'd been lying in bed trying to
go to sleep. She seemed too young for
Connor, whom Maddy placed in his
midthirties.

She thought of the box she'd left on the
porch and wondered how the young
woman would respond if she discovered
the package, so obviously from another
woman who was smitten with Connor.

Oh well, she thought. That was Connor's
problem, not hers. Heaven knew she had
enough of her own.

A loud thump pulled Connor from a sound
slumber. He squinted at the clock and
saw it was just past nine. He'd managed
to sleep in on his day off.

Correction: morning off. Monday was

the marina's slowest day, and he routinely left his capable staff to manage the docks. The same couldn't be said of the restaurant, however.

When Cheryl had said there was no one she could consider leaving in charge, she hadn't been kidding. And while Monday wasn't a particularly busy day, problems seemed to manifest when he wasn't there to oversee things. Plus, he needed to make the next week's schedule and be there for deliveries.

He'd have to arrive by eleven. But maybe he'd find time today to look over the résumés he'd received in response to his newspaper ad. Maybe he'd even fit in an interview or two and find the perfect person to temporarily fill Cheryl's position.

He couldn't keep up this pace indefinitely. It had only been three days since Cheryl left, and he was already exhausted. He was no longer a twenty-year-old who could burn the candle at both ends with little consequence.

He showered and dressed, scored a

fresh cup of coffee in the kitchen, and joined his sister on the sunny deck. Lexie was typing away on her laptop.

At the squeaky slide of the patio door she turned. "About time you got your lazy butt out of bed."

"Would've slept longer if someone wasn't thumping around the house."

"Sorry. It seems the harder I try to be quiet, the more apt I am to drop things." She returned to her laptop, her fingers clicking on the keys.

"Working on an assignment?"

"An eight-page paper."

She was taking a full course load over the summer, living with their sister, Tara, and her family. Lexie served as built-in babysitter to repay them for room and board, an arrangement that worked well for all of them—unfortunately. Connor could really use her help at the Landing right now.

Her fingers stilled. "Thanks for letting me crash here last night. I haven't had a full night's sleep in over a week."

"Lily still teething?"

She gave him a hopeless look. "I love my baby girl, but the child wails like a siren." She shifted her laptop. "I did the dishes and picked up the kitchen a bit. You should really hire a housekeeper or something."

"It's not that bad." Annie had always called him a clutter bug. But he suspected she secretly enjoyed picking up after him and fussing about it.

"Before I forget," Lexie said. "There was a package on the porch. It's from Tara. Too bad she didn't know I was coming. I could've saved her the postage."

"Right. She said she was sending some kind of oil for muscle aches."

Lexie laughed. "You're getting old, brother."

He rolled his eyes, but couldn't deny it when exhaustion left him feeling like he'd been hit over the head with a bat. He wished Tara had sent him something for that.

His sister was the nurturing sort, always sending him things in the mail. "You'd think she lived across the country instead of an hour away."

"Let her mother. That's what she does."

"I already have a mother."

"Well, she's all the way in Florida."

"Believe me, she does plenty of mothering from there." His mom and dad, happily married and busy with their ministry, checked in with him at least once a week.

"Any luck finding a replacement for Cheryl?"

"I got a couple résumés over the week-end. I'm hoping one will pan out."

"Maybe I can help out a few hours this weekend after I get this paper turned in."

He gave her a wan smile. "I'm really hoping to find someone by then."

"How long will Cheryl be out?"

He tipped his head back and closed his eyes, enjoying the warmth of the sunshine. "Not sure. They really don't know the severity of the stroke's effects yet. It could be a month or longer. I have to be prepared for that."

"It might be hard finding good temporary help, especially with things so up in the air."

"I know." He'd been praying fervently for the right person, though. Surely God would answer his SOS.

"Well, when you do find someone and have spare time again, there's someone I want you to meet."

Connor slid her a dark look.

"Don't you look at me like that."

"Did you get your oil changed?"

"Yes, I did, and stop trying to change the subject. I only have your best interests at heart."

"Why does everyone think they know what's in my best interest?"

"If by 'everyone' you mean your loving sisters, it's because we do."

"I think I'll stick to my own devices, thanks just the same."

"By that, you mean you'll continue to work long hours and close yourself up like a hermit in the evenings?"

"Finally on the same page."

"Connor..." She sighed softly, giving him a pitying look.

"Uh-oh, here it comes."

"It's been three years…"

"Yep, there it is." He took a long sip of his coffee, letting the warmth soothe his throat.

"I know you loved Annie, hon, but she's gone. She wouldn't want you to live the rest of your life alone."

"I'm well aware." He gritted his teeth and tried to keep his frustration from showing. He knew they meant well, but his sisters… They just didn't get it. And he hoped they never did.

"You're going to have to jump back into the dating pool at some point. Or at least ease back in, one toe at a time."

"Are we talking about dating or swimming?"

"You never were the cannonball type, but this is getting a little ridiculous. So…" She gave him a saucy look. "About this woman I want you to meet…"

"No offense, Lexie, but your friends are a little young for me."

"She's several years older, actually— thirty-two, to be exact. She's very kind, very attractive, and very personable."

"That's a lot of **verys**."

"Stop being difficult."

"If she's so wonderful, why's she still single?"

"So cynical. She was actually married until last year. She's divorced now and ready to start dating again."

"Sounds like a lot of baggage."

"First of all, Mr. Judgey, she's a very stable woman, and second of all, her husband was a jerk who cheated on her."

"And I'm sure there's no baggage at all from **that**."

She scowled at him. "Connor, you're thirty-five. Do you really think you're going to find a single woman your age without a little baggage? You're toting around at least a carry-on yourself. We all have issues, you know. That's just life."

He stared out to the hazy horizon where the white triangle of a sail was barely visible. He inhaled the air, letting it stretch his lungs before he exhaled it out.

He'd been with Annie so long. They'd been high school sweethearts, and he'd never even been with another woman.

He'd never say such a corny thing out loud, but she'd been his soul mate. His everything.

And then suddenly she was gone.

He'd never find that again. But did he want to spend the rest of his life alone? He missed Annie's friendship. He missed having a companion. And yes, he missed having a lover. The bar was so high, though, he feared no one else would truly satisfy him.

For some reason, the image of Louise's granddaughter, Maddy, formed in his mind. Shiny brown hair, moving easily around her shoulders. That long fringe of lashes, sweeping over her almond-shaped brown eyes. He imagined her generous lips stretching in a wide smile—something he had yet to see.

"So what about it?" Lexie asked. "Are you willing to meet her after your restaurant crisis is over?"

Connor shook the cobwebs from his head. "Who?"

Lexie gave him a look. "My friend Johanna...the one with all the **verys**?

Ringing any bells?"

Connor set his mug on the table between them. He knew he had to start dating eventually. He'd admit, if only to himself, that he was tired of being alone. He craved some form of what he'd had before, even if it couldn't be the same. And Lexie was right. Annie wouldn't have wanted this lonely existence for him.

He gave a put-upon sigh. "Fine. I'll do it."

Lexie squealed, clapping her eager young hands.

"But not until I find someone to fill Cheryl's spot," he said firmly. "And only this once." He had to set some limits or his baby sister would run all over him.

Undeterred, Lexie's smile was as bright as the sunshine. "I promise you won't regret it."

Connor scowled at his sister. He was definitely going to regret it.

CHAPTER 9

"Look at this," Maddy said, holding up the tiny sundress. It was their third day in the hot, stuffy attic, and it had been slow going.

Emma looked up from a dusty box. "Aw, that was yours, Maddy. I saw a picture of you wearing it in one of the boxes."

Nora was working quietly in a corner, black readers perched midway down her nose, sorting through a box of financial records.

Maddy envied her the unemotional job. She'd set aside a few boxes of her dad's things, not wanting to deal with them yet. There was a part of her that was very curious about her dad, since he'd died when she was still a child. She knew him only as a loving father. What kind of man had he been? What kind of worker? What were his dreams and aspirations?

Gram would be able to fill in the blanks, but she always got such a sad look in her eyes when Daddy came up in conversation. And Maddy was reluctant to bring up the touchy topic with her mother. She had to admit he'd been her "favorite parent," and she had a feeling that hadn't gone unnoticed by her mother.

Maddy tossed some old magazines into the recycle pile. They already had three large trash bags full of garbage and several full of Goodwill items. They'd set back a few things for themselves: photographs, seashells, pictures they'd drawn for Gram.

Gram called almost daily, and they updated her on their progress. She sounded more concerned about their relational progress, but a tense truce seemed to be the best Nora and Emma could manage. Gram would have to be all right with that because Maddy couldn't imagine either of them waving a white flag anytime soon.

Nearby, Emma stretched her neck, then checked her watch. "It's going on two. I'll go put something together for lunch. Turkey sandwiches and soup all right?"

Maddy's stomach gave a growl. "Sounds good. I didn't realize how hungry I was until you said that."

"I'll text you when it's ready."

After Emma left, Nora stood and stretched. "I never realized Gram was such a pack rat. She's kept financial records dating back to the seventies."

"Well, I didn't get that quality from her," Maddy said. "I'm lucky to find all my year-end information at tax time."

Maddy pulled out a store flier, her eyes quickly scanning the bathing suit ad that must've been from the fifties. Her gaze honed in on one of the models.

"Look at this," Maddy said. "Is that Gram?" She pointed at one of the four young women who were standing at the surf's edge, arm in arm. The one who looked like Gram in her younger years wore a yellow one-piece with a snug skirt.

"Well, I'll be. It sure looks like her."

"She never told us she modeled! She was gorgeous."

"Are there more?"

Maddy dug through the box. "Here's another." In this one she wore a blue two-piece with a boy-shorts bottom. Her long legs seemed to go on forever.

"Scandalous!" Nora said, laughing.

There were several other advertisements in the box. Maddy couldn't wait to quiz her grandma about her modeling days.

Connor shrugged into a clean shirt, struggling to pull it down over his still-damp stomach. One of his dockhands had a sprained wrist, so he'd spent most of the day gassing up boats. He couldn't show up at the restaurant smelling like gasoline.

He should put in a shower at the marina. He may as well live there at this point. He ran his fingers through his wet hair and decided to let it air dry. He grabbed his keys and wallet and left the house. When he was nearly back to his car, someone called out. He glanced up to see one of the granddaughters coming across the yard, flagging him down.

He met her at the edge of his property. She was the middle one, a real beauty with a friendly smile. Emma, he remembered.

"How are you doing, Emma?"

"Just fine. I'm sorry to bother you, but do you happen to know anything about appliances?"

"Sure, a little. What's going on?"

"I was making lunch, and the stove stopped working, both the oven and the cooktop. The thing's ancient; it's probably just finally bit the dust, but..."

"I think I know what the problem is."

He followed her to the house, making small talk along the way. She was pleasant and friendly, with a smile that reminded him of Louise's. Her younger sister could take lessons.

Once inside the kitchen, he went straight

to the wall outlet beside the stove and tried the can opener. As he suspected, it was dead.

"It's just a tripped breaker," he said. "This happens to your grandmother sometimes when she forgets and uses too many things at once. If you're using the stove and the microwave, you can't use anything else on this wall."

"Oh, good to know. Do you know where the breaker box is?"

"It's in the living room closet, but I'll get it."

As he entered the living room, the other two women were coming down the steps.

Maddy's eyes tightened at the corners as they connected with his. "Hello."

"Maddy. Nora." He nodded, then focused on the older sister. "Emma stopped me on my way out. She tripped a breaker in the kitchen."

He opened the closet and reached for the gray breaker box cover. It opened with a squawk. Locating the right switch, he flipped it, then closed the door again. "That should take care of it."

He trailed behind the sisters, heading back to the kitchen where he checked the oven.

"It works!" Emma said with a joyful smile. "Thank you so much. I didn't even think of checking the other outlets."

"Well, the stove probably is on its last legs," he said.

"Stay for lunch if you haven't eaten yet," Emma said. "It's only soup and sandwiches, but there's plenty to go around."

His stomach gave a hard twist. He hadn't eaten since the protein bar he'd downed on his way to the marina this morning.

"We insist," Nora said. "It's the least we can do. Right, Maddy?"

Maddy gave a strained smile. "Of course." She went to the refrigerator and pulled out a pitcher of tea.

He suddenly wanted to stay put, if only just to annoy her. The marina could do without him for another few minutes, and once supper hour rolled around he'd be too busy at the restaurant to eat.

"I'll take you up on that. Thanks."

Ten long minutes later they were seated at the table, Nora at the head, Emma and Maddy across from him. Pippy sat attentively nearby, clearly hoping for a scrap of food.

After Nora said grace, Connor dipped his spoon into the hearty-looking chicken noodle soup. A taste of the savory stew proved him right. The tea was sweetened just the way he liked and adorned with a sliver of lemon.

He made small talk with Emma, and Nora caught him up on their grandmother's excursions. He was glad Louise was having a good time with friends. She spent too much time alone. He hoped her granddaughters planned to hang around until her return.

They talked about their progress on the attic, and he offered his help once they got around to fixing the house itself. By then he'd have Cheryl's position covered —he hoped. The résumés he'd gotten so far had been dead ends. He wouldn't have trusted either applicant with a mop and a broom, much less a management role.

All the good summer help had been lined up weeks ago. He was going to have to broaden his reach with an online ad. He'd do that tonight, even if he had to do it after closing.

"So what is it that you do, Connor?" Maddy asked, pulling him from his thoughts.

The question itself was benign; it was her superior tone and the stubborn tilt of her chin that got under his skin. "I work at the marina, Maddy. Down at the end of Main Street."

Just the thought of the long night ahead made him yearn for his bed. He smothered a yawn.

"You look like you need a nap worse than you need a meal," Emma said.

"What d'you expect?" Maddy mumbled.

His eyes shot to hers. She watched her spoon dip into the bowl, come up with some silvery broth.

"I'm sorry—what was that?"

Her eyes flickered off his. "Well, when you stay out till all hours..."

"Maddy..." Nora gave Maddy a look that

clearly said, **What is wrong with you?**

Connor studied Maddy for a long moment, watching her squirm and enjoying it a little too much. "And how would you know what hours I keep?"

A flush had risen to her cheeks. "My bedroom window faces your way. Your headlights wake me up when you come home."

"Wait a minute…" Emma snapped her fingers. "Sullivan's Marina…I saw the sign a few days ago. You must be the new owner."

"Yes, ma'am."

Maddy's lips thinned as she arched a delicate brow.

He gave her a tight smile. She'd done nothing but judge him from the moment she'd laid eyes on him.

"The food's delicious, Emma." He finished off the toasted turkey sandwich. It really was tasty, stacked with meat and tomato and slathered with a mayo-based spread.

"Thank you," Emma said. "I love to cook, and unfortunately I like to eat what

I cook."

"Nothing wrong with that. If I cooked like you, I'd enjoy it too."

Emma's brown eyes lit up. "So, Sullivan's Landing...the new restaurant on the docks—do you own it too?"

"Oh, I noticed that the other day." Nora scooped up her last spoonful of soup.

His gaze toggled to Maddy long enough to see her haughty expression waver. "Technically it's not new. It used to be the Crab Shack. But yes, I own it now."

Heat prickled the back of Maddy's neck, and she resisted the urge to unfasten the top button of her blouse. Was the air-conditioning broken? What was the temperature in here anyway?

"Maddy was just saying we should stop there and try it out sometime," Emma said.

"You should definitely do that." He gave Maddy a forced smile. "Let me know the night, and I'll save you a good table. We have a nice menu and reasonable prices."

"Maddy manages a restaurant in

Charlotte," Emma said. "Pirouette. It's very prestigious. It's gotten reviews in some of the top epicurean magazines."

"Assistant manager," Maddy said.

"She's up for a promotion, though," Emma said.

Maddy winced. She felt Connor's gaze on her like a heat lamp but pretended avid interest in her sandwich.

"That a fact?" he said.

She heard something in his tone, like maybe disdain. As though he thought she was hiding something. Okay, she was hiding something, but still.

"Our Maddy's very well regarded in the local restaurant community," Emma said.

"She should be," Nora said. "She's devoted her entire life to the place."

Maddy squirmed as she finished the last bite of her sandwich. "All right, that's quite enough. I think it's time to get back to the attic—and let Connor get back to work."

Ten minutes later Maddy breathed a sigh of relief as they settled back into their sorting. She didn't know what it was about that man. All right, so he wasn't a beach bum. He still stayed out till all hours. Entertained women much too young for him. Had that ridiculous flop of hair.

"Why are you so prickly with Connor?" Nora asked. "He seems like a nice enough guy."

"I'm not prickly."

Emma laughed. "You are too. If Nora and I agree on something, you know it must be true."

Nora bristled as if that thought alone was unbearable.

"If I didn't know better..." Emma let the thought drag on unfinished as she un-wrapped a teacup, then wrapped it back up. She set the whole box aside and pulled another one from the dusty corner, sneezing hard.

"If you didn't know better...what?" Maddy asked.

"I don't know. It just feels like there's a little sexual tension going on there is all."

Maddy gave her a look of disbelief. "Sexual tension? That's ridiculous. I don't even like him."

Emma laughed. "On the basis of what? He helps out Gram, he was concerned enough to call us—"

"Or manipulative enough."

Emma spared Maddy a glance. "That again? Oh, come on. If he was a willing participant he only did it because he cares about Gram. You can't fault him for that."

"Leave her alone," Nora said. "You don't get to decide who she likes."

Emma stiffened, the words hanging between them, lingering in the air.

"No, you're right, Nora." Emma's eyes hardened on her older sister. "I don't get to decide who anyone likes."

Nora paged though a financial document, her nose twitching. "I'm not apologizing again, Emma. I was practically on my knees begging—"

"As well you should've been!"

Maddy held up a hand. "Come on, girls. You made a truce."

"I was as sorry as I could've been," Nora said. "I never meant to hurt you."

"Sorry doesn't change anything—and

what's that mean anyway? 'I never meant to hurt you.' You knew it was going to hurt me, but you did it anyway. You both did. That says everything right there."

Maddy pressed her lips together. They weren't putting her in the middle of this again. She'd made a concerted effort to bring about a resolution when she was eighteen and had failed miserably. She'd even managed to get them in the same room twice. But Emma was still hurt and angry with Nora, and any efforts Maddy had made to defend her had only made Emma angry at Maddy too.

Her efforts with Nora had been just as disappointing. Nora was finished apologizing to Emma, was tired of being the target of Emma's anger. She just wanted to move on with her life.

Feeling unaccountably tired, Maddy popped to her feet. "If you two want to go at it, fine. Tear each other apart. I'll be in my room."

CHAPTER 10

Three days later Connor pulled into his driveway, gravity weighting his body like a lead blanket. As he shut off the engine and extinguished his headlights, the distant sand dunes disappeared. Darkness pressed in from all sides. His eyes were gritty and dry, his lids heavy from lack of sleep.

His new sous chef had quit last night, leaving the kitchen shorthanded. He feared their chef was going to go elsewhere if something didn't change soon.

Saturdays were the restaurant's busiest night, and the food had been so slow coming out that customers left. The wait staff was weary of complaining customers, and Connor was just plain weary. He had to get this figured out.

His head against the headrest, keys clutched in his hand, he couldn't seem to make himself move. He closed his eyes, dreaming of bed just a short walk away. Then he thought of the long day ahead tomorrow and the one after that, stretching out, no end in sight.

Even after posting the position online the résumés weren't exactly flooding in. And those that were…He gave a heavy sigh and breathed yet another prayer for help.

He could ask Lexie to fill in, but she already had her hands full with classes and babysitting. If he pulled her away from Tara, he'd have a grouchy sister on his hands. He'd bought the restaurant. This was his responsibility.

He thought of Maddy next door and summoned the energy for a scowl. He'd forgotten she managed a restaurant. But he couldn't imagine why she would agree to help him when she couldn't seem to stand the sight of him. She also had a job on her hands already and a life to get back to.

Still...

She obviously had the expertise to get him through this crisis.

Connor woke with a start. His eyes fastened on the steering wheel as he became aware of the crick in his neck. He straightened from the car door, rubbing his neck.

The sun was just coming up, hiding behind a bank of clouds. If he weren't so achy and chilled he might've appreciated the swaths of pink and periwinkle on the horizon, heralding a new day. But the thought of another day only made him want to sink back into the oblivion of sleep.

What time was it? He winced as he shifted upright, feeling the pull of angry back muscles. He had to get a shower and get over to the marina. He opened the door and stepped out into the crisp morning air. His leg nearly buckled under him as his limb prickled with the fresh flow of blood.

He limped toward the porch, but on his way a movement caught his eye. On the back deck next door Maddy stood at the railing in a white robe. She stared off into the sunrise, a mug in her hand, her dark hair fluttering at her shoulders.

He remembered the restaurant crisis and his last weary thoughts before he'd fallen asleep in his car. Before he could reason with himself he changed his direction.

Maddy took a sip of her warm coffee, savoring the deep roasted flavor. There was a slight chill in the air, but the mere appearance of the sun on the horizon warmed her. She watched its slow ascent behind the clouds, enjoying the golden morning light. She'd come to appreciate these quiet moments before her sisters stirred.

She hadn't slept well last night. The tension between Nora and Emma had gotten worse after their words in the attic. They talked to Maddy but not to each other. She was tired of being caught in the middle and tired of rooting up memories she'd just as soon leave buried.

If only she could make her sisters behave like the adults they were. It was true that Nora's betrayal had been inexcusable, but it was so long ago. They were sisters, and everything had worked out after all. Hadn't it?

She drew in a deep breath of fresh morning air and let it out. In the distance a sea gull hopped along the beach and another soared overhead. The muted rhythmic sound of waves crashing the shore lulled her mind.

How many hours had she spent out on that strip of beach, searching for shells in low tide or building sand castles, complete with turrets and moats? With no other children living nearby, her imagination had been her best companion. Her mom or Emma would join her sometimes, offering ideas, helping in the construction.

Her daddy, always her biggest fan, would brag over her efforts. But no matter how wonderful her castles turned out, no matter how proud she was of her latest effort, it would be gone the next morning, flattened by the relentless tide.

Such was life.

She'd been close to her dad. All three of them were. He was affectionate, engaging, and—if Maddy were honest—had probably spoiled them a bit too much. Mama was the taskmaster who made sure they got their homework done and scrubbed behind their ears.

Daddy traveled for his job and was gone as many days as he was home. One might think the girls would've been closer to their mother, since she was such a staple in their daily lives; however, that old adage about absence making the heart grow fonder was true where their dad was concerned. When she was little she'd waited for him by the front window, anticipating his return.

Her parents' marriage had eventually failed, but she didn't blame her dad for that. Her mom was always the one harping on him to find a new job. She'd hated that he was gone all the time. Couldn't she see he was only trying to take care of them? He'd been such a good father. A good provider.

And knowing that had been making Maddy wonder lately why she'd had so much trouble finding a good man herself. No doubt the demise of her parents' marriage had had a negative effect on her view of love. But her dad had been such a good role model. How could a daughter of his end up with someone like Nick?

She thought of Nick now, imagining him lying in bed on this Sunday morning, sleeping in. He'd go to the late service at his church and then what? They'd always spent Sunday afternoons together, as it was the only day the restaurant was closed. Would he be spending it with Evangeline today? Maddy sighed. Did she even care anymore?

"Morning."

The male voice startled her, and her coffee sloshed over the rim onto her white robe.

She angled a look at Connor. His clothes were rumpled, his hair disheveled. He looked as though he was just getting home.

"Sorry." He came up the deck stairs wearing a penitent look. "Didn't mean to give you a fright."

She fished a Kleenex from her robe pocket and dabbed at the coffee stain, suddenly conscious of the fact that her face was bare of makeup, her hair snarled.

"No problem."

"You're up early."

"So are you—or are you just getting in?"

He gave her a long, steady look she couldn't quite decipher. In the golden light, his skin was tanned and flawless, interrupted only by a few days' stubble. And then there were those fathomless gray eyes.

"I've never seen such gray eyes." She hadn't meant to say it out loud or in that tone.

His eyes tightened at the corners. "You make it sound like a character flaw."

"Not at all." She took a sip of her coffee.

He sighed. "Look, Maddy. I know you don't like me, and that suits me fine. You don't have to. But I have a proposition for you, and I'd appreciate it if you'd hear me out."

Maddy got caught for a long moment in those gray tide pools. She pulled the lapels of her robe together and resisted the urge to run her fingers through her hair.

"Will you do that?" he asked. "Will you just hear me out?"

She hitched a shoulder. "I suppose."

He looked out at the horizon and scrubbed his hand over his face. "As you know, I own a restaurant and a marina. A week ago my restaurant manager had to take a sudden leave of absence—family emergency. Since then I've been trying to run the marina and restaurant both. It's not working too well.

"The restaurant really isn't my area of specialty. I won't get into all that, but suffice it to say, I'm desperate for help. I can't find anyone qualified to manage it, and to be honest, the place is falling apart."

Maddy watched as he leaned on the deck rail. His body seemed to sink wearily into it. So that's why he'd been out till all hours. He hadn't been running around with women—although there was still Miss Yoga Pants to consider. And the doodly-heart package left on her porch.

And now he was coming to her for help.

"I know you have things to do here and a life to get back to, but I was wondering if you'd consider stepping into the position—temporarily, of course."

The thought of working for him held no appeal. She pictured the restaurant—it had been aptly named the Crab Shack before—and imagined a loosey-goosey operation with untrained staff, sloppy service, and an uninspired menu.

She opened her mouth to respond, but he stopped her with a raised hand.

"I know the Landing is below your pay grade, but I'm willing to be generous. You could still help your sisters with the house during the day, and I'd take whatever you were willing to give in the evenings, for as long you're willing to give it."

He paused, looking at her with hope

and a hint of desperation.

She actually felt a little bad about having to say no. "Listen, Connor. I'm sorry you're struggling to find help, but I really don't think this is a good idea."

"What are your concerns?"

She chuckled uncomfortably. "So many..."

"Just throw them at me."

She squeezed the collar of her robe. "Well, we haven't exactly hit it off. I hardly think we'll be on the same page when it comes to running a restaurant."

"I'll give you complete control."

"**Complete** control? You don't even know me—or like me. How do you know I won't run your restaurant into the ground?"

"I know you manage a very nice restaurant, and I'm sure you could handle the Landing quite competently."

Such high praise. She raised a brow. "Did that hurt?"

The corner of his lip tucked in. "Little bit."

Hmm. A sense of humor. She took a sip

of her coffee, which had grown tepid. The sun was now hovering over the horizon, still shielded by low-hanging clouds.

She allowed herself to consider what it might be like, running the restaurant for a week or two. It was true she missed the hustle and bustle of restaurant life. She could even admit to missing that feeling of control—heaven knew she was in control of nothing here, with her sisters at each other's throats.

And that was another thing she wouldn't miss. Escaping the cloud of tension in the house was the most appealing reason to say yes.

"What are your other concerns?" he asked.

She paced a few feet away and settled on one of the wide steps leading out to the beach. "How will your staff respond to a new manager? Change of leadership can be very disruptive. Sometimes people quit."

"Trust me, they'll be relieved to have someone who knows what she's doing. I'm maybe not the most humble man, but

I know when I'm in over my head. I'm drowning here." He moved toward her and lowered himself to the step beside her. "Name your price, Maddy."

"That's a very dangerous thing to say to someone."

"I'm desperate."

"I'm getting that. How long will your manager be gone?"

"I'm not sure exactly. But I'll take you for as long as I can get you. It'll at least give me time to find someone qualified. Cheryl's done a great job managing the place. When she's there the place runs like clockwork. We've earned a good reputation around here, and I'm undoing all her hard work. I've already lost our sous chef. Cheryl's going to come back, and I'll have run the place into the ground."

"How in the world did you end up owning a restaurant?"

He gave a soft laugh, rubbing the back of his neck. "Long story. It's been two years, and it has been a great investment. I just need to get over this hump."

She pondered all he'd said. The man

clearly had no business running a restaurant, but that wasn't her concern. She had money set back—she wasn't a spendthrift. But with no new job on the horizon, adding to her savings was appealing. The bills back home hadn't stopped just because she'd come to Seahaven.

She gave him a sideways look. "And I'd be in charge? You wouldn't micromanage me or undermine me with your staff?"

He turned her way, and as their gazes connected a strange humming began inside. As if a live wire connected the two of them. She thought of what Emma had said about sexual tension and just as quickly shook the thought away.

"Why would I undermine you?" he asked. "If there's anything I've learned over the past week it's that I know nothing about managing a restaurant. And if you don't feel I'm holding up my end of the bargain, there's nothing stopping you from quitting."

Was she really going to do this? She liked the idea of a challenge. She was good at what she did, and he was clearly desperate. Her sisters might not like it, but maybe if she wasn't around to assist in the communication they'd find a way to talk to each other. Maybe she was actually in the way.

Plus, there was the money. She turned to Connor and named a fair weekly salary.

He froze in place, his lips parting and hope lighting his eyes. "You'll do it?"

Maybe she was crazy. Maybe she was in denial. But returning to work suddenly held a lot of appeal.

She gave a nod. "I'm willing to give it a try."

CHAPTER 11

Sullivan's landing was a bit of a mess, Maddy found when she arrived the next morning. Although Connor had asked her to cover dinner hours, she felt she could head off some potential troubles by arriving early enough to meet the staff and scope things out.

Her sisters hadn't been happy about Maddy's decision. More likely they weren't happy about being holed up at the house without their buffer. Well, it was high time they got over that.

Connor introduced her around and showed her the layout of the place before heading to the marina. She spent an hour acclimating herself to the menu and the delivery schedule that Cheryl had left behind.

The most immediate need was a sous chef. But after talking to the chef, Maddy agreed that one of the line chefs sounded promising. She called him in for an interview, and he seemed eager to prove himself. She offered him the position.

The hostess called in sick, and Maddy spent the afternoon filling in for her and generally getting a feel for the staff and customers and the lay of the land.

It was a casual place, she'd been right about that. But the menu was surprisingly original, the food unexpectedly tasty. Someone had taken a lot of care with it, and a steady flow of customers filled the harbor tables from lunch to midafternoon.

She couldn't be here from open to close every day, though, and she needed someone to lead the front of house through lunch hour. After a day of observation, she honed in on Amber, who worked the register. She had a good rapport with the customers and staff alike and seemed underutilized in her current position.

Amber jumped at the opportunity. Maddy gave her a crash course in her new duties during the slower afternoon hours and found the girl to be a quick study.

By the time dinner hour rolled around she had a full staff. As she helped set up the harbor tables she took a moment to appreciate the view. The bay was blue and calm today, the surface glittering in the sunlight. A sailboat moved through the channel and out into the open sea, its sails billowing with wind.

It was hot today, near ninety degrees, but the roof over the deck offered shade, and white fans spun lazily, moving the warm air. The deck jutted out toward the marina, where boats came and went throughout the day. True to his word, Connor had left her to her own devices, stopping in only once to ask if she needed anything.

Speak of the devil. She caught sight of him on a pier, unmistakable in his white baseball cap and white shirt. He was talking with a young woman with dark-brown hair. As Maddy watched, the woman tucked her short hair behind her ears and laughed at something Connor said. He reached down and swept her into a long, familiar hug.

Maddy turned away. She was here to run this restaurant, and that's exactly what she was going to do.

By the time Maddy got home it was almost one in the morning. She'd put in a long day, and all in all she was happy with how things had gone. The Landing staff seemed relieved to have her there. She saw areas that could be improved. The menu could be a little more original, and the staff was in need of better training. Just because it was a casual establishment didn't mean it couldn't be excellent. Though she doubted she'd be there long enough to rectify either situation.

She closed the bathroom door quietly and let down her bun. Her scalp practically purred in relief. As she removed her small loop earrings, she fumbled and dropped one. The earring clinked onto the counter, then onto the floor.

She bent over, perusing the area, then concluded it must've dropped into the trash can. Great. It was nearly full, of course.

She rooted through the tissues, finding an empty Visine box (Nora's), a Diet Pepsi bottle and gum wrapper (Emma's). She didn't know who the empty Oreo package belonged to. Okay, it was hers.

And there was the silver earring, way at the bottom. As Maddy reached for it, her eyes connected with another object, uncovered in her fumbling foray through the trash.

An oblong stick that had a tiny window containing a pink plus sign.

CHAPTER 12

By the time Maddy got up the next morning, Emma was knitting on the deck, Pippy curled at her feet. Maddy filled a mug and joined her sister.

"Morning," Emma said from one of the Adirondack chairs.

"Good morning." She'd hoped to sleep later, having gotten in so late, but her internal clock hadn't allowed it. "What are you making?"

"An afghan."

Gram had taught them all how to knit, but Emma was the only one who'd taken to it. "Already thinking about winter?"

"It's for a charity. They distribute blankets to homeless shelters. Plus, knitting keeps my hands busy so I don't eat too much."

"You always did worry about your weight."

"When you're five four you have to. I swear a single pound is enough to make my pants tight."

"You look great. Men like curves, you know."

Emma made a sound that could've been agreement—or not.

Maddy thought of the pregnancy test she'd found in the trash can the night before. It was likely Emma's. Years ago she and Ethan had decided not to have children, but that could've changed. It seemed more likely than Nora and Jonathan deciding to start over in their forties after they'd just reached the empty nest phase.

Maddy had lain in bed until almost two thinking about it. She hadn't yet heard Emma on the phone with Ethan. Or Nora with Jonathan for that matter, but Jonathan had always been such a workaholic.

"How'd it go at the restaurant yesterday?" Emma asked.

"Pretty good. The staff is competent enough, and I filled a couple holes. The menu is better than I expected. Someone put some thought into it. You'll have to come in and sample the lobster bisque. It's divine."

"And how did you and Connor get on?"

Maddy lifted a shoulder. "He hardly showed his face."

"So he was true to his word."

"He was." Maddy would give him that. She took a sip of her coffee and watched a sea gull drift on a current. "And how about you and Nora? I didn't see any blood on the floor when I came in last night."

Emma rolled her eyes. "She's so stubborn. I don't know how she lives with herself. I mean, she's the one who wronged me; you'd think she'd be at least a little remorseful."

Maddy tucked her hair behind her ear. Nora had been plenty remorseful back in the day. But Maddy wasn't about to get in the middle of this again.

"At least we got through a lot of boxes,"

Emma continued. "We're both eager to get this over and done with."

"And head on home?" Maddy studied her sister and thought she saw a flicker of something in her eyes.

"Of course."

She wished Emma would confide in her about the pregnancy. It had to weigh heavily on her mind, and she sure wasn't going to confide in Nora.

"How's Ethan holding up without you? He must be eager to have you back home."

"Sure. Of course. It's hard to be away, but we have to put this house to rights."

Maybe Maddy should just admit to having found the test. But if Emma wanted to tell her she would. Maybe she wanted to tell Ethan first. She obviously wanted to keep it from them or she wouldn't have buried the test in the trash.

But as Maddy scanned the quiet strip of beach she suddenly realized she wanted to be closer to her sister. She remembered the days when she could tell Emma anything, when Emma had been like a second mother to her. Now they were both adults, and Maddy longed for the close relationship that Holly had with her sister, Noelle. Sisters were supposed to share secrets. Sisters spilled the beans about things like positive pregnancy tests.

But she hadn't exactly been close enough with either of her sisters to expect this kind of vulnerability from them. And if Maddy were honest with herself, she was reluctant to share her own secrets. The part of her that longed for intimacy knew that sharing things was a big part of that. But there was another part of her that knew secrets had the power to tear people apart.

"We're separated," Emma murmured.

"What?" Maddy's eyes darted to her sister, unsure she'd heard right.

Emma's knitting needles clicked quietly. "For six months now."

"Emma...Why didn't you say something?"

She lifted a shoulder. "I'm sorry. I didn't want to talk about it with Nora around."

"I mean a long time ago. We've talked on the phone. You didn't say a word."

Maddy felt terrible that her sister had been suffering in silence. "I know we haven't been very close in recent years, but I hope you know I'm here for you."

"I guess I just didn't want to admit it."

She thought of the pregnancy test— it must be Nora's after all. Good heavens, a pregnancy just when she'd finally reached the empty nest. They were all in the middle of life crises.

Maddy touched Emma's arm. "Are you all right?"

"Oh, sure. I suppose. He moved into an apartment across the city. I used to get so annoyed, coming home to all his noise. His mess. Now the place is so clean and empty I hate coming home at all. I stay at work until I'm ready to drop. I jumped at the chance to come here when I got the call about Gram. And George was all right with me leaving the bakery awhile—I've been such a mess."

Her heart hurt for Emma. "Is there... someone else?"

Emma set down her knitting and lifted Pippy onto her lap. The dog curled up, snuggling against Emma's stomach. "I don't think so. He says there's not, and I believe him. In some ways it would be easier if there were. But no. We just...grew apart, I guess. We keep different hours, with me working so early in the morning, and he's been busy building a name for himself in real estate. We didn't make time for each other, ran out of things to talk about, yada yada."

"I'm sorry."

Pippy sat up in Emma's lap, looking to her owner as if sensing her pain.

Emma gave the dog a sad smile and stroked her neck, addressing the dog. "You're a good girl. We've been through a lot together, haven't we?"

"Are you trying to work things out? You've invested a lot of years in each other."

"Almost fifteen. Everything's up in the air right now. He calls it a break." Her fingers worked the needles nimbly. "It wasn't my idea, this separation."

Maddy studied Emma's face. "You still love him."

Emma paused her petting and looked at Maddy. Her eyes welled with tears as their gazes connected. "I do, Maddy. But you know what? I've only loved two men in my life—and they both left me. I don't know if it's worth the risk anymore."

Maddy's heart ached for her sister. "I know what you mean, Emma. I really do."

Emma's gaze sharpened on Maddy. "Are you and Nick having problems?"

Maddy gave a rueful laugh. She supposed it was time to come clean. "Understatement of the century. Nick and I are over. He—betrayed my trust."

Emma gave her a sympathetic look. "Oh, Maddy. I'm so sorry."

"Thanks. Love just never came as easily to me as it does to you and Nora. And then something like this happens..."

"When did it happen?"

"Right before I came here. I'm sorry I didn't tell you sooner. I was still reeling. And honestly, feeling like the only one of us who can't seem to maintain a romantic relationship."

"Well, obviously that's not the case."

"I guess things aren't always what they appear," Maddy said.

She thought of divulging the part where she'd lost her job, but couldn't bring herself to admit it. Her career had been the one thing in her life she was proud of—and now it was gone.

"I guess not," Emma said.

June twelfth was the hardest day of the year for Connor. When it rolled around he tried to stay busy, and so far he'd succeeded this year. He almost wished he were still working at the restaurant, because he wasn't looking forward to going home to an empty house. But he didn't exactly feel like company either.

His sisters had been calling all day long. They'd offered to come over, offered to take him out. He'd turned them down, but that hadn't stopped the calls. His best friend, Lamont, had also called, asking if he wanted to grab a pizza or shoot hoops. Connor finally turned off his phone.

He tossed the rope line inside the speedboat and gave the departing couple a wave. "Have fun out there."

"Thanks, man." The middle-aged guy expertly maneuvered the boat out of its slip and into the wake of a larger vessel.

Connor gassed up a Crestliner and made small talk with the owner. He and his wife were from Florida, just retired, and enjoying their first summer off.

He and Annie had been working toward that day. She was a planner, and though retirement was years away they'd talked about it often. She was a Florida girl, and Seahaven had never felt like home to her. It was too cool for her liking in the winter, and the water never got warm enough. She wanted to retire in the Keys where they could bathe in the sun until their skin wrinkled like raisins.

And Connor wanted to please her so he worked crazy hours at the marina, saving money by hiring fewer hands. He became single-minded about planning for their future. It was good for the business and good for their bank account, but bad for their marriage. He'd only later realized his tunnel vision tendencies.

His long hours made Annie feel neglected. They had many arguments about it, but he was so busy being right he dismissed her feelings. She was shortsighted, he told himself. He was looking out for the long term, couldn't she see that?

He swallowed hard against the knot forming in his throat. Why could he see so clearly now what he'd been blind to then? She'd needed his time. She'd needed him.

She'd also wanted a baby—and he'd failed to give her that too. It's not that he was opposed to the idea of children. He just thought there was plenty of time for that, and he discounted her feelings. The reminder was a punch in the solar plexus.

"You all right, boss?" one of his hands asked as Connor made his way up the pier.

"Fine." He managed a plastic smile and headed inside.

The familiar smells of new carpet and robust coffee failed to comfort him. He ducked into his tiny office and walked over to the window, shelving his hands on his hips. His breath felt stuffed inside lungs too small to hold it.

It didn't seem possible he'd been without her for three years. He should be all right by now. Everyone thought so, even if they didn't say it out loud. He knew he should be looking for another woman to fill the empty space in his heart, but he couldn't even bring himself to date.

It seemed as if he'd just been treading water since he'd lost her. Working. Marking time. If he could have her back he'd buy her that house in the Keys right now. He'd make her the mother she'd wanted to be instead of telling her to be patient. His eyes stung as guilt swamped him.

Connor had said to ring him if she needed anything, but Maddy couldn't seem to get hold of him this afternoon. She left the Landing's restroom, grateful for a breath of fresh air. She wasn't above the dirty job of stopped-up toilets—they happened when you served the public—but this particular job went way beyond a plunger.

She scoured her hands in the women's restroom, then let Amber know she was headed out for a few minutes. She had to get this figured out before the dinner rush.

As she walked toward the marina, the sun beat down from a clear blue sky, making sweat bead on the back of her neck. She didn't see Connor, but when she asked an employee he sent her inside.

The waft of cool air was welcome as she slipped through the door. The lobby was small, painted dove gray with white trim, and contained a few padded chairs and a high counter that featured an empty workstation and a dying geranium. Judging by the blisters on the stem and lack of blooms it was suffering from edema. She resisted the urge to move the plant to a sunny windowsill.

To one side of the desk was a short hall with two bathrooms and a drinking fountain. To the other side was a door labeled Office. It was open by several inches. She moved that way and peeked inside.

A desk took up most of the space. On top of it were numerous stacks of files and papers, a pencil holder, photos, boating magazines, and a laptop. Though the office appeared cluttered, it was organized chaos, and she suspected Connor could probably find anything at a moment's notice.

Her eyes drifted to Connor, who was facing the picture window that overlooked part of the marina. His head was bowed as if in prayer or distress, and she got the distinct feeling she was interrupting something.

As she shifted, the floor squeaked under her feet.

Connor turned.

Silhouetted by the light from the window, she couldn't see his expression. But the feeling that she'd come at a bad time persisted. "Sorry to bother you."

He cleared his throat and came around the desk. "No, come on in. Is everything okay at the restaurant?"

"More or less. I do have an issue I could use some help with, though." As he came closer she noted the vacant look in his eyes, the tightness around his mouth.

He cleared his expression with a benign smile and perched on the edge of the desk. "What can I do for you, Maddy?"

"I was wondering if you have a plumber you regularly use? The men's restroom..." She wrinkled her nose. "There's a... situation."

"Uh-oh."

"I tried to plunge it, but it's pretty hopeless. I'd like to have it in working order as soon as possible, obviously."

"Say no more." He was already searching through his phone contacts. "I have a guy who's pretty quick. Let me give him a call."

Maddy pulled out her phone. "If you give me the number I don't mind doing it."

He spared her a smile as he tapped the phone and held it to his ear. "He'll respond more quickly if I call...Hey, Darren, it's Connor Sullivan. How you doing?"

Maddy waited as he made small talk with a guy he'd apparently known awhile. When he got to the point she could tell from his end the plumber was coming right out.

Connor ended the conversation and pocketed his phone, then confirmed it with her.

"How's everything else going? The staff treating you all right? Any other problems I can help with?"

"The staff is great. A little younger than I'm accustomed to, but pretty competent nonetheless." She caught him up on the changes she'd made—promoting the line chef to sous chef and making Amber a shift leader.

"The cashier, huh? That didn't even occur to me. She's awfully young, isn't she?"

"She is, but she's quite capable, and she's a fast learner. She's also been there for two years."

He made a face. "I should've known that."

"Don't get me wrong, she's not ready to step into a managerial position just yet, but as a leader in training, she'll do just fine. The others like and respect her."

"Great. Glad to hear it. I, uh, have some time tonight if you need any help with the dinner shift."

She wondered if the brunette—or the blonde—had left him at loose ends. Then she remembered his defeated posture when she'd walked in, and was filled with mixed feelings. Who exactly was Connor Sullivan?

"The shift's covered, but thanks."

"Are you sure? I can bus a table with the best of them."

Maybe he just wanted to check up on her. See if she was running things to his liking. She couldn't help bristling a bit. "I'm sure. We're fully staffed tonight."

A shadow moved over his face, and something in his gray eyes pulled at her. "Great, great. So it's working out all right? You think you'll stick around a little while?"

"I don't see why not. You're keeping your end of the deal. But you'll continue to look for someone...?"

"Absolutely. The ad's still posted. I really appreciate your stepping in last minute."

"No problem. I enjoy the work." She moved toward the door. "Well, listen, I should get back."

"Darren will be there within the hour. He'll get you fixed right up."

"Thanks." She gave him a parting smile that wasn't as confident as it probably looked. Then she left the building and headed back up the boardwalk.

She couldn't figure out the man. As soon as she decided he was one way she saw something that made her question herself. Then again, after what had happened with Nick, was it any wonder she didn't trust her instincts?

She was thrown once again an hour later. She'd run back to the house to change her clothes before the dinner rush. As she was leaving the house someone was emerging from a white crossover in Connor's driveway. The brunette from the dock. She bent her upper body into the back seat and emerged with a Crock-Pot.

Maddy rolled her eyes. Apparently Connor had found something to do tonight after all.

CHAPTER 13

"Crab cakes on the fly!" Maddy called through the kitchen window.

A server had dropped a platter, leaving table five unfed and waiting. Maddy went to the table, assured them their meals were on the house, and went out to the deck to help the busboy with the recently vacated tables.

It was just into the dinner hour, and she was beginning to hit her stride. The staff was adjusting to her leadership, and she was feeling confident about the workings of the restaurant. She was beginning to enjoy the casual vibe with the country music and loud chatter.

On this Wednesday evening it was only

a half-full house, leaving her plenty of time to pitch in. She wiped down the nearest wooden table, vaguely aware of two women who'd been seated at table seventeen. The server had been sent on break.

Rather than pass the table to another server, she grabbed menus and approached the table. "Hi, welcome to the Landing." Her eyes connected with one of the women and her smile faltered.

It was the brunette she'd seen with Connor on the pier and again at his house yesterday with the Crock-Pot. Maddy's eyes went to the other woman, who was also familiar. The blonde. Ms. Yoga Pants.

At the same table. Together. Looking at her with curious eyes.

Maddy shored up her smile. "Um…Can I get you something to drink?"

"We'll just have water," Crock-Pot said.

Maddy dashed off to fetch their drinks. What in the world? Why were they here together? She had to be missing something.

A minute later Maddy delivered the

water. "Have you decided what you'd like, or do you need a few more minutes?"

"So you're Maddy...," Yoga Pants said.

Maddy eyed the woman. "Yes..."

Crock-Pot tucked her short hair behind her ears. "We're Connor's sisters." She began introductions.

His **sisters?**

One of them laughed, and Maddy realized she'd missed both their names.

"We've caught her off guard. He told us you rescued him from certain death."

"He's helpless when it comes to this place—I should know. I'm afraid it's my fault he got stuck with it."

Crock-Pot nodded toward Yoga Pants. "Lexie talked him into buying the restaurant a couple years ago. Then she bailed on him."

"I decided to further my education!" Lexie defended herself, clearly not for the first time.

"You seem to know your way around a kitchen," Crock-Pot said.

Maddy blinked. "I'm sorry, I missed your name."

"Tara. I'm the older of us girls."

Now that she was up close Maddy could see the resemblance to Connor. She had those brackets at the corners of her mouth when she smiled.

Lexie shared Connor's golden hair and gray eyes.

"There's a ten-year gap between Connor and me," Tara said. "He was so much trouble—or so we tell him—our parents waited ten years to try again."

"And a couple years later they went for one more," Lexie said.

"Because I was so delightful," Tara added.

"Well, it's nice to meet you both." She addressed Lexie. "You used to manage this place? Are you responsible for the menu? It's quite nice. I was pleasantly surprised."

"That was mostly Cheryl's doing, but I did hire the chef who created those brilliant dishes."

"And she fixed the place up," Tara said. "It was a real shack when Connor bought it. Then she ditched him to get her degree, and she's currently mooching off me."

"Excuse me." She addressed Maddy. "I'm her resident baby sitter."

"I'm just teasing," Tara said. "She's putting in her time."

Tara.

Maddy suddenly remembered the name in cursive letters on a package, accented with hearts. She wanted to plant her palm in the middle of her forehead.

"You're from Charlotte?" Tara asked Maddy. "You manage a restaurant there, I hear."

Connor had obviously shared some things with his sisters. Four eyes peered at her with curiosity. "Yes. I'm just here temporarily, getting the family beach cottage in order."

"We've met your grandmother," Lexie said. "She's so cute."

"She's in Boise at the moment, visiting friends."

"Good for her," Lexie said. "She seems like quite the character."

"Oh, she is," Maddy said.

"Well, I'm glad we got to meet you," Tara said. "We just wanted to pop in and see how things were going while we're in town."

"You don't live in Seahaven?" Maddy asked, forgetting for a moment the address on the package.

"No, Whiteville. Lexie and I came in for the night and are headed back after we eat."

"We didn't want Connor to be alone last night." Lexie bit her lip, her gaze drifting away.

Maddy had no idea what that meant, so she just nodded vaguely.

"It was really nice of you to help him out with the restaurant," Tara said. "He was running himself into the ground."

"Well, he needed a stand-in manager, and I had some time on my hands. I'm glad it worked out for both of us."

"Are you single, Maddy?" Lexie asked.

"Lexie." Tara nudged her sister and addressed Maddy. "Sorry. She's the impetuous one."

"Well, it was your idea to come check

her out."

A thump sounded under the table and Lexie jumped. "What? It was."

Heat flooded Maddy's face. "Connor's just a friend. Hardly even that. I don't think he likes me much, to tell you the truth. And that's just fine since I'll be headed back to Charlotte shortly."

The hostess sat a couple at the table next to them before Maddy could mention that the server was on break. Oh well, now was a good time to get back to work.

CHAPTER 14

Every year after June twelfth passed it felt as if a weight lifted off Connor's shoulders. Then, day by day, little by little, the weight returned. And by the time the day rolled around again it was just as difficult as it had been the year before.

Connor ran the caulk down the length of the window seam, then smoothed it out with his index finger. The sun was low in the sky, and a breeze blew across his deck, cooling his skin. A sea gull landed on the railing, studying him with marble-black eyes.

"No food for you. Get on with you, now."

The bird cocked its head.

Connor wiped the caulk on his old

T-shirt and continued the bead line. He was just smoothing it out when he heard a car pull up, followed by the sounds of car doors shutting and a young voice.

"Around back!" he called, but his voice was swallowed up by the wind and the crash of surf.

Lexie found him a moment later, niece on her hip and four-year-old nephew in tow. Logan caught sight of Connor and dashed ahead of Lexie, brown curls bouncing adorably.

"Uncle Connor, we're here! We're here!" The boy threw himself at Connor's legs.

The sea gull took flight.

Connor set down the caulk gun and ruffled Logan's hair with his clean hand. "I see that. How's my favorite nephew?"

"I brought my new dune buggy!" He held up the toy Connor had gotten him for his birthday, then dashed down the deck steps to the beach, his little legs working fast. "I'm gonna make a race track!"

"Don't you go past the dunes!" Lexie called.

"I won't!"

"He loves that thing." Lexie made herself at home on one of his Adirondack chairs, propping little Lily in the cradle of her elbow. The six-month-old held her own bottle and eyed Connor over her pudgy feet.

"Hi, baby girl. How ya been?" he asked.

Lily smiled at him around her bottle and continued drinking, her eyes steadfast on him.

Connor gave Lexie a wry look. "Baby-sitting tonight?"

"Thought I'd bring the munchkins over to keep you company."

His sisters had descended on his house only a couple days ago. He was still a little testy from that invasion.

"You guys ever think of calling?" He finished smoothing the line of caulk, feeling a prick of guilt for being cranky with her.

"What, am I interrupting your big Friday-night plans? Have you even eaten supper yet?"

"As a matter of fact, I have. I warmed up

Tara's stew."

She gave him a sideways look. "Any left?"

He rolled his eyes, going back to his caulking. "Help yourself."

But instead of going into the house she settled back in the chair, watching him.

He fixed a bump in the caulk and continued smoothing it, wiping his finger on his shirt when he was done.

"We stopped by the restaurant yesterday and met your friend Maddy."

He made a noncommittal sound, focused on his task.

"She's nice—and very pretty."

Connor pressed his lips together. "Don't you be getting any ideas. She doesn't even like me."

"Funny…She said the same thing about you."

He gave her a long look. "What'd you say to her? If you screw up this restaurant thing I'm not going to be happy. She's been a godsend, and if I have to go back to running it, I'm putting you in charge."

"Relax, we were just checking her out.

You'd mentioned her a few times—"

"My first mistake."

"—so we thought we'd see what all the fuss was about."

"There's no fuss. She works for me. Not interested. Period."

Lexie studied him until he felt heat crawling up his neck. A small part of him admitted that maybe that wasn't entirely true. Maybe she did intrigue him a little. But that was all.

"If you say so," Lexie said.

"I do." He grabbed the putty knife and scraped off a white flake of old paint he'd missed.

"Okay, so you're 'not interested' in Maddy"—she air-quoted the 'not interested' part. "That brings us back to my friend—the one with all the verys," she clarified before he could feign confusion. "I can give you her number, and I happen to know she's free this weekend and very eager to meet you."

He winced. Why had he agreed to go out with the woman? Maybe he could put it off yet again. He hated the thought of a blind date. So awkward.

"Don't try and get out of it," Lexie said. "I already told her you agreed to a date, and you'll hurt her feelings if you back out now. She's a very nice woman, and she doesn't deserve that."

Doggone it. Lexie was right. Anyway, wasn't he just thinking he needed to get on with his life?

Sometimes when his sisters were annoying, like now, he thought there were more than enough women in his life. Other times he remembered Annie and felt a hollow space inside he despaired of ever filling.

He wasn't a happy man—could hardly remember the last time he'd really laughed. He'd gotten accustomed to this gray existence. He'd been settling for a lesser life. But what if there was some-thing better for him? What if it was out there just waiting for him to wake up and reach for it?

An image of Maddy rose to his mind. The way she'd been a couple nights ago, darting around the restaurant, leading by example. Stopping to help a busboy when he got overwhelmed. When she'd caught sight of Connor at a table, her back stiffened a little. She gave him a tight smile and a little wave, but he was close enough he could see her eyes spark with irritation. No doubt she'd thought he was checking up on her. But he'd only been there for supper.

Those eyes hadn't been sparking on Tuesday when she'd stopped by the marina. They'd been soft and searching, and for the first time he'd noticed intriguing flecks of gold and green in them. He had the feeling there was much more about Maddy that he hadn't yet noticed.

He pushed away the thought. The woman didn't even like him. It bummed him out a little, but it was a fact. She wasn't his type anyway. Where Annie had been warm and carefree, Maddy was guarded and judgmental. He doubted he could find two more different women.

Lily babbled loudly, breaking into his thoughts.

"So will you call her?" Lexie said. "I kind

of told her you might."

He let loose of a sigh that seemed to come from his toes. "Sure, I guess." He had to start somewhere.

CHAPTER 15

Maddy spied Connor the next afternoon at the marina. She'd avoided this conversation for three days already and couldn't justify putting it off any longer. She worked her way down the boardwalk to the pier he was hosing off.

The afternoon sun blazed overhead from a clear blue sky, and a warm breeze toyed with her hair. She pushed it behind her ears.

There was the usual activity at the marina: a small boat coming in off the ocean, a dockhand gassing up another vessel. Working dockside, she'd become familiar with the sounds—the squeak of boats rubbing against the pier, the metal hardware pinging against masts, the distant hum of a motor. When she closed her eyes at night she still heard the sounds.

Connor was backing down the pier, waving the hose wand back and forth across the planks as he went. He wore a T-shirt that carried the marina logo, plus a pair of khaki shorts. His hair was pulled back into a ponytail, a few strands having come loose. A pair of tennis shoes completed the look.

She'd never been very good at eating crow. But lately, every time she thought of Connor, that feeling of regret and shame welled up inside.

"Hey there," she said when she'd drawn near.

Connor spun around, shutting off the flow of water. He pushed his sunglasses on top of his head. "Hey. How's it going? Everything okay at the restaurant?"

"Everything's fine. Running like clock-work, in fact."

She held out her peace offering—iced tea in a to-go cup that was already wet with condensation. "For you."

His brows rose and he gave her a brief puzzled look before taking the drink. He took a long sip through the straw. "Thanks. That hits the spot."

"It's a hot one today," she said inanely.

"It is. Darren take care of the plumbing issue?"

Maddy stuck her hands in her shorts pockets. "Yeah, he was great. Very fast and reasonably priced."

"Good, good." He nodded, and an awkward pause ensued. The hose dripped, water puddling at his feet. But he didn't seem to notice or care.

"I, uh, met your sisters the other day. They dropped by the restaurant."

"So I heard. A pair of busybodies, those girls."

Maddy thought about Lexie asking if she was single. It embarrassed her to think they might've also quizzed Connor about her. Especially given the way she'd treated him. He probably wanted to steer a wide path around her. If not for his crisis at the restaurant he would have done just that, no doubt.

"Listen, Connor...you have a minute? I hate to bother you at work, but our schedules kind of conflict."

Curiosity flashed in his eyes. "Sure. I have to move a boat down the bay. Come along?"

"Oh." She checked her watch. "How far is it?"

"Just down there." He pointed to the houses on the far end of the bay, maybe a half mile away. "We can walk back. Unless you need to be at the restaurant early today."

"No, that's fine." This would give them some privacy and ensure they weren't interrupted.

He wrapped up the hose, then she followed him to a small sailboat and he ushered her on board. She sat on the nearest bench. It was a nice vessel, shiny blue on the outside, crisp white on the inside. Comfortable, but not yacht-sized or as luxurious as a lot of the boats at the marina.

He set the tea in a cup holder and

loosened the ties from the cleats. The boat dipped as he came on board. He took a seat several feet away in the captain's chair and turned over the engine. The boat vibrated beneath her, and the steady hum of the engine filled her ears. He began moving it from its slip.

"The owners just got a new pier," he said over the wind as he navigated slowly into the empty bay. The boat rose and dipped on the small waves.

It had been a while since she'd been on the water. She hadn't realized she missed it until this very moment. "She's a beauty. I've never sailed before."

He tossed her a look, his escaped hair blowing across his face. "Is that right? I thought you'd be an old pro, coming in the summers like you did."

She lifted her shoulders. "No one in my family knew how. We only had a little fishing boat and a kayak. I took the kayak out a lot."

"We have kayaks at the marina. Come anytime and borrow one. But I'll have to take you sailing sometime—everyone should go at least once. There's nothing like it."

He was being much nicer than she deserved. Guilt pricked hard. "That's awfully nice of you. Especially given the way I've treated you."

He turned a curious look on her, holding her gaze for a long, intense moment.

"Listen, Connor." Maddy felt heat rising into her face as the words she needed to say thickened her throat. "I'm afraid we got off on the wrong foot, and that's my fault. I—I think I prejudged you. I know you didn't bring my sisters and me here under false pretenses. It seems I'm not terribly discerning when it comes to reading people. Men. I thought you were—" She pressed her lips together. If she wasn't careful she'd make it worse.

"You thought I was...?"

She sighed. "Well, you look...That is, I made some unfair assumptions based on your whole...beachboy vibe, I guess."

He quirked a brow. "Beachboy vibe?"

"And I noticed you coming home at all hours of the night, and then of course there were all the women."

He laughed. "All the women?"

She ran her sweaty palms down her shorts as her face went hot. "Your sisters. I didn't realize who they were until—"

"They showed up at the restaurant." He shook his head, still chuckling.

It was a nice deep laugh, the smile lighting up his whole face. He took a sip of tea.

"You can stop laughing now," she said, only partly teasing.

"All the women...," he repeated. "If you only knew how long it's been since I've even been on a date. Years, Maddy. Years."

He turned forward, navigating around an incoming boat, the remnants of that laugh lingering around his mouth.

She tried to get a better read on him, but he'd put his sunglasses back down. She let him focus on his driving until the boat had passed and he'd settled back in the seat.

"Thing is," she continued, "I recently had a bad experience with a man, and it's thrown me a little off my game. I guess you got painted with the same brush, and that wasn't fair of me. So I'm sorry."

He studied her thoughtfully as the boat sliced slowly through the open waters. "I think the judgment might've gone both ways, Maddy. I'm sorry as well. I was a little tough on you."

His lips tipped in a grin as a strand of hair blew across his face, and she couldn't help but smile back.

It was only a few more minutes before they were pulling along-side a pier that jutted out into the grassy shallows. He maneuvered the boat expertly into the boat lift and cut the engine.

When he helped her out onto the pier, his hand was warm and rough around hers. She stood off to the side holding his drink as he spun the metal wheel. It clicked and clanked as it turned, lifting the boat from the water.

"Okay, that should do it," he said.

"Do you have to stop in and let them know it's here?"

"No, they're not home right now."

He led her up the grassy slope of their yard and out to the quiet road that ran along the shore. They began walking toward the marina at a brisk pace. Tall trees cast long shadows over the pavement, offering a welcome reprieve from the hot sun.

"So..." He tossed a look her way. "A bad experience with some guy, huh?" He'd perched his sunglasses on his head again. His eyes looked silver in the shadows.

"You could say that. It's over now, but it was hard, and I'm still a little spooked."

"How long did you date?"

"About six months. We worked together at the restaurant."

"That can be a recipe for disaster—no pun intended. Do you still work together?"

She could brush off his question or she could be forthright. She hadn't even told her sisters, but somehow she felt she could tell Connor. Felt he'd understand in some way that her sisters wouldn't. Although now that she knew what Emma was going through with Ethan, she might have to rethink that.

"Didn't mean to pry. You don't have to talk about it if you don't want to."

"It's all right. I managed the front of the house at Pirouette. Nick was the beverage manager. Our general manager was set to retire, and I was up for the promotion. Honestly, it was just kind of assumed—by everyone, I think, not just me—that I'd get the job. I worked hard. That place was my entire life."

The neighborhood was silent except for the nattering of a nearby squirrel and the bits of gravel crunching under their feet.

"Nick and I started dating around Thanksgiving. He pursued me relentlessly for weeks, but I was...reluctant. Not on account of him specifically—he seemed nice enough—but it's my nature to be a little guarded. I don't let people in easily." She tossed him a smile. "You might've noticed."

The one he returned made her toes curl in her sandals.

"Anyway, after a while I started trusting him. I let him in, let down all my barriers and allowed myself to fall in love. At least I thought I was in love. I'm not so sure now." She shook her head. "I don't know why I'm telling you all this. I haven't even told my sisters this much."

"Maybe you just needed to get it off your chest. It won't go any further."

She believed that. The Connor she was only beginning to see wasn't the type to gossip behind someone's back. He'd listened thoughtfully so far, and it felt good to be heard. She thought of Emma hiding her separation. And Nora, keeping her pregnancy under wraps. What drove the Monroe sisters to keep secrets from each other? Something to ponder... another day.

"So...," she continued. "Fast-forward to May twenty-ninth. My relationship with Nick had been exclusive for months and had grown quite serious. The GM was set to retire in June, and I walked into the GM's office to find Nick and the owner, Evangeline, talking about me. He was running me down, and it was obvious from what she was saying that she was promoting Nick instead of me. After hearing this, while I stood mute and in shock, he kissed her. It was quite the intimate embrace, let me tell you. Clearly not their first."

The image made her chest feel hollow all over again. But was that heartbreak she was feeling? Or simple disillusionment?

He gave her a sad smile. "I'm sorry, Maddy. That must've been very hurtful."

"Evangeline didn't even know we'd been dating, because Nick had convinced me to keep our relationship on the down low at work. I'm pretty sure he was only playing me, playing Evangeline, the whole time."

"May twenty-ninth...That was the day I called about your grandma."

"Right. That's why I didn't answer your calls. I kind of fell apart after what I saw. I wanted to hide from the world. I was so...hurt and angry."

"Who wouldn't be?" He drained the rest of his tea, making a slurping sound as he reached the bottom.

"By the time my best friend, Holly,

dragged me from my sleep-drugged coma, you'd already left quite a few messages."

"Did you confront that tool you were dating? Quit your job?"

Maddy shoved her hands in her pockets. "Not really. They saw me, realized what I'd seen and heard. I left and haven't spoken with either of them since."

"Man. He got off way too easily. Want me to beat him up for you?" He glanced at her, looking half serious.

Maddy gave him a wan smile. "I'm not sure which was more hurtful—the way he stabbed me in the back professionally or betrayed me personally. The fact that it all seemed so premeditated, that I was blind to it, is what's stuck with me the most. It's made me really unsure of myself."

"I get that." His voice was low and rumbly. "It's one thing to distrust others, but when you can't trust yourself, it throws everything into question."

She glanced at him, then fell into his warm gaze, feeling wonderfully understood. "Exactly."

He brushed his hair back. "Listen, Maddy, we've all been mistaken about people a time or two. It sounds like this Nick was a real con artist. And that's on him, not on you."

"That's exactly what Holly says."

"That doesn't make it any less hurtful, I know. But something I've always hung on to...When I can't trust others and I can't trust myself, I can always trust God. He'll work it all out, you know?"

"Yeah. I think I lost sight of that for a while."

She'd left God in the dust quite some time ago, in fact. She'd been so busy trying to prove herself at work. And then Nick came along, and he was yet another distraction.

"Don't beat yourself up, Maddy. God's still right where you left Him."

The thought washed over Maddy like a cool waft of water on a hot summer day. Connor was right. She gave him a sideways glance, wondering, not for the first time just who this man was. Sometimes people were not at all who you thought they were. But she was starting to see that sometimes this was a good thing.

Their brisk pace had slowed to a comfortable stroll as they continued along Bayview Drive. Connor felt Maddy's eyes on him, and heat rose on the back of his neck as the moment lengthened.

Finally he returned the look. "What? Why are you looking at me like that?"

She squinted thoughtfully, tilting her head. "I don't know. I've only known you a couple weeks now, and everything I thought I knew about you was wrong."

He lifted a shoulder. "I'm no big mystery. Pretty ordinary, really."

"Your sisters don't seem to think so."

His sisters again. He rolled his eyes. "My sisters are little pests."

Maddy smiled, her eyes coming alive. "That's what little sisters are supposed to be. I should know—I am one."

"They're needy little suckers, and they butt in all the time. They hover like mother hens—especially since I lost Annie."

He winced. Now why had he gone and said that?

"Annie?"

"My wife. Late wife." Well, now that he'd gone and spilled the beans..."This week was the third anniversary of her death, so it's been a little rough. You might've noticed I was distracted when you came by my office the other day."

Maddy's eyes softened. "I'm so sorry. That's what your sisters meant when they said they didn't want you to be alone this week."

He gave a wry grin. "Exactly how long was this conversation between you and my sisters?"

"Not long at all. They were only explaining why they were in town the other day. You don't have to talk about it. I just— I'm trying to get a picture of who you are, I guess. Now that I know you aren't a beach-bumming womanizer."

A laugh rumbled out, foreign and pleasant, surprising him. That was twice now. "Well, I can see I have nowhere to go but up."

Her sheepish smile charmed him. "The bar was pretty low, I'll admit."

They shared a smile, and his gaze roved quickly over her face. He took in the pleasant planes, noticing her small shapely nose, her sun-kissed skin, and the generous curve of her mouth.

He pulled his eyes away, following a spotted plover that hopped across the street. It flew off at their approach.

He was a private person. He'd never worn his emotions on his sleeve, but he didn't think Maddy did either, and she'd been vulnerable with him. He could share a small piece of himself.

"Annie and I were married for ten years. She passed away suddenly three years ago—an aneurysm."

"I'm sorry. I can only imagine how hard that must've been."

Maddy had obviously suffered regrets about things she'd done—falling in love, trusting someone unworthy of that trust. He wondered if she knew that regrets from things left undone could be just as painful. Maybe even more so.

"My dad died suddenly when I was twelve." Then she quickly added, "I know it's not the same thing."

"Both are huge losses. That's pretty young to lose a father."

"It was a shock—hard on all of us."

Their stories weren't similar, not really. But they had some things in common. They both knew love could be a wonderful thing, and that losing it could shatter a person in two.

"Whew," she said, smiling at him. "This is some heavy conversation we're having today."

"You're easy to talk to," he said, suddenly surprised at how much he meant that.

"Tell me about your family," she said. "Your parents. Are they still living?"

"Yes. My folks are great. My dad pastors a church in Jacksonville, Florida, and my mom is a social worker, though she's planning to retire soon. We talk or FaceTime regularly, and they come here a few times a year at least."

"How did you and your sisters end up in

North Carolina?"

"This is where we grew up. Dad pastored a church in Whiteville, and Mom stayed home with us. Well, she worked part-time. We were blessed. How about you? I only know a little about your family from your grandma."

"Right. Well, we were raised in Charlotte—spent our summers here, of course, at the beach cottage. My mom stayed at home with us, and my dad was a salesman. He traveled around the state. During the summers we'd come to Seahaven, and he'd travel from here. We hated that he was gone so much, but the flexibility was nice."

"That must've been great, having summers here."

"It was." Her smile fell, and her eyes dimmed until there was something wistful in her expression. "Until it wasn't."

Her grandma had made many references to their family dysfunction, but she'd carefully left out all the details. He'd prayed for the sisters before he'd even set eyes on them. He'd been curious, but now he suddenly wanted to know everything about Maddy, including her family history.

"I'm sorry," he said. "Your grandmother mentioned a splinter in the family."

"That's putting it mildly. The last summer here was a total disaster. It blew our family to smithereens, and I'm afraid we still haven't recovered. I'm not sure we ever will."

He gave that a moment's thought. "Maybe this summer will be a healing one."

"Well, it hasn't gotten off to the best start. Neither of my sisters is willing to give an inch."

"That can always change."

She seemed to fumble with her thoughts. Maybe having trouble putting them into words.

"I don't know how," she said finally.

"Well...our God is a God of miracles. He set the stars in the sky, created every living being, and parted the sea." He nudged her arm. "It's not the how, Maddy. It's the Who."

Her eyes searched his until heat began to climb his neck again. Had he been out of line? Heaven knew he didn't have it all figured out. He couldn't even get his own life together. Who was he to give advice?

She was shaking her head, a befuddled expression on her face. "Who **are** you, Connor Sullivan?"

He chuckled, rubbing the back of his neck. "Aw, I'm just a man, Maddy. Nothing special."

She studied him for a moment longer. "I'm not so sure about that."

Her words warmed him from the inside out. He felt soft inside in a way he hadn't felt in a long time. In a way he'd never thought he'd feel again.

When his feet hit gravel he realized they'd already reached the marina parking lot. How had that happened? It seemed as if they'd only just stepped from the boat.

He found himself reluctant to part ways with her. There was still so much he wanted to ask about her and her life.

But they both needed to get to work.

She came to a stop as they neared the turnoff for the restaurant and turned his way. Her softening toward him was evident in her relaxed expression, in her open posture. He'd somehow won her over in the last fifteen minutes, and it made him feel ridiculously heady.

"This has been nice," she said, those doe-brown eyes fixed on him. "Just talking."

He couldn't stop the smile from blooming on his face. "It has."

"Again, Connor, I'm sorry for misjudging you. I hope you can forgive me and that maybe we can be…friends?"

"Water under the bridge. And I'd love that, being your friend. Maybe I can take you out on the water again soon and actually put up the sails this time." The offer rolled off his tongue before he'd had a chance to mull it over. Even so he felt no regret. Only hope.

"I think I'd like that." She glanced at her watch.

"You'd better get in there before a chef

quits or a toilet overflows."

The corner of her mouth ticked up. "You never know what's going to happen, do you? I'll see you later, Connor."

"See you, Maddy."

He was walking down the boardwalk with a silly grin on his face when she called his name.

He turned, walking backward.

Her long hair whipped in the wind, and the smile on her face made his heart stutter. She gestured at the restaurant. "Feel free to stop in anytime. You know, if you feel the random urge to bus a table or something."

He gave his chin a lift as he raised his hand in a wave. He just might do that.

CHAPTER 16

July 12, twenty years ago

The summer was turning out much better than Maddy had expected. It seemed Jonathan had to work a lot, leaving Emma free to hang out with her.

They'd taken the ferry to Bald Head Island and tooled around on a golf cart for an entire day. They'd taken the kayaks out in the bay and around Pelican Point. And they'd made many ice-cream runs, even though Emma often complained that she'd never fit into her wedding gown.

Maddy also got to help with the planning of the wedding. It was going to be held in January at their church in Charlotte. That

Emma trusted Maddy's input made her feel all grown up. Mama, Gram, and Nora pitched in also, the five of them often huddling over a kitchen table that was filled with invitation samples, bridal magazines, and menus. Maddy couldn't believe all the minute details involved in planning a single day. If she ever got married, she was going to elope! Emma hoped to get the bulk of the planning done over the summer so she could focus on school once August came.

Jonathan seemed only too happy to let them handle the plans, coming around every so often to drop a kiss on Emma's head and applaud her decisions. His job was planning the honeymoon, and he was keeping all those details to himself.

The only negative was that the busyness was making the summer pass too quickly. And as much as Maddy was enjoying her time with Emma, it seemed as if the family was all too often going in opposite directions.

Daddy, of course, traveled a lot, although he made time for each of them when he was home. The only time they were all together seemed to be Sundays, when they attended Gram's church. Nora also seemed scarce, although to be fair, much of Maddy's activities with Emma involved the sun, and ice-cream outings didn't interest Nora, as she'd never had much of a sweet tooth. Was it the wedding planning, Maddy wondered, that had thrown everything off? Or the presence of an outsider in the house?

Maddy shook the thought away and stared out the window as Emma drove them down the road toward the hair salon. Maddy was getting her hair cut today. She'd grown it out long, but it was a pain, always blowing in her face. And ponytails made her head hurt. She'd found a picture of a woman with a long bob in one of Emma's magazines and thought that might do the trick.

The picture! Maddy stuck her hands into her pockets, but they came out empty.

"What's wrong?" Emma asked from the driver's seat.

"I forgot the picture."

"You can just describe it, can't you? We're almost there."

"Please, can we go back? I don't want her to get it wrong. What if she messes it up?"

"Maddy."

"We're early anyway. We'll still be on time."

Emma sighed. "Fine." She slowed the car and turned around in the bicycle shop's parking lot.

A few minutes later they were back home. Emma pulled the car along the curb and Maddy jumped out.

The house was quiet except for the strains of jazz Jonathan always listened to while he worked. He called it big band music and was always making them listen to songs that had been popular way back in Gram's day.

As seemed to be the case recently, everyone was otherwise occupied today. Gram and Mama had gone grocery shopping, and Daddy was traveling. Jonathan was working in his bedroom, and Nora was undoubtedly lounging in the shade somewhere with her nose in a book.

Maddy took the stairs quickly, not wanting to irritate Emma further by dillydallying. She'd left the picture in the bathroom where she'd been trying to imagine what she'd look like with eight inches lopped off. She was a little nervous—she didn't want to look even younger.

She slid past her own bedroom door, then into the bathroom. There it was, by the sink. She snatched it up and turned just as a familiar lilt of laughter sounded over the strains of a saxophone.

Maddy paused outside the bathroom door, looking farther down the hall to Jonathan's door, which was partly open.

"So I hear you're the favorite grandchild." Jonathan's tone was teasing.

"Not true. Gram is very fair—she spoils us all."

"I've been a witness to that, but from what I've seen I think your dad is just as guilty of that as your grandmother."

"Maybe so. Mama certainly seems to think so."

"You have a nice family, Nora. I envy you the siblings. I always wanted brothers."

"Not sisters?"

He chuckled. "Um, no."

Nora emitted a giggle.

Maddy frowned at the doorway. She'd never in all her life heard that sound come from Nora. She edged closer to the door, peeking in carefully. She saw Nora's legs—she was stretched out on her stomach on the bed, directly across from where Jonathan usually worked at his desk. The singer continued warbling the melody.

The conversation had moved on to their parents, and Nora was talking. "They argue sometimes—mostly about Daddy's traveling. I wish Mama would just accept it. I mean, we miss him when he's gone, but when he's here, he's really here, you know? She could do a lot worse."

"Emma said she harps on him a lot. But at least they're still together." There was a warmth in Jonathan's voice that she'd only heard when he talked to Emma.

Maddy's stomach twisted. It didn't

sound as if Jonathan was working at all. And it didn't seem right that Nora was alone with him in his bedroom, on his bed no less. On the other hand, he and Emma were obviously in love, and Nora would soon be his sister-in-law.

The subject soon changed to books, and Maddy listened a few minutes longer until Jonathan mentioned he was getting hungry. At the squeak of the mattress, Maddy turned and padded quickly down the stairs, not wanting to get caught spying.

"What on earth took you so long?" Emma asked as soon as Maddy had sunk into the bucket seat beside her.

Maddy reached for her seat belt and stretched it across her body, clicking it into place. "I, um, couldn't find it at first."

But as Emma put the car in gear and pulled away from the beach cottage, Maddy had a terrible feeling she'd found a lot more than she'd been looking for.

CHAPTER 17

Present day

Maddy slipped through the back door and stepped out onto the deck. She squinted against the sun, which glared blindingly on the water.

Emma was already on the deck basking in its light, her short hair springing in all directions. She wore a white V-necked T-shirt and pink pajama shorts that were scattered with little cupcakes.

She tossed a fond smile over her shoulder, her eyes going to half-moons. "Happy birthday, little sis!"

"Let a girl wake up before you hit her with all that energy." Maddy took a sip of hot coffee before sinking into the chair next to Emma's and adjusting the robe over her bare legs.

"How's it feel to be another year older?" Emma said.

Thirty-two. How had that happened? "Not altogether wonderful, if I'm honest."

Especially if she took stock of the current state of her professional and personal lives. But for some reason her thoughts slid instead to Connor and the nice conversation they'd had the day before.

"You're a virtual baby," Emma scoffed. "Still young and fresh, no signs of aging. Still turning heads. Talk to me again after you hit the big 4-O, turn invisible, and have to diet for a month to lose a single pound."

Maddy gave her a wan smile. The only signs of aging Maddy could see on her sister were laugh lines. Those didn't even count.

"You're still gorgeous, Emma. I'll bet you turn heads all the time."

"Well, I was all but invisible to Ethan, I

know that much." Emma waved away her own words. "Enough about me. It's your birthday! What are we doing to celebrate today?"

The door creaked open, and Nora slipped out onto the deck, already made up. She'd paired her white shorts with a bright purple top that complemented her auburn hair and fair skin.

Pippy stood, her tag jingling as she shook, then she approached Nora.

"Good morning," Nora said, stooping to sweep Pippy into her arms. "Happy birthday, Maddy."

"Thanks."

"Did you see the package that arrived yesterday?" Nora asked.

"It was from Holly. She sent me a basket of beach stuff to 'remind me to relax.' "

"Sounds like she knows you all too well." Emma's gaze shifted to Nora. "We were just discussing birthday plans. Let's take the day off. We could go to Bald Head Island or go kayaking or whatever you want. It's your day."

"I think I want to go to church," Maddy

said impulsively.

Some of the things Connor said had hit home. She'd been hit-or-miss with church at home on account of her work hours, and the sisters hadn't attended at all since they'd come to Seahaven.

"Okay," Emma said. "I'll go with you."

"I guess I will too," Nora said. "It's probably the same people we knew from before. I wonder if they still have that old organ—and the woman who played it—the one with the white granny fro."

"Oh, she was ancient then," Emma said. "She can't still be alive, can she? Remember that usher with the glass eye? It always felt like he was staring me down."

"I was so scared of him when I was little." Maddy sipped her coffee, trying to wake up. "Then when I was five or six he helped me tie my shoe, and I realized he wasn't so bad after all."

Nora scratched Pippy behind the ears, and the dog's eyes all but glazed over. "Gram dated him for a while."

Emma gasped. "She did not."

"I didn't think Gram dated anyone after

Gramps passed," Maddy said.

"I don't think she dated much," Nora said. "But I know she went out with him at least once—she mentioned it to me."

"She and Gramps had the perfect relationship," Emma said with a sigh. "I don't think anyone else could live up to him."

Nora humphed. "There's no such thing as a perfect relationship."

Maddy lifted her mug in a mock toast. "Hear, hear!"

"What do you want to do after church?" Emma asked.

"You know what?" Maddy said. "At the risk of sounding like an old fuddy-dud, I think I'd just like to relax and take a nap. These late hours at the restaurant are getting to me."

"You should do that," Nora said. "I think I might go for a jog on the beach, if it's not too hot when we get back."

"You? Jog?" Emma smirked. "Isn't golf or tennis more your style?"

Nora ignored the scorn in Emma's tone. "I like the endorphins it gives me. I can take Pippy along, if you don't mind. She might like it. She seems like the adventurous sort."

"She's never gone running before," Emma said. "She might tire easily."

"I don't run very far or very fast. Just a mile or so."

"Suit yourself. Just keep her on a leash, or you'll be the one doing the chasing." Emma's gaze drifted to Maddy. "So how about if we take you out to supper tonight? We can dress up and make a night of it."

"That sounds like fun."

"Where do you want to go?"

Maddy had been wanting to experience Sullivan's Landing as a customer, but hadn't had the time. Maybe this would be the perfect opportunity.

"Not the Landing," Nora said firmly. "It's your day off."

"For heaven's sakes, no," Emma said. "No work today. How about that fancy restaurant on the other side of the bay— the Harbormaster? They filmed a scene from that Nicholas Sparks movie there, and I heard someone raving about it at the coffee shop."

"It's awfully expensive," Maddy said. She'd looked up the menu online. It was important to know the local competition —even though the Harbormaster was above the Landing's pay grade.

"Oh, it's a special occasion." Emma raised a saucy brow. "Besides, Nora can afford it. Can't you, Nora?"

Maddy gave Emma a look. She wished they'd get beyond these snarky comments.

Nora's lips thinned, and her mug clattered on the glass table as she set it down. "Of course. Wherever you want to go, Maddy. It's your birthday, after all."

That evening a pretty hostess led the sisters across the Harbormaster's dining room. The restaurant wasn't yet crowded as they'd skipped lunch and decided on an early supper.

The table for four was swathed in white linen, impeccably set with sparkling silverware, and situated by a glass wall overlooking the quiet bay. Soft music played in the background, mingling with the low hum of conversations. The savory smell of grilled steak hung in the air.

Chilled by the air-conditioning, Maddy slipped on her light-weight sweater as she settled into the leather chair. She let her gaze rove objectively around the front of house. The building was old but recently refurbished. They'd kept the scarred, wide-planked floor, but it was scrupulously clean. Old brick walls gave the room added character, and antique chandeliers dangled from the lofted ceiling, giving off a dim glow that made the space feel intimate.

The staff seemed efficient and friendly. They wore white oxford shirts and black trousers. The long-haired servers wore theirs back in a bun or ponytail, and they were all clean-cut and well-groomed.

"It's really charming, huh?" Emma said.

"Definitely a different vibe from the Landing," Maddy said. "More formal and sedate."

"Well, I for one can't wait to try the crab cake appetizer. And we have to save room for dessert," Emma said. "I want to try out their pastries. They have a sampler."

"I'm sure they don't compare with yours." Maddy opened her menu and winced at the prices. They were even higher than she remembered.

Nora was perusing the menu too, twin frown lines etched between her brows. She bit into her bottom lip.

"There's a landlubbers section at the bottom," Maddy told Nora. She'd never cared much for seafood.

Nora's frown disappeared, and she gave Maddy a smile as she closed the menu. "I saw that. The chopped steak looks really good. I think I'll get that. What are you getting?"

"That's just a glorified hamburger," Emma said. "Did you see the coffee-crusted filet mignon? I'll bet it's to die for."

"That's too heavy for me." Nora straightened the silverware. "I snacked a bit this afternoon."

The server came by and took drink orders. Emma and Maddy ordered one of their specialty teas, and Nora stuck with water.

When the server left, Maddy's gaze drifted to movement beyond Emma's shoulder, focusing on a man several tables away. She recognized Connor's profile, even though he was clean-shaven, and his hair was slicked back in a style she hadn't seen on him before. He wore a gray plaid button-down shirt and khakis, another first.

Across the flickering candlelight from him was an attractive woman with a long brown bob and sideswept bangs. Her features were small and dainty, her halter-style black dress complementing her tanned, slender shoulders.

The woman laughed at something Connor said and brushed her bangs to the side in a feminine gesture that for some reason gave Maddy a pang of jealousy.

No, not jealousy. Confusion. They were obviously on a date. And hadn't Connor told her just yesterday that he hadn't been on a date in years? What was up with that? Why would he lie to her?

She'd only known him a couple weeks,

but he'd seemed so genuine when they were talking. On the other hand, she knew better than to trust her own intuition. He could be a complete con artist for all she knew.

"Did you hear me, Maddy? What are you looking at?" Emma turned and looked over her shoulder.

Maddy took a sip of the tea the server had apparently brought while she'd been distracted.

She looked up in time to see that Emma had caught Connor's attention. Too far away to engage in conversation, they all exchanged waves.

Maddy froze as Connor's eyes connected with hers. Some emotion flickered on his face. Guilt? Or maybe just chagrin at having been caught in a lie?

Maddy gave him a stiff smile and turned her attention to her sisters. She made an effort to engage in conversation about the house and the needed repairs.

When the conversation dragged on, Maddy turned her thoughts to Gram's overgrown flower beds. She had big plans to restore them to their former glory. She would do a thorough weeding, thin out the perennials, prune the rosebushes. She wanted to add some colorful annuals too. Some red zinnias and yellow lantanas for the sunny spots. Pink and white impatiens for the shaded areas.

The server returned, took their orders, and scurried back to the kitchen. For the next while Maddy made sure to keep her eyes away from the table behind Emma. It was harder than she wanted to admit.

She didn't know why the situation upset her at all. Maybe because she'd believed him and he'd fooled her. She shook her head. Would she ever learn? She should just give up men and become a nun. Too bad she wasn't Catholic.

She was too caught up in her thoughts to notice Connor's approach.

He appeared at their table, towering over them, a spicy scent wafting around her. "Hello, ladies. Fancy meeting you here."

"**Fancy** is the perfect word," Emma said. "This place is beautiful."

He turned his attention to Maddy, his

eyes searching hers. "Hi there."

She hated the way her heart stuttered at his attention. She offered a strained smile. "Hello."

"It's Maddy's birthday today," Nora said. "We're out celebrating."

"She's thirty-two," Emma added.

Connor's brows rose as his eyes slid to Maddy, searching. "Is that right?"

"Mmm." Maddy straightened her silverware.

"Well, happy birthday, Maddy. I hope you're having a great day."

"So far, so good."

"I also wanted to let you know I'd be happy to help out on the house repairs. I'd started painting the exterior before your arrival but got sidetracked by the restaurant. Now that Maddy's freed up my schedule, I have some time on my hands."

"That'd be great," Emma said.

"Thank you," Nora said.

"We were just lamenting our lack of handyman skills," Emma added.

The server approached with their

appetizer, and Connor stepped back to give her room. "Well, I see my friend is headed back to our table. I'll let you ladies get on with your celebration. Just wanted to stop over and say hi. Have a nice supper."

Maddy made room on the table for the large oval plate. Three crab cakes were artfully arranged in a puddle of yellow sauce and topped with sprigs of parsley. A fan of lemon wedges completed the presentation.

"Ooh, look at those," Emma said. "They look scrumptious."

Savory smells wafted her way, but Maddy's appetite was gone.

"You can have mine." Nora scooped up a cake and set it on Maddy's plate. "I've never been a big fan."

"Thanks." Maddy dug into the crab cake and tried to appreciate the blend of flavors. It was moist and perfectly seasoned, and the sauce complemented the crab flavor.

"Mmm." Emma's eyes were closed as she chewed. "So good."

"It's a relief to have the house officially cleaned out," Maddy said, her mind still on that conversation with Connor. "Hopefully the repairs won't take us long."

"Wishful thinking," Nora said. "Connor will only have so much time. We'll have to muddle our way through most of it. Have you noticed that the porch is lopsided? Any idea what to do about that?"

"There's always YouTube," Emma said. "You'd be surprised what you can learn just by watching videos."

Maddy's gaze flickered over her shoulder to Connor's table. The woman was talking, her fingers clasped loosely on the table. Connor leaned forward on his elbows, gaze focused, listening intently.

Maddy's heart gave a heavy thump. He affected her, and she didn't like it. She didn't realize until now how many times she'd thought of him since they'd talked yesterday. How many times she'd repeated his words in her mind. How many times she'd pictured that bracketed smile and those warm gray eyes, trained so steadily on hers.

She'd thought he listened closely because he wanted to know more about her. Now she saw he was just a good listener, period. It was his nature to make other people feel interesting and captivating.

Yes, that was it. For a few minutes yesterday she'd felt captivating. And she hadn't felt that way in a long time. Nick had been attentive at first, but less so as their relationship progressed. Looking back, his attentiveness had probably been a big act.

She finished her crab cake, hardly even tasting it. Emma had finished hers too and was scraping up the last of the sauce from her plate.

"You can have the other one," Maddy said.

"No, it's all yours, birthday girl."

"Really," Maddy said. "I have a big meal coming, and if we're doing dessert, I'm going to have to stop now."

Emma gave a cheeky smile. "Well, we can't let it go waste, now can we? That'd be a crime."

The waitress appeared at their table, a

bottle of champagne in her hands. "Ladies, a bottle of Dom Perignon, our finest champagne."

"No, thank you," Nora said. "We're fine."

"It's actually a gift—from the gentleman." She gestured toward Connor.

He was wrapped up in conversation with his date and didn't notice their attention.

"Well, isn't that nice?" Emma said as the server proceeded to fill Nora's glass.

Maddy winced, thinking of Nora's pregnancy. She shouldn't be drinking even if she was only barely pregnant. Surely she knew that; it hadn't been that long since she was pregnant with Chloe. Maybe she wasn't actually planning to drink it.

Emma waved the server off her glass. "None for me, thank you."

Emma didn't drink at all, and though Maddy rarely indulged, she allowed the server to fill her glass halfway. She didn't want to be rude. It had been a gift in her honor, after all.

She caught Connor's eye just then and raised her glass, giving him a nod. Her sisters waved their thanks.

Nora lifted her glass in a toast. "To Maddy—another year of success and prosperity and all the best life has to offer."

"Hear, hear," Emma said, raising her tea.

Success and prosperity. Those things were starting to seem empty. In her heart of hearts she wanted someone special to share her life with. And yet, romantic relationships were unpredictable and ultimately disappointing. It was a paradox she hadn't yet figured out how to resolve.

They clinked glasses, and Maddy took a sip of the champagne. Its effervescence made her eyes water, and the pungent flavor was quickly lost on her as she watched Nora lift the glass to her lips and take a sip.

"Are you sure you want that?" Maddy asked.

"Of course," Nora said. "Why wouldn't I? Do you have any idea how much this stuff costs?"

"It's just—" Maddy's eyes toggled to Emma and, finding no help there, back to Nora. "I thought you didn't care for champagne, that's all."

"It's not my favorite, but I'm not going to turn away a gift. What do you think of it?"

"It's good." Maddy's stomach tightened as she watched Nora take another sip. "Kind of fruity, I think, but I'm no expert."

"It is fruity. A little smoky too. Very nice."

Over an hour later Maddy took her last bite of raspberry cheesecake and dabbed her mouth with the linen. The service had been spot-on and the food delicious, from her perfectly seasoned salmon to the delightful sweet potato casserole. The chef at Harbormaster knew his business.

Nora had drunk a whole glass of champagne. Before her sister had a chance to refill her glass, Maddy asked the server to recork the bottle so they could take it home.

Connor and his date had left as the sisters were served their desserts. He merely waved good-bye, then placed his hand at the small of the woman's back as he'd ushered her from the restaurant.

"I'm stuffed," Emma said. "The pastries

were delicious."

"Which was your favorite?" Maddy asked.

"The apple turnover, I think. Although the raspberry one was really unique."

"I liked the chocolate," Nora said.

"Me too," Maddy said. "But I liked the cheesecake best of all." It had come with a single flickering candle, which she pretended to make a wish on.

The server stopped by the table, making sure desserts had been perfect. She left the bill folder and recorked champagne on the table and left with their empty plates.

Nora opened the bill folder and reached into her purse. She'd seemed a little off tonight. Quiet. Maybe it was the pregnancy hormones.

Emma set her napkin on the table and reapplied her lip gloss. "Expensive, but worth every penny. Of course, that's easy for me to say since I'm not picking up the tab."

"It really was delicious," Maddy said. "Thank you, Nora, for the meal."

"Of course. I'm glad you enjoyed it." Nora stuck her credit card in the bill folder, and the server snapped it up almost immediately.

Emma checked her watch. "It's still early. Do you want to do anything else?"

"I'm so full I can hardly move," Maddy said.

Emma put her hand on her stomach. "I'm right there with you. I ate way too much."

"We still have almost two hours of daylight left. I wouldn't mind getting some work done on the house."

"But it's your birthday!" Emma said. "We should do something fun."

"It's Sunday night," Maddy said. "The town's pretty much shut down. Besides, the sooner we get the house done, the sooner we can all go back to our lives, right?"

She balked at her own words. What life? She had no job, no boyfriend waiting for her. Only an empty apartment.

"That's true, I guess." Emma probably wasn't eager to get back to her problematic relationship with Ethan.

Nora, who hadn't weighed in, was the only one who really had a life to get back to, but she seemed in no hurry either.

They decided they'd do some of the smaller jobs around the house tonight and save the painting for later.

The server approached the table and set the bill folder down by Nora and spoke in a hushed voice. "Um, I'm sorry, ma'am, but the credit card wouldn't go through."

"Oh no." Nora pulled out her purse and removed her wallet. "I'll have to call home later and see what's going on. Maybe there was a fraudulent charge."

"I hate when that happens," Maddy said, trying to smooth things over. "Your card gets canceled abruptly, and then you have to change all your auto-pay bills over to the new card. Such a hassle."

"Oh dear." Nora was visibly rattled. "I only brought the one card on this trip. And I don't have enough cash on me."

"No worries." Maddy reached for her purse. "I'll get it."

"You will not," Emma said. "It's your

birthday. I've got this."

"I'm so sorry," Nora said, her creamy skin now mottled with pink. "I can't believe this is happening."

The server hovered awkwardly, waiting for Emma to withdraw her credit card.

Maddy thought it odd that Nora had only the one card with her. Even she traveled with three credit cards, and she hardly had Nora's amassed wealth.

Other things had tweaked her curiosity lately too. Nora, who normally enjoyed life's finest, was buying a lot of generics at the grocery. Her contact with home had been infrequent. Maddy overheard her on the phone with Chloe sometimes, but she hadn't noticed any calls between her and Jonathan at all. Could there be trouble in paradise?

"I'll pay you back," Nora told Emma as the server scurried away with the bill.

"You'd better," Emma said, her laughter breaking the tension. "That was my entire grocery bill for a month!"

CHAPTER 18

When Connor got home he changed from his date clothes into his khaki shorts and T-shirt. He headed to his desk, grabbed his bills, and sat down at the kitchen table.

The date had been a disappointment. It wasn't Johanna's fault. She was nice enough and very attractive. She seemed like a nice Christian woman. She didn't talk too much or have an annoying laugh or complain about her ex—even though, according to Lexie, she had reason to.

They shared a love of boats and spent quite a while on that topic. She talked freely about her faith, spoke kindly about the people in her life—including Lexie—and found her work as an advisor at the university fulfilling.

And though he'd enjoyed their conversation, he couldn't seem to dredge up any romantic interest in her. Especially once he'd noticed Maddy and her sisters across the dining room. From that point on, his mind had wandered often. Mostly toward Maddy.

He'd only just yesterday told her he hadn't dated in years, and here he was out on a date. He hadn't missed her guarded greeting and the absence of that infectious smile he'd witnessed on their walk back to the marina. Given that she'd recently been burned where men were concerned, her reaction wasn't surprising. He felt bad about the misunderstanding, especially since it was her birthday.

He also felt guilty for not giving Johanna his undivided attention, even though she hadn't seemed to notice. Their good-bye at her door had consisted of a platonic hug. She thanked him for the evening, and though he thought she'd probably go out with him again if he asked, he made no offer. Because of that the date had ended awkwardly.

Maybe he hadn't given her enough of a chance. His dating experience was limited, as Annie had been his first love, but he remembered what a connection was supposed to feel like.

And with Johanna it just wasn't there. He hadn't hung on to her every word the way he had with Maddy the day before. He hadn't been tempted to touch her hand, just to see how soft her skin was. He hadn't even noticed the shape of her lips, much less wondered what they might taste like.

He ripped a finished check out of the checkbook and placed it in the envelope. Johanna had already texted to thank him again for the nice evening. He'd texted back something polite and non-committal. He wasn't sure what he was supposed to do next. He didn't want to hurt her feelings.

A repetitive sound was drifting through the open windows, like someone was trying to pull-start a lawn mower. Connor got up to look.

Maddy was in her backyard bent over her grandma's old Toro. That thing hadn't been run in heaven knew how long. Connor usually did their grandma's mowing after he finished his own, but lately he'd neglected it.

He slid on his flip-flops and left his house by way of the back deck. It was a pretty evening, the temperature mild, a light breeze blowing in off the sea. An egret, poised between their properties, took flight at his approach, its legs extending behind him like long black sticks.

The sputtering motor drew his attention. Maddy was giving the pull-start renewed effort, one tennis-shoe-clad foot braced on the mower's frame. She wore a pair of yoga shorts and a long gray tank top that crisscrossed in the back, exposing sun-kissed shoulders. Her ponytail bobbed with her efforts.

The smell of gasoline wafted his way. "You're flooding it," he called.

Maddy didn't seem to hear him over the noise.

"Maddy!" he called again.

She turned, breathing hard, a sheen of perspiration glistening on her forehead. A frown pulled at her brows, tugged at her lips. "You scared me."

"Sorry 'bout that. You've flooded the engine. You need to let it rest awhile."

Maddy let go of the pull cord, and it whipped back into the mower. "Stupid thing."

He took a closer look at the mower. The throttle was open, and the spark plug was attached. He checked the oil and found it full. "Did you prime it?"

"Of course."

"Put gas in?"

She gave him a look.

"Okay, well, I don't think this thing's been used in years. It probably needs some work done."

He hadn't imagined her guardedness at the restaurant. She was downright prickly. "I usually just run my mower over your grandma's lawn when I finish mine. I've let it go the past couple of weeks, but I can do it tomorrow after work."

"That won't be necessary." She wheeled the mower and pushed it up the grassy slope and onto the concrete walkway alongside the house.

"You can let it rest fifteen minutes or so and see if you have better luck, or I can lend you mine. It's a lot newer and easier to maneuver."

She brushed off her hands. "Thanks, but I'll wait."

Connor studied her face—the tightness at the corner of her eyes, the persistent frown, the stubborn set of her chin. "Suit yourself then."

He found himself missing the way she'd looked at him yesterday, tilting a smile up at him, those amber flecks sparkling in her eyes. He hated that they'd had a misunderstanding.

"Listen, Maddy, I wanted to explain about tonight. I know how that had to look after what I said yesterday—"

"You don't owe me an explanation, Connor."

With two sisters and a mother, he was pretty good at reading women. "Is that a fact? Because you seem a little cross with me."

She gave her head a shake, and the quick hitch of her shoulder said, **I have no idea what you're talking about**. But her bland smile was too carefully arranged, her couldn't-care-less counten-ance forced. He'd seen this look before on every woman in his life.

Maddy wiped a hand across her sweaty forehead, wishing Connor would just leave. His persistence to explain made her feel foolish for caring so much. Probably made her look jealous. And she wasn't. She had no reason to be jealous.

"My sister set me up with a friend," Connor continued.

"That's fine." Maddy waved away his words. "Really. None of my business. She seemed great. Did you have a good time?"

The planes of his face hardened, a shadow flickering in his jaw. He looked toward the crashing surf. His profile was striking, she had to admit. A strong forehead, perfectly proportioned nose, and that wavy hair stirring in the wind.

When he looked back at her, his gray eyes were like storm clouds, threatening rain. "Obviously it's not fine. Please hear me out. I don't want you to think I lied to you; it's true that I haven't gone on a date in years. That was my first since my wife passed away. Lexie thought it was high time I get back out there, and she set me up with a friend. That's all."

A fist tightened around Maddy's heart at the raw honesty on Connor's face. A flood of warmth spread through her limbs. If she'd felt foolish before, she felt like a complete idiot now. Her eyes fell to the mower.

"After what you've been through recently I just wanted to clear the air with you." He bent his knees until he made eye contact.

There was something earnest and searching in his gaze. As if he wanted to see clear down to her soul. It drew her like a magnet, and she was helpless against its pull.

"Are we okay?" he asked. "You believe

me?"

She let out a breath she didn't know she was holding. "Sorry I was a little edgy with you."

His mouth relaxed in a rueful smile. "I get it, Maddy. You're just learning to trust again—both yourself and others. That can make a person wary. You don't really know me, but I don't make a habit of lying. If you hang around long enough, you'll see that's true."

"Fair enough." Her heart was palpitating at his focused attention. She pulled her gaze away from his and shifted the topic. "Thank you for the champagne tonight. That was thoughtful."

"You're welcome."

"I'd only ever had the cheap stuff you get at New Year's Eve celebrations. There's a big difference."

"Glad you liked it. I hope you had a nice birthday."

"I did. The meal was delicious and my sisters behaved. That's about as much as I can ask for."

"The least they could do for your

birthday."

"And your date?" Maddy hated herself a little for asking, but she had a perverse desire to know. "It seemed to be going well."

"Yeah... She was nice." He nodded slowly, but there was uncertainty in his tone.

"She's a friend of Lexie's? She looked older than your sister."

"Not really a friend. Johanna is her advisor at the university." His lips turned up in a wry grin. "They got to talking, and Lexie became convinced she'd met my perfect match."

"Well, you never know. Maybe she is."

"I don't think so. But how do you go about getting that point across to a perfectly nice woman after only one date, huh? Help a guy out. I'm a little out of practice here."

"Not a match made in heaven then?"

"She's great, really she is. Just not for me, you know? Is it all right to just let it end a quiet death, or do I have to tell her that? Please say I don't have to tell her that."

Maddy chuckled at the obvious dread on his face. "You're just a big softie, aren't you?"

"Don't you be telling anyone now," he said, all Southern charm.

"Are you sure you've given her a fair chance? It was only one date. Maybe it was just an off night."

"No, she was great, but there was just —no connection. We could be friends, I think. Except I got the feeling she might want more than that."

Maddy winced. "Awkward."

"Very."

They shared a commiserating smile.

"In that case, I think you can just let it die quietly unless she persists. At that point you really should say something."

He made a face, sticking his hands into his back pockets. "Ugh."

"Hey, I didn't say it'd be fun. But the only other option would be ducking her calls, and that's unkind. It's not really fair to let her waste her time and energy if you're not interested."

"You're right, you're right." He tucked in the corner of his mouth, shaking his head. "Why exactly did I jump back into the dating pool again? I'm having trouble remembering."

"I'd say the water's warm, but that'd be a big fat lie."

His low chuckle stirred something inside her, as did the way his eyes warmed as they studied her for a long, breath-stealing moment. His gaze drifted over her face with a flicker of male appreciation.

"I enjoyed talking to you yesterday, Maddy," he said softly.

"Me too." She kept a casual tone, though her pulse fluttered at his words.

She was attracted to him, she'd admit that much to herself. She thought he was a good guy. And she believed him when he said he hadn't lied to her.

But this couldn't go anywhere. The misunderstanding tonight had brought it all back, a stark reminder of her recent heartbreak and all the reasons she had boundaries in place. She wasn't ready to go there again just yet.

"Maybe we should set up a time to go sailing soon. I think it'd be a lot of fun."

She reached for an excuse. "I don't know when we'd go, with our schedules."

A look of surprise came over his face. "Oh. I meant to tell you. Cheryl called this afternoon. Her dad is faring better than expected, so she's planning to come back later this week. Sorry... I should've called you right away."

She deflated a little at the thought of losing the job at the Landing. "Oh. No, that's fine. I'm glad he's going to be all right."

The restaurant had kept her mind off of what had happened back home and given her a break from the tension here at the beach cottage. It was fun to do something she was skilled at. It gave her purpose. She was going to miss that.

Maddy forced a smile. "I'm sure you'll be glad to have her back."

"You've done a great job; Cheryl's going to be thrilled to see it all in one piece when she gets back. It was falling apart under my leadership, I can tell you that much."

Maddy hitched a shoulder. "We all have our gifts. I'm sure your marina would be a disaster under my direction."

"Speaking of the marina..." He gave her a charming smile. "How about that sail?"

She laughed. "Nice segue."

"Wasn't it? I can finagle a Saturday off with a little advance notice. The boat belongs to a friend of mine, but he doesn't use it much."

Maddy was more tempted than she wanted to admit. She made the mistake of meeting his gaze. The storm clouds were gone. Now the gray looked as soft as kitten's fur, and that bracketed smile coerced.

Darn her fickle heart.

"No pressure, Maddy. It doesn't have to be a date...just a man and a woman going out for a sail."

Maddy lifted a brow. "Don't you have enough women in your life already?"

He chuckled. "You'd think, wouldn't you? I've always had great women in my life—don't tell my sisters. I like them to think they're a burden."

She smiled at the warmth in his tone.

"Fact is, I'm probably more comfortable with women than most guys are." He looked at her through lashes that looked golden in the light of the setting sun. "So what do you say? You could bring your sisters along if you like."

"Um, no. I would not like."

He looked at her askance. "Okay…"

"All that tension between them can be very uncomfortable."

"Sounds like a story I need to hear sometime. Perhaps during a leisurely sail…"

She chuckled. "You're relentless."

"One of my finer qualities."

"Hmm, I'm not sure about that. But I guess a day on the sea does sound like a nice escape." Her heart pounded at the thought of hours alone with Connor. She hoped she wasn't making a mistake.

"It'll be a blast, you'll see. We'll make a day of it. I'll do all the work, and you can sit back and enjoy going wherever the wind takes us. This Saturday work for you?"

"That should be fine." Maybe it would rain. Did she want it to rain?

"All right then. It's a plan." He clapped his hands together, and his gaze dropped to the mower. "Now, why don't we see if we can get this old machine up and running?"

CHAPTER 19

Maddy waffled back and forth all week about whether or not going sailing with Connor was a good idea. She reminded herself it wasn't a date. She even mentioned the outing to her sisters, striking just the right casual tone.

It hadn't fooled anyone. Least of all Maddy herself.

In the end she decided to leave it in God's hands. Good weather: good idea. Bad weather: bad idea. And when Saturday dawned bright and sunny, she told herself it must be an answer to her prayers.

Now, as she settled on the bench at the stern of the boat, she found herself second-guessing even God.

Connor looked like male perfection as he readied the boat, going about the business as if it were second nature. He wore a pair of black and turquoise trunks and a white T-shirt that the wind molded to his skin. His hair was tied back with a leather strap, and his sunglasses shielded his eyes from the sunlight glaring off the water.

Maddy tucked a loose wisp behind her ear. "Can I help with anything?"

"Almost done. Just sit back and relax. There are drinks in the cooler." He nodded to it. "Help yourself."

Maddy fished a bottled water from the ice, and by the time she was seated again he had the boat untied and was back onboard. He took his place behind the big wheel at the stern.

The motor rumbled beneath her as he put it in gear and maneuvered from the slip. The boat steadied as it sliced through the calm bay. Her white sleeveless blouse billowed in the wind.

The week had flown by. Connor had come over to paint the exterior of the house on Tuesday and Thursday while the sisters painted inside. Maddy, worried about Nora and the paint fumes, suggested she start in the kitchen and dining room, where there were many windows they could open.

Thursday had been Maddy's last day at the Landing. Cheryl returned to work yesterday, and Connor had texted to say she was delighted with how smoothly the restaurant was running.

Without the restaurant Maddy would have extra time, and the house would come along more quickly. But she found herself reluctant to return to the problems awaiting her back home.

"Doing all right over there?" Connor asked over the wind.

"Perfect." She smiled up at him. She was sitting adjacent to where he stood, clearly in his element behind the captain's wheel.

The sun was high overhead so she tilted her face to the sky and closed her eyes, enjoying the warmth on her skin. Between the house and the restaurant she hadn't had much downtime recently. Maybe a few hours of leisure was just what she needed.

She tuned in to the cries of nearby sea gulls and the sound of the wind cutting across the sea. The rumbling engine, lapping water, and gentle dipping motion had a soothing effect.

She drew in a breath of salty sea air and let it out, mentally disconnecting with life on land as the boat whisked her away from it. Just for today she'd leave her worries behind and surrender to the wind's wiles.

When she opened her eyes, Connor's gaze was fixed on hers. His lips were turned up, as if he sensed—and approved of—her thoughts. Feeling the moment of connection, she returned his smile and looked out to the horizon. They were passing through the inlet that led to the open sea.

Once they left the shelter of the bay, the wind kicked up, the waves ruffling the water's surface. There were other boats out and about. Sailboats and fishing boats, people out enjoying the beautiful summer day.

A few minutes later Connor moved out from behind the wheel. "Ready for some sailing?"

"Absolutely. Anything I can do?"

"Why don't you just observe today? A lot can happen, and quickly. The only thing you need to know about is the boom." He gestured to the horizontal pole under the main sail. "It can come flying across the boat, and you don't want to be in its way."

"Got it."

He raised the mainsail, and it started flapping like crazy in the breeze. Next he raised the front sail and went about securing it. He obviously knew what he was doing, and she watched closely in case she got the opportunity to help next time.

Next time?

She brushed the thought away—no worrying allowed today.

Connor continued adjusting both sails, and the boat began moving. He checked the wind direction with the ribbons that were tied to one of the cables.

She was content to watch him work with the shifting wind. Sailing wasn't a lazy man's sport, she could see that. But Connor wasn't lazy. He seemed to love the work. His muscles flexed and shifted with his movements. He checked on her from time to time, making sure she was content, a smile lingering around his lips.

Eventually Maddy decided to recline on the bench and enjoy the ride. They were sailing toward an island he knew of. Connor had packed a picnic lunch, and she already found her stomach growling, but the sun warmed the back of her eyelids and the motion of the boat lulled her.

"Maddy?"

Her eyes opened, blinking against the harsh sunlight.

Connor hovered over her, his form silhouetted by the sun. "We're here, sleepyhead."

Maddy eased upright, feeling sheepish. "I fell asleep. I'm so sorry."

"Don't be." He turned to grab their

supplies. "I'm glad you were able to relax."

She followed him off the boat, looking around. The boat's sails were down, and they were already tied off at an old wooden pier. There wasn't a single soul in sight. The island was small enough that she could see both ends from their position at the end of the dock.

He helped her off the boat, and she freed him of the picnic blanket.

"Where are we exactly?"

"Not too far from Fort Fisher. Just a little scrap of land an old friend showed me a while back. Good fishing here too, but I'm more interested in food right now."

"That makes two of us." She checked her watch, surprised to see she'd been asleep for over an hour.

The old pier creaked and swayed under their feet. The water beneath them was shallow and clean, little fish flittering around. The pier ended on a narrow strip of sand, not wide enough to be a public beach. It extended toward a slope covered with seagrass, scrub brush, and low-growing coastal plants.

When they stepped off the pier Connor kicked off his sandals, and she followed suit.

"This place is deserted," she said as her feet sank into soft white sand.

"It's a private island."

Maddy raised her brows. "Who owns it?"

"Same friend who owns the boat." He shared a smile.

"Do they have a house here?" She didn't see one, but she couldn't see above the sloped dunes.

"Nope. He wants to keep it natural." Connor set the cooler down in the sand. "He's a great guy, kind of eccentric. He could sell the land for a fortune—he's had offers—but he's not interested."

"How do you know him?"

"Through the marina—he's a customer."

Someone had laid a sitting log on the beach close to the base of the dunes. There was a fire pit nearby and evidence of a recent fire.

Maddy spread the picnic blanket in front of the log while Connor opened the cooler and began pulling out the food. There were sandwiches, thick with meat and fillings and wrapped in plastic, a quart of creamy-looking coleslaw, a small tray filled with strawberries and cheese cubes, and last, a perfectly round minia- ture cheesecake.

"Save room for dessert," he said.

"Do you actually think we're going to be able to eat all this?"

"I plan on giving it my best effort." He lowered himself in the sand, using the log for a backrest.

Maddy did the same, leaving plenty of space between them. After a quick blessing he offered her her choice of sandwich.

She took the ham and left the turkey club for him. "I know better than to come between a man and his bacon."

"I knew you were a smart woman."

Maddy took a bite of the sandwich and groaned in approval. It was from Harvey's Deli and slathered with their famous homemade sauce.

"They know how to make a sandwich,

right?"

"It's delicious." She took a bite of coleslaw and reveled in the tangy/spicy flavor. "I can see my dilemma right now will be trying to leave room for dessert."

"That's the only kind of dilemma you should have on a day like this."

"I enjoyed the sail, even if I slept through most of it. It's like a different world out there. It felt natural to leave behind my worries. I used to kayak, of course, but it's not quite the same. Maybe because I never went too far from shore."

"That's exactly how I feel out on the water, more so even on a sailboat when I'm working with the wind and sea. I'm disconnected from life when I'm out there. From the fast, everyday pace of the world." He gave her a wry grin. "Not to overly romanticize it."

"No, I get what you're saying. Well, except the at-one-with-wind-and-sea thing. All the adjustments you make to the sails—it seems like a full-time job."

"It's not for everyone, but I enjoy the challenge."

She took another bite of her sandwich and watched a piper scuttling across the beach. Water lapped the shores rhythmically, washing up only several feet.

"So," she said after washing down a bite with a sip of water, "how'd you come to own a marina? Is that what you always wanted to do?"

"Actually, I wanted to be a wide receiver in the NFL." He shrugged. "But those dreams were shot when I couldn't even get a football scholarship. I went to community college for a semester, then I overheard my uncle talking about a friend who needed dockhands at his marina. It sounded like a dream after sitting in the classroom.

"I could tell my parents weren't too happy about it, but they wisely let me chart my own course. Ray hired me, and I moved to Seahaven—this dingy little garage apartment. I liked working outside. And though much of the work was the same every day, it was different enough to keep it interesting.

"Dockhands came and went, and before

I knew it, I was Ray's longest-standing employee. I sort of became his right-hand man. Then as he started getting older he wanted more time off, and he made me manager. He was about my dad's age, but he was really different. Kind of gruff. Hardly ever let loose a compliment, but when he did, it mattered, you know?"

Maddy smiled at him.

"I kind of felt bad for him. His wife had died years before, and they didn't have kids. I think he thought of me as a son."

There was a long pause before he continued. "One morning he didn't show up to work. He'd had a heart attack, apparently in the middle of the night."

"Oh no." Maddy winced. "I'm so sorry."

"It was a shock. I'd never lost someone that close to me, and as far as I'd known he hadn't had any health problems. He was active and wasn't overweight." His brow furrowed as he took a bite of cole-slaw. "The next week I found out he'd willed the marina to me."

Maddy's jaw went slack. "Wow. That

was very generous."

The corner of his lip tucked in. "He never said a word. But that was just like him."

"And you've been running it ever since. And expanding..."

"I'm not sure buying the restaurant was the wisest thing I've ever done, but Lexie can be very persuasive. And as long as Cheryl's running things, I'll keep it." He took a long drink from his water bottle. "Your turn. Why the restaurant business?"

She felt a smile tugging at her lips. "Because it's like hosting a perpetual party—and I get to run the show. I guess I've always been industrious. When I was little my parents sometimes invited their friends over for dinner, and I'd run around getting drinks for everyone and waiting on them. The adults thought it was cute, so I got a lot of attention. I tried the same thing when my sisters had friends over, but they mostly just wanted me out of their hair.

"The restaurant industry was a natural fit for me. When I was sixteen I got a job as a server at Waffle House. After I graduated I went to Virginia Tech and got my hospitality degree. I thought I might end up in hotel management, but I got an opportunity to intern at a four-star restaurant in Roanoke and fell in love with the restaurant industry." She held up the last bite of her sandwich. "And it doesn't hurt that I love great food."

"It feels good to find where you fit."

"It does. Of course I'm at loose ends at the moment, but—"

"You'll find a place. You're very good at what you do, Maddy."

Her face warmed at his appraisal. "Thank you. I'm sure it'll all work out. It just feels very uncertain at the moment."

"What do your sisters do? Emma runs a bakery, doesn't she?"

"Yes, in Denver. Food again—maybe my family has issues," she said dryly.

He chuckled, a low rumble in his chest. "Don't we all."

"Nora's from Boston, a stay-at-home mom—or she was when her daughter was younger. Chloe's in college now, and

Nora fills her time with charities and such. Her husband, Jonathan, is a mortgage broker, self-employed, and they do quite well."

"I gathered as much from the Mercedes."

She thought of that baby on the way and wondered if Jonathan knew yet and how he was taking the news. How would Chloe feel about having a sibling who was so much younger?

"We both have big age gaps with our siblings," Connor said. "Were your sisters like second mothers to you growing up?"

"Sometimes. More so Emma than Nora. But neither of them wanted me hanging around their friends."

"I'm afraid I was guilty of that too. They were little pests. I didn't really appreciate them until I was out of the house and came back to visit."

"You seem pretty close now."

"We are. But when they were young I was often stuck babysitting, and I resented it. I used to swear up and down I'd never have children." A grin tugged at his lips.

"Do you still feel that way?"

He looked away. A shadow fell over his eyes, and his smile gave way to gravity. Maddy wondered if she'd brought up a bad subject. He and his wife had been married ten years, after all. Plenty of time to start a family.

He blinked and the look was gone. "Nah, I'd like to have kids someday. Until then I'll just enjoy my niece and nephew."

Maddy took a bite of strawberry and savored the sweet flavor. "So how did things end up with your date? Did you have to let her down easy?"

"Johanna? No, thank God. She texted me after the date, but things just kind of fell off after that. Lexie told me she'd had a good time and would be agreeable to another date. But I think my sister could tell I just wasn't into her."

"I'm surprised she didn't try to talk you into giving her another chance."

He chuckled. "Oh, she did. But I can put my foot down when I need to."

"Yeah, you don't strike me as a pushover."

"Well, I admit, when both of my sisters

are on me about something, it's sometimes easier to just roll over and give in."

"I can imagine."

He finished off his coleslaw and set his
plate aside. "Ready for the cheesecake?"

She put a hand on her stomach. "I'm
already full. That sandwich was huge."

"Oh, come on, just a little piece..."

He unboxed the presliced cheesecake
and grabbed a plastic knife, poising it
above a slice. "This okay?"

She put her hand on his, moving the
knife until there was just a sliver of
cheesecake left. His hand was big and
warm under hers. She pushed down, and
they sliced it together.

Their gazes connected for a long
moment. She was starting to become
rather fond of his eyes. Had she thought
them colorless? They were all kinds of
interesting with varying shades of gray
and those flecks of silver. They were
expressive too. Stormy or soft or just
steady and quiet.

Her gaze fell to the golden scruff on his
jawline, and she wondered if it would feel

soft or bristly. And also what did it mean that he'd shaved for his date the other night and not for this?

It means this isn't a date, that's what it means.

She withdrew her hand and cleared her throat as an awkward moment settled between them.

Connor plated her sliver of cheesecake and handed it to her. "That's hardly even a bite."

"I'm not used to eating this much for lunch. It was delicious, though. Thank you."

She took a small bite. It was slightly sweet and pleasantly creamy. The buttery graham cracker crust had a hint of ginger, making it rather extraordinary.

He took his own hefty slice, and they ate in silence awhile, watching the pipers scuttle around on the beach.

"So," Connor said a few minutes later. "Tell me about your mom. Are the two of you close?"

"She lives in Georgia, and she's re-married. I wouldn't say we're close. We talk on the phone now and then. Visit occasionally."

"Part of that rift your grandma has made reference to?"

"Something like that."

Maddy didn't want to talk about her family. She'd only ever given Nick the CliffsNotes version, and he'd been satisfied with that. Of course, he hadn't really cared about her.

She savored another bite of her cheesecake, refusing to let the topic bring her down.

"Sorry," he said. "Didn't mean to pry about your family business."

"It's okay. I just don't want to think about it today. It's too perfect a day."

That made him smile. He set his plate aside. "You're right. In fact, I think I'm ready for a swim. I don't know about you, but I'm getting a little hot."

"I'll be right behind you."

He stood and tugged off his T-shirt, dropping it onto the blanket.

She watched him stride toward the water, her mouth going dry at the sight of

him. He had nice broad shoulders that
tapered down to a trim waist. His arms
were sculpted, his legs trim, and all of him
was tanned and gorgeous. His calves
bunched into hard knots as his feet
worked through the sand, cutting over
toward the pier. He hopped onto it, broke
into a run, and did a cannonball off the
side.

CHAPTER 20

Maddy turned onto her stomach, cradling her head in her arms. The sun beat down on her damp back, warming her. She and Connor were drying off after their swim. The water had been cold, but she'd soon forgotten that as they frolicked in the sea.

He dozed beside her, and Maddy lay listening to the soothing sounds of the ocean, enjoying the play of breeze off the water. She liked that he felt comfortable enough to drift off. There was something flattering about that.

She let her gaze rove over him while he slept. He lay on his stomach too, one arm folded under his head, turned her way. Sand dotted his back, and freckles spotted his shoulders. His forearms were covered with a smattering of golden hair.

His face was peaceful, his long lashes sweeping down over sun-kissed cheeks. His lips were parted in sleep. He had a nice mouth. His lower lip was full, his upper lip dipping in a distinct cupid's bow just about the right size for her index finger. Hidden in the golden stubble on his chin was a subtle cleft she hadn't noticed before.

There was something boyish about him in sleep, all that virility at rest. He'd been through so much. Her heart gave a tug. He'd lost a dear friend and the wife he'd obviously loved very much—both suddenly. He must be strong to get through all that. Her own troubles were nothing in comparison.

The wind blew a damp strand of hair over his face, and before she could stop herself she reached out and brushed it away.

His eyes snapped open, connecting with hers.

Maddy's pulse skittered as she drew her

hand away. She'd been caught staring, caught touching him.

His eyes softened on hers as he stared back. "How long was I asleep?"

"Not long. Fifteen or twenty minutes."

He propped his head up with an elbow, and his eyes roved over her face, taking his time.

Turnabout was fair play, she supposed. Though she was conscious of the fact that the ocean had washed away the bit of makeup she'd applied that morning. Her hair lay in damp tangles down her back, and her cheeks were probably blotchy from the sun's heat. But the way he was looking at her made her feel beautiful.

"You have freckles on your nose," he said with a little grin.

She made a face, wishing he'd noticed her thick eyelashes or high cheekbones instead.

"They're cute," he said, and she could tell he meant it. "They make you seem more approachable."

She huffed as though affronted. "Are you saying I'm aloof?"

He quietly continued his visual observation. "Your other features are strong and beautiful. Wide-set, serious eyes... high cheekbones...perfect mouth."

Her breath hitched at his lazy perusal. Every inch of her skin felt hypersensitive, especially her lips as his gaze lingered there.

"But those freckles...They soften the whole effect." His voice was like warm honey. "I like them."

He seemed content to lie there and stare at her, so she stared right back. She wasn't sure she could stop herself. There was something so quiet and steady about him. He took care of her grandmother and obviously doted on his sisters. He was the kind of man people depended on, the kind who came through without making a fuss.

"I had fun today, Maddy." There was a rough texture to his voice.

"Me too."

His eyes searched hers. "I can't tell you the last time I enjoyed someone's company so much. I know we agreed this wasn't a date, but...I'd really like to see you again."

Her heart thumped heavily against the packed sand beneath her. No fair, she thought. He'd caught her off guard, on her hiatus from life, when she'd decided to leave her worries and fears behind.

"I like you," he continued. "I know you're just out of a bad relationship. But we could take it slow. Casual, even, if you want."

This didn't feel casual. This felt serious and real and like the kind of thing that could swell up and swallow her whole. She took a deep breath, her ribs pressing into the ground.

"You're too quiet," he said. "Tell me what you're thinking."

Her thoughts spun for traction. "I won't be here much longer, Connor. My life's in Charlotte." It wasn't the real reason, but it was easier, more tangible.

He tipped a smile. "That's not so far away."

She expected more of a rebuttal. Long-distance relationships weren't easy.

Especially one that was only just starting. And it wasn't as if she had much of a life left there anyway, but he didn't point that out.

"Why don't you tell me what's really on your mind."

He'd read her so easily. She stared at him a moment longer, remembering the heartache in her not-too-distant past. Attraction could lead to love and love led to...nothing good. The familiar fear bubbled up inside, a low boil, roiling beneath the surface. Her chest tightened until her breaths felt restrained. She kept all of it from her face.

"Tell me." The tenderness in his gaze was her undoing.

"I'm...a little afraid, I guess." Her voice was a thready whisper.

It was too honest. She dropped her gaze. She didn't know him well, and he was only talking about a date, after all. He hadn't asked for her hand in marriage. He was going to think—

He set his hand over hers and waited until she made eye contact. "I know,

Maddy. I understand. You've been hurt. It's been a long time since I've entertained the idea of a woman in my life. The last time didn't end well. I know it's a risk, opening your heart to someone. Even just letting yourself hope again..."

He did understand. Her stomach tightened at the thought of his loss. Of course he'd be scared too. Compared to him, her breakup was nothing. And yet, her heart felt as if it were going to explode in her chest.

"But I feel like there's something here worth exploring, and I think you feel it too. Will you at least think about it?"

Hadn't she just been thinking about how trustworthy he'd proven himself to be? He'd been nothing but honest with her—very honest, actually—going back to when he'd told her he'd let her run the Landing without interference.

Her heart implored her to say yes, but her brain flashed a warning signal. She couldn't pull her eyes from his, and the longer she looked at him, the more those warning signals seemed to fade into the distance.

"Yes," she said. "I'll think about it."

His lips tipped up, barely a smile. "We'll go at your pace."

"I said I'd **think** about it." She teased him with a smile.

"Well, hurry up and think," he said, his gaze falling to her lips for a long, drawn-out moment. " 'Cause I'm dying to kiss you."

Before she could even digest the comment, Connor sprang to his feet. He brushed off the sand and held out his hand, wearing an infectious grin. "Now, come on, woman. It's time to go sailing."

CHAPTER 21

Maddy slipped inside the house, closed the door, and leaned against it. Connor had insisted on walking her to the door. The mood had shifted after their conversation at the beach. Though they'd had a leisurely sail back, things were less light-hearted, their serious conversation lingering between them.

I'm dying to kiss you.

Even now his words made her stomach flip. She wanted that too, more than she cared to admit. But was dating Connor the wise thing to do?

She didn't know. She was tempted. Oh, how she was tempted. She pictured him as he'd been on the sail back, feet planted in a wide stance behind the captain's wheel, hair fluttering behind him, glistening in the sunlight. It had dried wavy and beautiful, unlike her own, which now hung straight and limp over her shoulders.

A creak sounded nearby, pulling Maddy's attention to the staircase. Nora descended in a stained T-shirt, carrying two gallons of paint. Her auburn hair was pushed back with a lime-green headband.

Pippy leaped down the stairs one at a time. The dog had taken to Nora since she'd started taking her jogging.

"You're back." Nora studied Maddy, then lifted an amused brow. "Someone had a good time."

Maddy straightened from the door. "Yeah, I did actually. It was fun."

"Well, I hate to take that flush off your face...but you got an interesting phone call while you were gone."

"Who was it?"

Nora set the paint cans on the drop cloth. "That idiot you were dating—Nick?"

Maddy's stomach dropped, the glowy

feeling inside extinguishing instantly. She hadn't heard a peep from Nick since that awful scene at Pirouette. Of course, she'd blocked him from her phone and erased his contact information. How had he even found her? Only Holly knew where she'd gone.

But Holly's sister worked at Pirouette... worked for Nick now.

"What in the world could he want?" Maddy said.

"I told him you were on a date." Nora grinned impishly. "I rather enjoyed that."

When she'd filled her in on their break-up a while back Nora had been outraged. Maddy had wondered if Nora realized she'd done even worse to her own sister.

She followed Nora to the kitchen. There were drop cloths along the newly painted walls, blue tape sealing off the wood-work. Emma was on the deck talking to someone on the phone.

"Did he say what he wanted?"

"No." Nora pulled a tub of Moose Tracks from the freezer. "Want some?"

"No, thanks."

"He left his number, though, and wanted you to call him back."

Maddy huffed. "Fat chance. He's the last person I want to talk to."

"I figured as much, but I wrote down the number anyway. You ought to call him back just to give him an earful after what he did to you."

Maddy shook her head. She'd only recently stopped brooding about this. She didn't want to dredge it all up again. Better to just move on and put it from her mind. She must be ready; her mind was full of Connor these days.

"I guess ignoring him works too," Nora said. "But he struck me as the kind of guy who doesn't give up." She dragged a generous scoop of ice cream from the tub. "So...you and Connor, huh? He seems like an upstanding guy."

Maddy opened her mouth to respond.

"And don't you tell me it wasn't a date —you should've seen the look on your face just now. I'd hazard a guess you're already a little smitten with our neighbor."

Maddy grabbed a water bottle from the

fridge. "I like him just fine, but I don't think I'm ready for anything serious quite yet."

Nora lifted a shoulder. "So just go out and have some fun."

"That's exactly the sort of thing that leads to something serious."

"Would that be so awful?" Nora capped the ice cream and licked a finger. "You deserve someone nice, Maddy."

"I'm the career girl, remember? Romantic relationships aren't my specialty."

"Nonsense. You can have both. Everybody needs love, and you're as capable as the next person."

Was she? She felt like maybe something was wrong with her. She knew her outlook on love wasn't good. It was hard to be content in a relationship when you were always waiting for the other shoe to drop. She'd felt that way through most of her relationship with Nick.

And then the shoe had dropped, proving her right.

Look at her parents, look at Emma. Even Connor. Did love ever end well? She supposed it had for Nora.

Maddy's gaze drifted to the deck where Emma leaned on the railing, still on the phone, her voice lost in the wind.

"Who's Emma talking to?" Maddy asked.

Nora settled at the table with her ice cream. "Ethan, I assume. She's been out there awhile."

Maddy hoped she was right. Maybe Emma and Ethan could work out their problems and save their marriage. But Maddy couldn't mention that. Emma had never told Nora about the separation—yet another layer of secrets between the sisters.

CHAPTER 22

July 27, twenty years ago

Maddy couldn't sleep. She was hot, and the overhead fan was only moving around the stifling air. Plus, her mind wouldn't shut down. She pushed the sheet to the bottom of the twin-size bed. Opening her eyes, she spotted the lumpy shadow of Emma in the bed next to hers. Nora was on the farthest side, by the open window. The sisters had to share a single room this summer since Jonathan was here.

Maddy's pajamas were damp with perspiration, and her mouth was dry. She got out of bed and crept from the room, nearly tripping over a pair of sandals. The house was quiet, save for Daddy's snoring and the low hum of the window air conditioner in Gram's room.

Maddy's bare feet picked up bits of sand on the steps. The third step creaked beneath her. Gram complained about all the sounds the old house made, but Maddy liked the familiarity of those creaks.

All was dark downstairs but for the moonlight filtering through the sheer curtains. It was enough to see her way to the refrigerator for a glass of iced tea.

It was cooler downstairs, but Maddy knew the temperature hadn't been the real reason she was tossing and turning in bed. She had a lot on her mind. It hadn't been the slow easy summer of years past, and it wasn't just because they were planning Emma's wedding.

First there was that moment she'd witnessed between Nora and Jonathan a few weeks ago. Maddy hadn't told anyone she'd found them in his room, talking so easily together. She'd told herself she was being stupid, and that worked most of the time. But at night, when she stilled, it niggled uncomfortably in the back of her mind.

Then there was Mama and Daddy. She couldn't quite put her finger on what was amiss there. The other day she'd noticed that, though they carried on normal conversations with everyone else, they rarely talked directly to each other.

Ever since she'd noticed that, she'd been paying close attention. They hadn't spoken to each other once, except for idle requests like "Please pass the salt" or "Where are the car keys?"

She'd almost brought it up to Emma, but her sister would just say Maddy was imagining things. Her sister had wedding on the brain, that much was for sure. It was all she and Mama and Gram ever talked about.

Maddy took a drink, enjoying the smooth flavor of Gram's sun tea as it slid down her parched throat. She could hear the muted crash of waves hitting the shore, and the familiar sound drew her to the windows.

Outside starlight flickered against a

black canvas, and the full moon looked like a big white ball, suspended in the night sky. It shot a beam of silvery light across the ocean's surface.

A movement on the beach caught her attention. At first she thought it was just the waves washing ashore, but the motion had been nearer to the house than the shoreline. She cupped her hands against the window, and her eyes caught on a shadowy bundle just past the last low dune.

She squinted, going still, to see if it moved again. The bundle took more form as her eyes adjusted to the light. Someone was sitting out there. No, two people, she saw as they parted.

Emma and Jonathan, she realized. Who else would it be snuggled up on the beach? Their neighbors were old, and no one would be walking the beach at this late hour. But hadn't Emma been in her bed? It hadn't just been a lump. She was almost certain of it. Her chest tightened with dread.

Maddy watched a moment longer, but it

was too dark to make out their identities. She had to know for sure. She was moving toward the kitchen door before she could have second thoughts.

As she took the deck's steps to the sandy footpath, a cloud skittered over the moon, darkening the landscape. She made the trip down the path by memory. The wind was loud in her ears, and the crash of the surf was a lonely sound tonight.

The sparse lawn gave way to rolling hills of soft sand. She was nearly to the last dune when the clouds parted, casting a pale blue glow over the beach.

The couple was huddled beneath a blanket, merged into one shadow now. Maddy recognized Jonathan's silhouetted profile, the brim of his ball cap, and the sharp slopes of his nose and chin. She must've been mistaken about seeing Emma in bed. The couple was kissing, sharing a rare private moment.

Maddy suddenly felt like an intruder. Her sisters were right. She had a big imagination, and she was snoopy to boot. She turned to go.

But as she did, her eyes caught on something she hadn't noticed before. The woman's hair waved in the wind, flying out behind her, much longer than Emma's. It was well past the woman's shoulders, and the red strands glistened in the moonlight.

CHAPTER 23

Present day

Maddy dipped her brush into the aqua-colored paint and slathered it on the Adirondack chair. The old paint had eroded to an ash gray, and the chair was in sore need of a fresh coat. The evening sun was low in the sky, though the temperature was still well into the eighties.

Emma worked beside her on another chair, a little sloppy with her strokes, in Maddy's opinion.

"Where's Nora?" Emma asked. "I thought she was going to finish the kitchen tonight."

"She went to the grocery." Apparently

Nora hadn't yet solved the credit card situation, as she'd borrowed forty dollars from Maddy. Was something more going on with Nora's finances? Part of her wanted to ask. Another part wanted to let it go.

"I talked to Gram earlier when you were at the hardware store," Maddy said.

"How's she doing?"

"Having a fantastic time with her friends from the sound of it."

"That's good. When's she coming home?"

"She's very noncommittal, but I got the idea it would be at least another week or two."

"Did she press you about Nora and me?"

Maddy slanted a look at Emma. "Of course. I told her the truce was holding up, but she's not satisfied with that, as you well know."

"Well, I don't know what to tell her. I guess this is as good as it's ever going to get."

Maddy prayed she was wrong. "I updated her on our progress with the house. I think she's going to put it on the market as soon as she gets back."

Emma sighed. "That's kind of sad. There are so many memories here."

"Not all of them good, though," Maddy reminded her.

Her eyes drifted past the chair and toward the dunes where she'd spied Nora and Jonathan making out on the beach so many years ago. Maddy and Emma were currently sitting on the very deck where their family had splintered apart.

"Believe me, I know," Emma said.

"But you're right. Once upon a time we were happy here, and the three of us were close. I miss that, Emma."

"Were we close?" Emma asked. "Sometimes I think things weren't as wonderful as we imagined. They certainly weren't between Mama and Daddy. I mean, we knew they argued sometimes, but I didn't think much of it. Maybe there was always stuff going on down deep, and that last summer just exposed it all."

The thought bothered Maddy, made her skin feel too tight. "What do you mean?"

"Well, Nora for instance. You know she was always Daddy's girl."

They rarely talked about their dad. There was still so much hurt there.

"Gram favored her too," Emma continued. "That became very obvious that last summer."

"She was the first grandchild—that's not uncommon. But you were always Mama's favorite."

Emma dipped her brush in the paint. "I don't know about that."

"Oh, come on," Maddy said, not unkindly. "You favor her the most. She always took your side and went easiest on you."

Emma seemed to consider that. "Maybe back then it was true. She was definitely there for me after Nora betrayed me. It seemed like she really understood what I was going through. Like she was on my side. That's why it hurt so much when she went to Nora and Jonathan's wedding. It felt like a stab in the back. **Three** stabs in the back—one from each of them."

"I know it was a terrible time, Emma. But Mama was in a difficult spot. She was going to hurt one of you no matter what she did."

Emma was silent for a long moment. "I guess every family has its complications."

"Do you hear from her much...Mama?" Maddy asked.

"Every month or so, I guess."

Maddy huffed a laugh. "More often than I do."

"Yeah, but every time she reaches out she begs me to reconcile with Nora. I think that's the main reason she calls. It feels like it's all about Nora and what she needs. Well, what about what I need? What about Nora apologizing to me?"

Nora had begged for Emma's forgiveness back in the day. But after a while she'd grown weary of being rebuffed. Had put her back up and gotten riled up herself.

"I know what you're thinking," Emma said. "But should her apology really count when she went ahead and married my fiancé anyway? Actions speak louder than words, Maddy—and both of their actions said plenty."

Maddy was sorry she'd brought it up. They'd been over this ground so many times already.

"How is everything between you and Ethan, if you don't mind my asking? Have things gotten any better? I've been praying for you."

"Thanks." Emma seemed as relieved as Maddy for the change of topic. "I actually think the distance has been good for us. I'm starting to realize I gave up on us too easily. Before he left he tried to tell me he was unhappy, and I didn't want to hear it. Then he left, and I just—It hurt so much. It took me right back to Jonathan's rejection, and I felt so unwanted, by my own husband. It reawakened all those feelings."

"Oh, Emmie. I'm sorry."

"So I just closed down. I shut him out, refused to listen to what he was trying to tell me. I was afraid. But I'm starting to think his leaving was his way of trying to wake me up. Make me listen. Little did he know it would have the opposite effect.

"Yesterday on the phone...he told me he still loves me. I really needed to hear that. He's said it before, during our separation, but I wasn't listening—again thinking that actions spoke louder than words. All I saw was that he'd left me, and it tore me up inside."

"It sounds as though being away has given you some perspective."

"It has. We're talking more often, trying to work it out." She opened her mouth as if she had more to say, but she closed it again.

Maddy offered a smile. "That's hopeful. I'm glad for you. I always thought you and Ethan were good together."

"I do love him. And I've missed him so much. But I've been too afraid to be vulnerable with him. I don't know if we'll be able to work things out, but I'm going to try. It's worth the potential disappointment."

Maddy let the words sink in. They reflected her own situation with Connor, her own fears. Was it worth it? Emma seemed awfully sure, despite the pain she'd endured.

"Speaking of romantic relationships," Emma said after they'd painted in silence a few minutes. "Have you heard from our friendly neighborhood hottie since yesterday?"

"Sure haven't."

She was a little surprised Connor hadn't called or texted. Their time on the beach had been foremost in her thoughts the past twenty-four hours. She couldn't get the image of that crooked grin, those steady gray eyes, out of her mind.

But maybe he'd only been caught up in the moment. Maybe he regretted pressing her about dating him. Maybe his own fears had kicked in. He had even more reason to be cautious than she did.

"What are you going to tell him? Do you want to go out with him?"

Maddy gave a rueful laugh. "Have you met him? Of course I want to go out with him."

"And yet I sense an unspoken but behind that last word."

Maddy used the tip of her brush to smooth out a drip of paint on the arm of the chair. Nick had tried to call again this morning. She'd recognized the number on the caller ID and hadn't answered. He'd left a message asking her to return his call, but she deleted it. She used to love listening to him talk. He had a faint Boston accent and spoke with such passion. Now she only heard his arrogance.

"If you're not careful," Emma said, "fear can rob you of the most wonderful gifts life has to offer. I'm not saying that's Connor, necessarily. But it could be. You won't know until you give it a chance."

Emma made a lot of sense. "I'm praying about that. But it's easier said than done."

"Oh, believe me, sister. This I know."

"Got an extra paintbrush?" The baritone voice startled Maddy.

Connor was rounding the deck, that infectious smile widening his lips.

Maddy hoped he hadn't heard their conversation. There was no indication from his expression that he had.

"Know what?" Emma popped to her feet. "You can have mine. I just remembered a, um, creak in the stairs that needs immediate repair."

"You leave those creaks be." Maddy impaled Emma with a look, but her sister was too busy handing her paintbrush to Connor to notice.

He wore a pair of khakis and a stained blue Sullivan's Marina T-shirt that stretched taut over his broad shoulders and around his biceps.

Once Emma disappeared inside, Connor took her place on the deck and gave her that roguish grin. "Well, that worked out rather nicely."

"What?" She quirked a brow. "Your devious plan to get me alone?"

"Is it devious? Can't a guy just want to flirt in private?"

She slid him a look. "I thought you came to lend a hand."

"I'm an efficient guy. I can do both at once."

"I have no doubt." She thought he could handle a good deal more than that with those soulful eyes and charming grin. Maybe he wasn't the player she'd thought him to be, but he probably did have all the local women in a tizzy.

He dipped his brush and went to work. "So how was your day, Maddy? Did you get a lot done around here? I noticed the flower beds. They look great."

"Changing the subject?"

"Trying to, if you'd just let me."

"You're in a cheeky mood."

"I'm in a **good** mood." He gave her a sideways look. "I've been looking forward to seeing you all day."

Her heart squeezed tight. Okay, maybe that made up for the fact that he hadn't reached out to her.

"You got nothing?" he asked, boldly searching her face.

Her face warmed under his perusal. She didn't know what to say. Truth was, she had missed him today. She didn't know how that was even possible.

"You know you missed me," he teased.

"Someone needs to get his ego in check."

He chuckled. "All right. I'll let you off the hook this time. I've got a story to tell you anyway." He proceeded to tell her about a young man who'd approached him a couple months ago, asking to use the marina to propose to his girlfriend.

"It's going down Thursday," he said. "The anniversary of their first date, which happened to be a boat ride from the marina. He doesn't own the boat anymore, but that's where he wants to do the deed.

"He's going to set up lanterns and stuff. His family's going to light them and scatter rose petals down the pier, then disappear before they arrive."

The story warmed her heart. "That's very romantic. It's good of you to participate."

"You kidding me? You should see this guy—he's head over heels. If she says no it's going to break my heart."

His brows drew together, a focused look on his face. But she didn't think it was the painting he was caught up in as much as his own thoughts.

"You're actually nervous for him," Maddy

said.

He gave a mock scowl. "It's not easy for a guy to lay it all on the line like that. I know it's the modern age and all, but you women have it so much easier."

"Oh-ho." Maddy laughed. "Is that a fact?"

"Well..." He had the grace to look chagrined. "Minus the whole pushing-a-live-human-from-your-body thing. It's hard for a guy to put himself out there. No one likes rejection."

"Yes, but, traditionally speaking at least, men get to make the decisions. When to ask her out. When to kiss her. When to propose. Unless the woman wants to take the lead, she's stuck waiting, and that's no fun either, mister."

"Oh yeah?" He gave her a searching look, his sparkling eyes and slanted lips putting her on notice. "Let's recall our conversation from yesterday and talk about who's waiting for whom, hmm?"

Heat flooded Maddy's face, and she dipped her brush in the paint to avoid his eyes. "Touché, Mr. Sullivan."

"I wasn't trying to score a point, only provide a nice little segue. So...have you given any thought to our conversation?"

She shook her head. "You're a tricky, tricky man."

"I prefer to think of it as crafty."

"You're awfully good with words for a man who works with boats, I'll say that."

"If I were that good we'd be on our first date right now instead of slapping paint on a couple of chairs."

Her lips twitched. Truth be told, she'd thought of little else since yesterday. She knew what she was going to say—it was all over but the words. If she hadn't known it before, she knew it now, sitting side by side, having fun even while doing a mundane chore. Connor intrigued her too much to say no. She had to know where this could go even if she also feared finding out. Worry fluttered in her belly, a thousand butterflies stirring to life.

"I don't like that little dash between your eyebrows," he said, his tone light. "Something tells me it precedes a negative response, so maybe I should just cut my losses and change the subject."

They'd been teasing and playing, but she didn't want to play games. Not about this.

She turned toward him, catching his profile. "You're not going to get a no, Connor."

He did a double take that ended in a long, searching look. His brows disappeared beneath the long bangs sweeping across his forehead.

"Is that a yes then?"

Maddy looked at him a long moment, her pulse fluttering at the sweet hope on his face. She gave a nod. "That's a yes."

CHAPTER 24

Connor felt ridiculously nervous as he raised his hand to knock on Maddy's door. His muscles were twitchy, and his mouth was dry. He felt like a seventeen-year-old boy asking a girl to prom.

But Maddy already meant a lot to him. She drew him. She intrigued him. She was all kinds of special. Chances with women like her didn't come around often.

God, please don't let me blow this.

It was his last thought before the door swung open, revealing a beautiful Maddy. She wore a halter-style black dress that made the most of her subtle curves. Her shiny hair cascaded in waves over her bare shoulders. Her skin glowed in the evening sunlight, and her brown eyes were as inviting as melted chocolate. But it was her lips, painted red and perfectly lush, that stole the show.

"Wow," he said. But what he thought was, **You are so out of your league, Sullivan**.

Her lips curved. "Wow, yourself."

He didn't hold a candle to her in his black pants and button-down shirt.

Her sisters had made themselves scarce, and Maddy already had her purse, so he escorted her to his car and opened the passenger door. He watched her long, lithe legs disappear into his Infiniti and swallowed hard.

They'd decided on supper at a restaurant in Wilmington. The thirty-minute drive and leisurely meal would give them plenty of time to talk. Not that they hadn't done some of that as they'd worked on the house this week. But for the most part he'd been perched on a ladder, painting the exterior.

"So give me the full scoop on the proposal," Maddy said once he'd backed from the drive and they were on their way. "'She said yes' isn't going to cut it, in case you were wondering."

"The kid stopped by the marina today, over the moon. Apparently the night started a little rough—trouble getting her there on account of some reservations she'd made. They nearly got into an argument over it on the way to the marina. But then she saw the setup, realized what was about to happen, and all was forgiven."

Maddy laughed, the sound filling his car like a rich melody. "Did she cry?"

"That's not a question a man thinks to ask. But he did send me a few pictures." He handed her his phone and directed her to the texts.

"Aw, it's beautiful. Who knew a marina could look so romantic."

"Hey," he said teasingly.

"There are so many lanterns and twinkle lights. He obviously put a lot of thought into it. What a blessed girl." When she finished thumbing through, she set his phone down.

"I think they'll be very happy together," Connor said.

"It was nice of you to help make their moment special."

"It was fun. I offered to get it on video for them, but he wanted it to be private. I don't blame him. I don't care for those public proposals either."

"How did you ask your late wife to marry you?" she asked, then quickly added, "Sorry. You might not want to talk about that."

"I don't mind. I'll tell you anything you want to know." He thought back to that day. It seemed so long ago. "There was this park we went to a lot. I asked her there. I probably didn't do it up as much as I should've, but she really wasn't the grand-gesture type."

"I'm sure she loved it. She said yes, after all." Maddy gave him a warm smile.

"That she did." He didn't want to go on about Annie. He was no dating expert, but that definitely seemed like a first date no-no.

"Tell me about Nick. What first attracted

you to him?" Then he winced because he'd just brought up her ex.

"His '67 Mustang?" she joked, then made a face. "No, honestly, looking back, I really have to wonder."

"You don't have to talk about it. That's probably not first-date material either, is it? I'm a little out of practice."

She shrugged. "It's our date. We can make it whatever we want. Nick was nice looking, so that didn't hurt. I think I was flattered by his persistence. He was very charming, and I admired his confidence— although I have to say I see it as arrogance now. Hindsight."

"It can be very illuminating."

"Can't it?"

"He never got around to explaining himself or trying to apologize?"

"Nope, although—full disclosure—he's tried to call twice this week." Her gaze drifted out the passenger window. "I don't want to talk to him. I'm sure he and Evangeline are working together quite happily now. He got exactly what he wanted."

"He'll get his due. You don't treat people like that and not get what you have coming eventually."

"I'm trying not to wish him harm. I know I need to let it go."

"Sorry. I guess I should be advising you to forgive and forget. But I'd kind of like to string the guy up myself; I can only imagine how you must feel."

"Actually, I'm doing all right. I no longer wish I'd smacked him upside the head when I saw him with Evangeline."

He smiled. "Progress."

"Distance has given me a little perspective, I think."

"That's good."

Maddy tossed him a grin. "I'll bet you were murder on your sisters' dating lives. Did you beat up all their boyfriends?"

"Not all of them." He tipped a grin. "Tara always had pretty good instincts when it came to men, but Lexie's gotten herself mixed up with some real losers."

"I feel for her. Sometimes losers come disguised as nice guys. Nick's a real con artist—I see it now. I guess Evangeline will have to figure that out for herself."

"Why didn't you rat him out? She might've fired him and given you the promotion after all."

Maddy's gaze swept down, and he detected a bit of a flush on her cheeks.

He signaled a turn, checked for traffic, and accelerated around the bend. He hadn't realized the question would be such a stumper. But clearly he'd stumbled upon something uncomfortable.

"It embarrasses me to say this," she said quietly. "But I made a mistake when I applied for the position at Pirouette. I falsified something on my résumé—in my employment history. I knew Evangeline might not check them all out since she was in a hurry to fill the position. And there was a lot of competition..." She gave her head a shake. "There's no excuse—it was plain wrong."

Connor could see she regretted her actions. He knew all about regret. "We all make mistakes, Maddy. Sometimes you have to extend yourself some grace."

"I almost told Evangeline on several

SUMMER BY THE TIDES

SUMMER BY THE TIDES

occasions over the years. She was a reasonable person, and the guilt was eating me alive."

He put two and two together. "You told Nick."

She spared him a glance. "Yes. If I'd gone to Evangeline and told her what he'd done, he would've thrown me under the bus. I would've lost my job anyway. Besides, by the time it was all over I figured I'd probably gotten what I deserved."

"I don't think God works like that. He's not into retaliation."

"No, but there are consequences for our sins. You can't deny that. The Bible is full of examples."

"Well, Nick doesn't get off the hook so easily in my book. And it doesn't sound like he has an ounce of regret about the damage he did."

"Probably not, but he's not a Christian either—although he claimed to be. I knew better. And frankly, I wasn't where I should've been spiritually. If I were I never would've gone out with him to begin with."

"Hindsight," they said simultaneously

and shared a smile.

He admired her for admitting her mistake to him. It had taken a lot of courage and vulnerability, and knowing she was guarded by nature, that meant a lot to him.

"For what it's worth," Maddy said, "I've learned from my mistake. It turns out I have a fresh start, and I'm willing to put in the work to get where I want to be. No more shortcuts."

"That's good, Maddy."

"Did I scare you off?" There was a teasing note in her voice.

"Did you mean to?" he asked. He let the question hang for a minute. When she didn't reply he said, "You're a hard worker, Maddy. I've seen you in action. I respect that about you. I have no doubt you'll get where you want to go."

"I've noticed you're not exactly a deadbeat yourself. You must've put in a lot of effort to impress Ray so much that he'd leave you his business."

"I believe in giving it your all. My parents raised us to earn our keep and pull our weight and all those other principle-oriented clichés." He thought of Annie and gave a sad smile. "But I also tend to have tunnel vision sometimes. That's not a good thing. I'm working on it, though."

"We're all works in progress."

"That we are. Thanks for telling me what you did, Maddy. You didn't have to."

"Figured you should know what you're getting yourself into." She said it jokingly, but he had a feeling it revealed a seed of truth.

"Our mistakes don't define us—thank God. If they did we'd all be up the creek."

Maddy let out a breath she didn't know she'd been holding. Her heart was still palpitating in her chest. She was still mortified by what she'd done to get that job, and she'd been afraid Connor would view her differently once he knew.

She remembered telling Nick about her résumé and couldn't help but distinguish between the two men's reactions. Nick had high-fived her and said, **Whatever it takes, babe**. She should've known then and there what kind of person he was.

Instead, she'd allowed his approval to soothe her guilt. Connor's reaction hadn't affirmed her actions, but he'd also shown her grace.

Conversation continued to flow easily on the drive to Wilmington, and before she knew it they were pulling into a diagonal parking spot along Main Street. She could hardly believe they were already here.

Connor ushered her into the restaurant, a hand at the small of her back. Delectable smells filled the air: grilled steak, a hint of garlic. The hostess led them across the dining room.

The lighting was perfect, falling from rustic urban chandeliers onto white tablecloths. The low buzz of conversation and clattering of silverware blended with the sultry jazz piped in from invisible speakers. An adjacent room boasted high ceilings and a scarred wooden floor that tilted a bit, ending at a brick wall. It was there that the hostess seated them, then left them to look over the leatherbound menus.

A few minutes later Maddy's mouth was watering at the entrée descriptions. "Everything looks so good. Do you have any recommendations? Have you been here before?"

"No, I haven't," he said. "My best friend, Lamont, recommended it. I'll tell you, it's a little intimidating to choose a restaurant for someone in the business."

"What? No, I'm not hard to please. Besides, you're in the business."

He gave her a wry look over his menu.

Maddy laughed, her gaze flittering over the entrée selections. "I really don't eat out very often, but I admit I'm impressed by the chef's creativity. Look at the blackened scallops. 'Served with a spring mix atop sweet-and-sour sauce, garnished with candied walnuts and bleu cheese crumbles.' Yum."

"Sounds like someone's made a decision."

"Oh, I don't know. Did you see the cioppino? And the Chilean sea bass? It all sounds so good."

"Well, you've narrowed it down to

seafood at least. That's further than I've gotten. I can't get past the smell of the steak."

When the server came to the table she shared the dinner features. Maddy was sold on the blackened scallops, and Connor settled on a very large rib eye.

"Your sisters seemed to be getting along pretty well this week," he said once their server sashayed away. "At least while I'm around."

"They're...behaving. But nothing's been resolved, believe me. Much to my grandmother's dismay."

"She's been gone awhile. I've only lived next door a couple years, but I've never known her to take a long trip like this."

"I think she's giving us space to work things out. Frankly, I'm surprised Emma or Nora didn't take a hike a long time ago. I've been praying for reconciliation, but neither of them is willing to budge."

"And there you are, right in the middle."

"It's never been my favorite place." The server came and brought their drinks, then slipped quietly away. "You've never asked what happened between them."

He took a sip of his Coke. "Figured it was none of my business. Must've been a doozy to still be festering after all these years."

She searched his face. She could trust him with the truth. He was fair, and look at the grace he'd already shown her. Plus, they could definitely use more prayers. And maybe she could shed one more layer of guilt while she was at it.

She folded her arms on the table. "That last summer we spent in Seahaven, Emma brought her fiancé, Jonathan. I turned twelve. We were busy that summer, planning the wedding."

She went on to tell him about the times she'd caught Nora and Jonathan alone together. "I realized later I should've said something to Emma. Or confronted Nora about it. But I didn't, and because of that..." She shook her head, her chest tightening. "Things took a terrible turn."

His eyes softened on her. "That must've been awful for all of you—especially Emma."

"I wished so many times I'd confronted Nora that first time I saw them alone together. Maybe I could've prevented the whole thing."

"It wasn't your fault, Maddy. You were only a child."

She remembered what Holly had said about her burying her head in the sand. She'd been running from conflict even then. "When it all blew up I could tell Nora felt terrible. But they'd fallen in love. It was just awful."

It had been Maddy's first experience with love gone wrong. Watching her sisters suffer had been terrible. And seeing firsthand how the ensuing conflict ripped her family apart had been enlightening in the worst way.

She didn't want to think about that night anymore. She fast-forwarded through her memories. "Long story short, the two of them got married a few months later, and Mama and I went to the wedding. Emma still harbors resentment about that. She feels we took Nora's side, but I think she's forgiven me because I was so young. Mama's a different story, though. And that's just the start of what happened that summer. We haven't been close since then—any of us."

"But Emma's married now, right? It's been years; life goes on."

"Emma's marriage is actually on shaky ground at the moment, just between you and me. And Nora seems to be at a... crossroads of some sort. I don't know what's going on with her. We could all use your prayers."

"You've got them. Your grandma isn't the only one who wants reconciliation, you know."

"I know. But I have two very stubborn sisters."

"Well, don't you lose hope. God can handle stubborn, believe me."

It was dark by the time they pulled into Connor's drive. Maddy'd had a wonderful evening. Dinner was delicious, and they never ran out of things to talk about. She filled him in on her job search. She'd put in several applications in the past couple weeks.

Connor was a good listener, the perfect gentleman, and she couldn't deny he was also nice to look at across the candlelit table. He'd shaved for their date, and though she enjoyed an uninterrupted view of the cleft in his chin, she also found herself missing that bad-boy scruff.

She stepped out of his car, and they walked across his lawn toward her place. The night was quiet, save for the muted chirping of crickets and the distant crash of the surf. A lone light lit the porch, but the windows were dark.

"They must've gone to bed early," Maddy said.

"I can't imagine it's much fun for them without you here as a buffer."

"I'm sure it isn't. Even so, every time I leave them alone, I come back hoping they got things sorted out."

"One of these days they will." He took her hand loosely in his.

His palm was warm and rough against hers. She felt the touch in every cell of her body. If a mere touch could affect her so, what would his kiss do? Was she about to find out?

Her heart palpitated in her chest, equal parts anticipation and fear. She knew he was a good man—nothing like Nick. But she'd been hurt one too many times.

Connor walked her up the porch steps. The handrailing was sturdy now, thanks to his handyman skills, and the front door sported a fresh coat of red paint.

"The place is really coming along," he said, as if reading her mind. "You're going to run out of things to do soon."

He must be wondering when she'd be going home. She'd been wondering the same thing. "I want to stay until Gram comes back, at least. I'd like to spend a few days with her."

"I'm sure she'd like that," he said.

As they reached the door, he let go of her hand and tucked his own into his pockets. The golden light fell over him, whispering over the angles and planes of his face, glinting off his hair. It flashed on the golden tips of his lashes and made his eyes sparkle with silver flecks.

"Thank you for tonight," she said. "I had a very nice time. The food was wonderful —and so was the company."

The corner of his mouth kicked up. "No regrets?"

She quirked a saucy brow. "Not yet..."

He chuckled. "Uh-oh. Now I—as the guy—have to figure out what that means exactly. Will a kiss make her regret the evening, or will she be disappointed if he leaves her with only a hug?"

"And it's the part where I have to wait and see what he wants to do..."

"Isn't it obvious?" His soulful eyes searched hers for a long breathless moment. "He wants to kiss her."

Her throat closed up, making her next words barely audible. "She'd like that very much."

His gaze fell to her lips.

She forgot to breathe while she waited for his lips to touch hers. When they did, she instantly forgot where she was. Forgot everything but the feel of his mouth, warm and soft, on hers.

He stepped closer—or she did. His

hands came to her waist, and she moved her palms up the hard planes of his chest. He kissed her as though he had all the time in the world. As though he were savoring her. The thought made her insides melt a little. His touch, reverent and undemanding, kindled a fire inside. Connor Sullivan knew how to kiss a woman.

His hands clenched at her waist an instant before he drew away.

The cool evening air pressed in on her, and a breathy sigh escaped. Her fingers were tangled in his hair, she realized as her eyes fluttered open. And they were unsteady as she let them glide down his chest.

She'd seen many looks in his expressive eyes, but this sleepy-eyed gaze won top spot in her favorites list. She'd put that look there, she thought, amazed.

"Okay, then...," he said shakily.

Maybe she wasn't the only one whose knees were about to buckle. She withdrew her hands but couldn't pull away from the look in his eyes.

"That was…" He seemed at a loss for words, shook his head.

"Yeah," she said with a tremulous smile. "It really was."

CHAPTER 25

Washing the draperies was on Maddy's to-do list on Wednesday. Judging by the dust puffing from her armload of curtains, it had been a while. She felt a tickle in her nose an instant before she let out a big sneeze.

Her eyes drifted out the living room window as she passed through. It was beautiful out today, but a tropical storm was brewing in the Caribbean, and a likely path had it coming their way in a couple days.

Emma and Nora had gone to the grocery to stock up on basics and to the hardware store for batteries and flashlights in case they lost power. In addition they were getting new cabinet pulls, lightbulbs, and a new seal for the bathroom faucet. Might as well get more work done around here, impending storm or no.

Their grandma was going to be tickled pink with their progress. She was finally flying home tomorrow—just in time for the storm, it sounded like. The walls were freshly painted in neutral colors, and Connor planned to finish the exterior Sunday.

Connor. She couldn't help the smile that curled her lips as she dumped the curtains into the washing machine. He'd been around a lot this week, lending a hand. They'd worked and talked and laughed. But it seemed as though her sisters were always nearby—there hadn't yet been a second kiss.

She couldn't get the one they'd shared off her mind. She went to sleep thinking about it and woke up thinking about it. She was also pretty sure it had filled her dreams.

They were falling into a new routine. He'd started texting her good morning, and they shared a few texts in the afternoon. After work he came over for supper, and they went to work on the house again.

The doorbell rang as Maddy closed the washing machine, and Pippy ran to the door, barking. Maybe it was Emma and Nora, their arms full of groceries. Although it didn't seem as if they'd been gone that long.

She rushed to the door, lifting a feisty Pippy into her arms, and swept it open. Her lips parted at the sight of the man on the front porch. He was dressed business casual in khakis and a slim-fit shirt.

Nick.

Maddy's breath escaped, her stomach diving for the floor. He looked exactly the same, that dark hair flopping over his forehead, those ice-blue eyes warming on her as a smile lifted his lips.

"Hello, Maddy," he said.

She gave her a head a shake as if he were a mirage she could make disappear. But no, he was here in Seahaven. On her porch, nothing but a screen between them. And he was smiling as if he hadn't recently betrayed her in every way possible.

Of course Maddy had chosen this morning to throw on her ugliest paint-stained T-shirt and oldest pair of shorts. She hadn't bothered with makeup either and had thrown her hair into a sloppy bun that was now falling down around her face. It bothered her most that she even cared.

"What are you doing here, Nick?" She sounded hard and unyielding. Good.

He gave her his boyish grin. "Aren't you going to invite me in?"

She tilted her head, making no move to do so.

"Come on, Maddy. We need to talk— and you won't take my calls."

"Can you blame me?"

He had the grace to look sheepish. "No, I can't. I don't blame you at all, but I came all the way here. You might as well hear me out, right? I want to apologize, okay? I owe you that much, right?"

The man made a good point. Still, her

sisters weren't here, and she didn't want him in the house. "Go on around to the back deck. I'll be out in a minute."

"Thank you." He turned to go, that familiar gait making all this feel very real.

She needed a minute to collect herself. She couldn't even define the emotions coursing through her. Her insides were going haywire, her heart beating against her ribs, and her breaths struggling to keep up. It seemed surreal that he was here, at her grandmother's cottage.

She made her way to the back of the house, resisting the urge to improve her appearance. All the words she'd mentally spewed at him after his betrayal rose in her mind. How good would it feel to hurt him as he'd hurt her?

But the check in her spirit reminded her that retaliation wasn't right. And those fiery feelings were no longer there anyway. So she breathed a prayer for wisdom and forced herself to pour him a glass of iced tea. She added one for herself just so she'd have something to do with her hands.

Leaving Pippy inside, she slipped out the door. He'd seated himself in one of the aqua chairs and she wished, uncharitably, that the paint was still wet.

"Thanks," he said as he took the glass. "What a great place. How come you never brought me out here?"

She sat in the chair next to him, glad it was a good few feet away, because she suddenly wanted to smack him. "I asked you several times. You said we were too busy."

"Well..." He slanted her a grin. "I'm sorry we didn't. We probably could've used the break from work."

"And my grandmother could've used the visit." She was cross with herself for not coming without him.

"Of course."

He turned in his chair, and her gaze fell to his squared-off knees, then down to his immaculate brown shoes. He was fussy about his shoes, shining them nearly every time he put them on.

"Listen, Maddy..." The smile was gone, replaced by a hangdog look. "I know I owe you a big apology. What I did was wrong."

"Which part, Nick? You not only be-trayed me with Evangeline, you stabbed me in the back professionally. You knew I was counting on that promotion, and you deliberately took it from me."

"I know." He gave a nod. "That was... pretty despicable of me. All of it."

"Did you ever care about me, Nick? Or was I only a pawn the whole time?"

His eyes widened. "No, absolutely not. Is that what you've been thinking? Maddy, of course I cared about you. I hope you believe that. When we started dating you were so...refreshing. And we had so much in common. I loved hanging out with you. I never thought I even had a chance at that promotion.

"Then a few months ago Evangeline..." He gave her a sheepish look. "She kind of hit on me one night after work—and I rebuffed her. I did, at first...But she wouldn't give up. Then she told me she was considering me for the promotion, and I just got so caught up in it all. You know how ambitious I am—and you're just as bad, Maddy..."

His pointed look left no doubt that he was thinking of her falsified résumé. Nice.

"I never told Evangeline about your résumé," he added.

Well, give the man a gold star. Who knew if he was even telling the truth? Had Evangeline really come on to him or had it been the other way around? Maddy couldn't imagine her former boss doing any such thing, but she'd probably never know. Nick knew she'd never ask Evangeline, so he could say anything he wanted.

Maddy didn't even need to know the truth. She'd pretty much put this whole debacle behind her. Though clearly the forgiveness part was still a work-in-progress.

"Okay," he said. "I can see you don't quite trust me, and you have good reason not to. Can't blame you. But it's true. I never said an unkind word about you until that day you walked in. I knew how badly you wanted the promotion, but she wasn't going to give it to you anyway. So why shouldn't it go to me?"

"That's not the impression I got from her when Joe announced his retirement. She told me I was first in line."

"Her opinion changed over the next couple months."

Maddy gave a rueful laugh. "No doubt."

He raised his hands. "I had nothing to do with that. You know Allison never liked you. She bent Evangeline's ear every chance she got."

"Allison is a hostess who couldn't even show up to work on time. Why would Evangeline listen to her?"

"Allison is no longer there for that very reason, but she was a little drama queen behind the scenes. She stirred up some of the others and got them on her side. You had a mutiny on your hands and didn't even know it."

She wouldn't put it past Allison, but then, she only had Nick's word. Noelle had never mentioned any of this to Holly. But then, Allison had probably left Noelle out of her games since her sister was best friends with Maddy.

"You ran a tight ship, and Allison didn't like following rules. That's on her, not you. But Evangeline took her complaints more seriously than she should've."

And Maddy guessed Nick had done nothing to defend her. But what did it matter now? Water under the bridge. The job was long gone, and she and Nick were over.

"What do you want, Nick?" she asked wearily. "Why are you here?"

"I told you, I owe you a big apology. I'd like your forgiveness, though I know I don't deserve it."

He had more to say. She could hear it in his voice. "And..."

"And..." He gave her a charming smile. "I have an opportunity I wanted to share with you. Something right up your alley. I'm not sure if you've got another job lined up yet, but when I heard about this I thought of you immediately."

"A job?" She remembered what she'd overheard him saying to Evangeline and couldn't hold back. "What about my 'tendency to get frazzled'? My 'inability to handle responsibility'?"

"Ah, Maddy, I was an idiot. I know that, okay? Cut a guy a break. I'm trying to make up for it. That's why I came. A buddy of mine is launching a restaurant in downtown Charlotte. I told you about it. He had the managerial staff lined up, but the general manager position fell through. I convinced him you'd be perfect for it."

"And you think I'd be interested?" In something Nick had set up with "a buddy of his"?

"It's a great opportunity, Maddy. I considered taking it myself."

"What about Pirouette? You just got that position." Stole it, but who was counting? "And what about Evangeline? You were just going to leave her hanging out to dry after she promoted you?"

"That's why I decided to stay. But Evangeline and I were never serious, Maddy. We're not even together any-more. I work for her now—that's it." He tilted a look at Maddy. "She's just not you, babe."

She bristled. "Don't call me that."

"Come on, Maddy. I wasn't going to get into this today, because I think we need to focus on the job opportunity. But I do miss you; I'm just going to leave that right there for now. Have you accepted another position somewhere?"

Maddy blinked at the emotional whiplash. "Not yet, but I have my feelers out. And to be honest, Nick, I'm a little skeptical about your involvement in this opportunity."

He put up his hands, palms out. "I'm not involved, not really. I'm just the broker of the deal, and I don't need an answer today. Just think about it. It's a great opportunity, and you shouldn't let your emotions get in the way of that. You should know they have a great up-and-coming chef onboard—Louis Antoine Marseille."

Maddy did a double take. She'd read an article about him in **Food and Wine** magazine. He'd graduated from Le Cordon Bleu in Paris and had worked with some of France's best chefs. He was a great catch, and it showed the owner was serious about excellent cuisine.

"I told you it was a great opportunity. The job's not going to be available forever, though. Miles wants to lock down the management in the next couple weeks." He set down his iced tea. "Take a walk on the beach? I can tell you more about it."

Maddy hated to admit it, but she was tempted. Even despite the drawback of Nick's involvement, it could be a real career boost.

CHAPTER 26

Connor had forgotten what this felt like… being happy, having hope. He'd gotten so accustomed to the dark cloud hanging over his head that it had become his normal.

Maddy had changed all that. Who could've known that the woman he'd thought snarky and judgmental was actually the answer to his prayers? The reason he was driving down the road with a goofy grin on his face.

It's just the beginning, he reminded himself, trying to temper his expectations. Although they'd spent a decent amount of time together, he'd only known her a matter of weeks. And his hope felt out of proportion with the beginner status of their relationship.

And then there was that kiss. She'd been so soft and warm and responsive. And man, did he love the sweet scent of her hair. He craved it when he was away from her.

He shifted in his seat, eager to see her. So eager he'd left work a full hour early, something he couldn't remember doing before. It was time he gave his top dockhand, Brandon, a little more responsibility. The kid was capable and eager to prove himself.

His thoughts jumped to the jobs still needing done at the cottage. He'd agreed to handle the things the sisters didn't feel comfortable with: fixing the plumbing, changing out the linoleum in the laundry room, and replacing a window that had a failed seal.

If they were productive tonight, maybe he could talk Maddy into a walk on the beach. He was eager to get her alone, eager for another chance to kiss her.

He pulled onto Bayview Drive, wondering how quickly he could shower and change. Silly, maybe, since he was only going to get dirty again, but the smell of fish clung to him, and he wanted to smell good for Maddy.

As he approached his place his eyes fell on a red car in the driveway next door. The Monroe sisters had company. As he grew nearer he realized it was an old Mustang—a late sixties model, if he wasn't mistaken.

He remembered Maddy's comment from their date, and his stomach fell to the floorboard. He pulled into his drive-way and sat there a moment, looking next door.

Had she been expecting a visit from Nick? She hadn't said anything.

The Mercedes was gone, but Maddy's car was there. Likely Emma and/or Nora was gone. That meant Maddy might be alone with Nick. Connor had no reason to be concerned about her safety—just because he was a tool didn't mean he was dangerous.

A few minutes later Connor went inside

his house and went through the motions: taking a shower, washing his hair, getting dressed. His mind spun a mile a minute. Worry churned in his gut. What did Nick want with Maddy? Was she okay?

When he got downstairs he grabbed his cell phone and pulled up Maddy's number. He'd just make sure she was all right.

But moments later the phone rang into voicemail. He hung up without leaving a message. Why would Nick have come all the way to Seahaven? She'd said he'd been trying to reach her. Was he here to make amends? Did he miss her, want her back?

Connor walked into the kitchen where he could see the cottage through the window. He'd feel a lot better if he knew one of her sisters was there.

The landline. He found their grandma's number under his contacts and called it. He wasn't sure what his place was. He recognized the jealousy twisting his gut, but she wasn't his girlfriend. They'd only had one official date.

The phone rang five times before going to voicemail. Darn it. He ended the call and squeezed the back of his neck. Why wasn't someone answering? It was possible they'd all left in the Mercedes. But that was also unlikely.

He was going over there, he decided, charging toward his back door. He hated to make things uncomfortable for Maddy, but her safety came first. It was worth the bit of awkwardness his appearance might cause. If she was fine, he'd excuse himself.

But when his feet hit the deck, his eyes caught on movement down by the beach. He immediately recognized Maddy's dark hair trailing in the wind. She walked beside a man he could only deduce was Nick. He was several inches taller than she was, dark hair, sleek looking.

Connor's lungs deflated, leaving him with a hollow feeling. If someone had asked him yesterday what Maddy would do if Nick turned up on her doorstep, he would've sworn she'd shut the door in his face.

Instead, she appeared to be taking a leisurely stroll on the beach with him. He could barely see them now, over the dunes, walking together, more closely than he would've liked.

Clearly Maddy felt they had things to talk about. Closure? Or was that just wishful thinking on his part? Maddy and Nick had a long history. They'd been in love— or Maddy had been—while Connor's relationship with her was brand-new.

Still, he couldn't believe she was giving Nick the time of day after what he'd done. Connor watched from the deck, hands on hips, energy churning through his body, until he couldn't see them anymore.

He'd never felt this way before. Annie had been the first girl he'd been serious about, and she'd never given him reason to feel jealous. He put his palm against his chest where his heart actually ached.

Enough of this. He took out his phone, opened the last incoming call on his phone, and waited until there was an answer.

"Hey," he said in greeting. "Still want to shoot hoops tonight?"

"Sure," Lamont said. "Thought you had other plans."

"They fell through." He'd never actually said he'd be over to help the sisters tonight. And obviously Maddy had other plans now. "See you in ten?"

"Sure thing."

Connor ended the call. He suddenly couldn't wait to burn off some steam.

"Dude." Lamont hunched over, hands on his knees. "Take it easy on a brother. I haven't played in weeks."

"You're just sore I'm beating you for once." Connor slapped the ball against the concrete. The local park was nearly empty tonight, the humidity chasing everyone away. They'd both lost their shirts five minutes in, and now sweat rolled off their bodies.

Lamont drew a forearm across his forehead. "Why do I get the feeling I'm in the middle of some kind of therapy right now?"

Connor put up a shot from the three-point range, and it sank through the net with a **swish**.

Lamont scowled. "Man, you're killing me. Something happen today? Your sisters getting on your nerves or something?"

"My sisters are on my nerves twenty-four/seven." He put a body on Lamont. Had to get up tight on the man. He wasn't tall, but he was scrappy.

Lamont pivoted, faked him out, and put up a shot. It banked off the board and dropped through.

"Lucky shot."

"It's that girl, isn't it? What, she go back home or something? Leave you all alone and heartbroken?"

Connor grabbed the ball and dribbled out. "She's still here."

"Well, something's eating at you. You haven't played like this since—"

Connor gave him a dark look. He did not want to talk about the days following Annie's death. His friend had the good sense to drop it.

Lamont shrugged. "Just saying, man. You're a hot mess."

They played in silence for another forty minutes, until Connor was flushed with heat, his lungs full and achy. Lamont had put up a good fight, but Connor had beat him by four. He'd played like a maniac. Too aggressive, though Lamont gave as good as he got. Connor was going to pay for this tomorrow when he rolled out of bed—he wasn't eighteen anymore.

They headed for the wooden picnic table where they'd left their stuff. Connor sat on top, uncapped his water. His breaths were ragged, his throat so dry he downed the water in one long drink. Squirrels nattered from a nearby tree, and children squealed from the playground equipment. A hot breeze ruffled his hair, stirring up the earthy smell of his own sweat.

"You ever going tell me what's eating at you, or are we just going to pretend all that"—he nodded toward the court—"didn't happen."

Connor wondered if Maddy and Nick

were still walking the beach. Had he tried to kiss her? The thought rankled. Connor had wanted to walk the beach with her tonight. Had wanted to kiss her again.

Now she was potentially doing both with her ex-boyfriend. Unreal. The Maddy he knew would sooner slap the guy than kiss him, but there was a lot he didn't know about Maddy. And she'd admitted her instincts weren't the best. She'd described Nick as a con artist, and he hated the thought that she might be sucked right back into his web.

"You two have a fight or something?" Lamont asked.

Connor slid him a look. "What's with all the touchy-feely stuff tonight? Been watching the Hallmark Channel again?"

"Hey, my lady loves that channel—and I love my lady. Can't fault that logic."

"Guess not."

Lamont and Brianna, dating for over a year now, were probably headed for an engagement soon. They were a fun couple. Connor had thought about asking Maddy to double with them sometime soon.

He still felt like trash even after burning off the excess energy. Maybe he did need to talk about this thing with Maddy and Nick. It was eating his lunch, and better Lamont than one of his sisters. He hadn't even told them he was dating Maddy; they'd never leave him alone about it.

He capped his empty water bottle with a sigh. "So, when I got home tonight, her ex-boyfriend's car was in her driveway. Her sisters were gone, and she didn't answer her phone when I called."

"Huh. He's not from around here, is he?"

"He's from Charlotte, like Maddy. Came all the way out here to see her—that can't be good, right?"

"Give her some credit. He cheated on her, you said. She don't want none of that."

Connor wished he could make himself believe that. "That's what I thought, man. Next thing I know she's taking a stroll on the beach with him."

"A stroll on the beach, huh? Well, that

could be closure, could be anything, could be nothing."

Connor pictured the two of them, side by side. "Didn't look like nothing. Maddy said she hadn't talked to him since the breakup, then here he is, showing up at her door."

"You don't think she was lying about it, do you?"

"No. She wouldn't do that."

"See? Probably just closure. Maybe you should just ask her what's up with this guy."

Connor had come to the same conclusion over the past exhausting hour and a half. "You're right. Just put it out there."

Lamont gave him a long, searching look. "She's getting to you, huh?"

"Like nobody's business." He just hoped he hadn't already lost her. He gave Lamont a chagrined look and held out his hand. "Thanks for letting me blow off some steam."

Lamont grasped his hand. "Hey, man. What are friends for?"

CHAPTER 27

Maddy let loose a soul-deep sigh as Nick pulled from her drive. She had not expected that. Her mind was spinning with all he'd said, the words swarming around her brain like a dozen bees, refusing to settle anywhere.

To further confuse the matter, she wasn't sure what to believe—if things had happened with Evangeline the way he'd said. If Allison had really sabotaged her promotion.

She decided to put that on the back burner. Did it really matter at this point? And then there was the whole "I miss you" thing. He'd never circled back around to that. But she could see the interest in his eyes, in the way he'd found excuses to touch her as they walked along the shore.

She wanted none of that. It was the only thing she was sure of right now. She couldn't be with a man she didn't trust. And she no longer felt toward Nick the way she once had. That had been made crystal clear by his visit. She was glad he'd come, for that reason alone. It had offered such clarity.

She checked her watch. Connor had been off work for over half an hour, but his car wasn't yet in his drive. She'd been trying to rush Nick along, not wanting an awkward confrontation between the two men.

Movement caught her eye, a car. It wasn't Connor's, but the Mercedes. Nora pulled into the drive and came to a stop. Maddy went to help her sisters with the groceries.

"Who was that?" Emma nodded toward Nick's Mustang, only now just disappearing from view. They must've seen him pulling from the drive.

Maddy lifted the trunk and grabbed a

handful of bags. "That was Nick."

Emma did a double take. "**Nick** Nick?"

"The very one."

"Don't tell me he's come crawling back," Nora said.

"I hope you told him to go jump off a bridge."

Maddy hadn't yet confessed to losing her job, and this didn't seem like the time to bring it up. "I'm not interested in picking up where we left off, and I think I got that message across loud and clear."

Emma nodded in approval. "Good for you."

"I hope you got to slug him," Nora said.

"Tempting," Maddy said. "But he did apologize, and I've decided to give forgiveness a try." She kind of liked the peace that came with it.

"Bear in mind," Emma said as they walked through the house, "granting forgiveness doesn't mean granting trust. One is given, and the other is earned."

Tension sprouted between the sisters as they set their groceries on the counter. The subject of betrayal had once again resurrected unresolved feelings. The tension lingered in the air as they put away groceries. Emma was probably dealing with her residual anger, Nora with guilt that had also morphed into anger over time. What a mess it all was.

Maddy sensed their truce was on shaky ground, and she was afraid to say anything for fear of causing the stress fracture that would make everything collapse.

When the groceries had been put away, Maddy grabbed the burnished bronze cabinet pulls they'd selected from the hardware store. "I like these. They'll freshen these old cabinets right up."

"I thought they'd look good with the new faucet," Nora said in a perky tone, obviously relieved for the tension breaker. "I'll put them on tonight."

"Where's Connor?" Emma asked. "He's usually here by now."

"I'm not sure. He never really said he was coming over, so maybe he has other plans tonight." Maddy checked her phone and saw she'd missed a call from him while Nick was here. "Oh, he tried to call earlier."

She wandered to the back door as she returned his call. But a moment later his voicemail kicked on.

"Hey, it's Maddy," she said when prompted to leave a message. "I guess I missed your call earlier. We never really talked about tonight, so I'm not sure what your plans are, but would you mind coming over when you get home? If it's not too late, I'd like to talk. Okay, well, I guess I'll see you later."

Connor stepped from the shower—his third of the day—and pushed the damp towel on the floor out of the way. His muscles quivered from overuse on the court. He'd grabbed a bite to eat with Lamont, and they'd gone back to his apartment and watched part of the Braves game. They'd been down 5–2 in the fifth inning when Connor left.

He couldn't seem to care about his favorite team tonight. He had Maddy on his brain.

He cleared the fog from his mirror and

rubbed down his hair with a dry towel. He hadn't bothered shaving this morning, or yesterday for that matter. He suspected Maddy liked the scruffy look, though she hadn't said so. He'd caught her looking at his jawline, however, and thought he saw a flicker of approval in her eyes.

He went to his room and grabbed some clothes that were lying across his dresser. When he collected his phone he saw Maddy had left a voicemail. He touched the screen, filled with equal parts hope and dread, and listened to her message. Her tone gave nothing away. But she wanted him to come over, wanted to talk. That didn't sound good. His stomach was in knots by the time the message ended.

It was going on ten o'clock, but unlike her sisters, Maddy usually went to bed after eleven. Rather than text her that he was coming over, he decided to just show up at her door.

His legs weren't as steady as he would've liked as he covered the uneven ground between their houses. He told himself his muscles were fatigued from his workout. But the dread roiling in his stomach told a different story. He was a wreck over this.

They'd only had one date, he reminded himself. They sure hadn't gotten into serious territory yet. They weren't in love. They weren't even a couple. They'd only known each other five weeks and had spent half of that time disliking each other.

Yet even with all these marks in the **easy come, easy go** column, the one item in the **heartbreak ahead** column outweighed them all.

"I like her," he said out loud. "I really like her."

More than seemed possible given all the items in the first column. But that didn't change the fact that it was true. These things didn't always make sense on paper.

If she was calling it quits it was going to hurt. Heck, it hurt just thinking about it. He felt as though he were on his way to the gallows as he entered her yard and looked up at the kitchen window, a lone light spilling through it and onto the deck.

The warm wind tousled his damp hair as he took the steps up the deck and spotted her sitting at the table, a mug of something cupped between her hands. The stove light cast a golden glow over her face, softening her features.

Did she look like a woman who'd just stood strong against her ex-boyfriend or a woman who was about to break another man's heart?

Before he could decide which it was, she caught sight of him, and he forced his lips upward.

Her instant smile gave him a jolt of hope. She rushed to the door and opened it. "Hey there."

"Hey. Got your message."

She wore a paint-stained T-shirt and a pair of shorts. No makeup that he could see, and the freckles on her nose were making an appearance. In short, she was the prettiest thing he'd ever seen. His heart stuttered at the thought he might lose her.

"Let's go outside," Maddy said. "It's finally cooled off a bit. Do you want something to drink? Or eat? Emma made some lemon poppy seed muffins that are to die for."

"No thanks. I just ate."

He followed her across the deck, where she lowered herself onto the steps leading down to the beach. He sank down beside her, leaving a gap between them.

The crash of the surf was distant, the tide going out. Moonlight glimmered on the water, a blue cone widening toward the shore. Overhead the sky was like black velvet, twinkling with a million stars.

His gaze fell to Maddy. The shadowy night revealed little of her expression, making him wish they'd stayed inside.

"So what did you do tonight?" Her question was casual. "Anything fun?"

"I shot hoops with Lamont, grabbed a bite to eat, watched the game at his place."

"That's nice. That's great you have a close friend."

"He's been by my side a long time. Been through some tough stuff together."

"Those are the best kind. I don't know

what I'd do without Holly. I miss her. Texting and phone calls just aren't the same."

"Yeah, I get that. Did you get much done on the house?"

"Not as much as I would've liked."

No doubt. He could tell she was stalling for time, trying to find a way to bring up Nick's visit. Maybe he should just put her out of her misery. But before he could open his mouth, she spoke.

"So listen, Connor. I wanted to tell you about...Well, Nick came to see me this afternoon—my ex-boyfriend."

Connor dug the toe of his sandal through the sandy soil, making a deep horizontal line. "That so? What did he want?"

"Well...I guess mainly he wanted to apologize for his behavior."

Apologize for cheating on her? For stealing her promotion? For manipulating her emotions? How did one go about such a feat?

"And how'd that go over?"

She breathed a laugh, ducked her head. "It was good to hear, I'll admit, after waiting all these weeks. Not that I'd been holding my breath, mind you. But I'm working on the forgiveness part, and knowing he's sorry helps. I'll get there eventually."

He searched her face, desperate to know what was going on in her head. He had a feeling there'd been a whole lot more to their conversation.

"Is that all he wanted?"

With her toes she extended the line he was drawing in the sand. "No. Actually, it wasn't."

He braced himself. Drew another line parallel to the one he'd drawn before.

"He said he knows of a job opportunity for me."

He slanted a look her way, unable to stop himself from saying, "Didn't he steal your last one?"

She helped him with his line, their toes touching for a brief instant. "A friend of his is opening a restaurant in Charlotte. The chef's well known, and it seems like a promising opportunity. It's the GM position—same one I was trying to get at

Pirouette."

"A friend of Nick's? That doesn't concern you?" He couldn't keep the disbelief from his voice.

"I'd have to meet the man and judge for myself if he's someone I'd want to work for, of course."

He scratched his neck.

"I have to consider this, Connor. I don't have another offer yet, and my savings are dwindling."

He clamped his lips together and dug a vertical line with more force than necessary. He didn't want to think about her having a connection to that dirtbag, even a professional one. And he couldn't help but think this job opportunity was just Nick's way of trying to manipulate his way back into her life.

"Is that all he wanted?" Connor squeezed the words past the ache in his throat. Part of him wished he could call back the question. Especially when a lengthy pause ensued.

Maddy finished the line in the sand. They'd made a tic-tac-toe grid.

"He said he misses me. But that was about the extent of that conversation."

His heart skipped a beat as he stared off to the darkened horizon. He forced a casual tone. As if her answer wouldn't break his heart a little. "And you, Maddy? Do you miss him?"

She turned toward Connor. He could feel the heat of her gaze on the side of his face. He surrendered to it, turning to meet her eyes. The breeze tousled her hair, teased him with her sweet scent. She made his heart ache.

"No. I don't miss him." Her lips turned up a little, searching his eyes. "I don't miss him at all."

His breath left his body in a quiet **whoosh**. That was all he needed to hear. What he'd longed to hear all night, ever since he'd seen her and Nick on the beach.

She looked down at the sand and drew a circle in one of the corner spaces.

He smiled at her action, feeling almost giddy inside. He didn't want to play games. They were on the same team. He

SUMMER BY THE TIDES

drew a circle in the opposite corner.

She gave him a look of surprise, then her eyes twinkled in the darkness. She drew a circle in the center square.

He dragged a straight line through the circles and met her gaze.

"We win," she said softly.

He hoped they would. "Listen, Maddy, I have to be honest about something..."

She tilted her head, her smile falling at the gravity in his voice. That crease formed between her brows, and he hated that he'd put it there.

"What's wrong?" she asked.

"Nothing's wrong. I just wanted to tell you I came home this afternoon. I left work early and was planning to come over and help with the house. But then I saw you and Nick together on the beach and..."

"Oh."

"I've been fretting ever since, and when I got your message a few minutes ago, I thought you were going to tell me the two of you were back together."

Her eyes widened. "What? No. Absolutely not."

Her vehement denial made hope rise to the surface like a submerged buoy. "I know we only just started going out, and I don't want to freak you out, Maddy, but...I really don't want to lose you."

He braced himself, hoping he hadn't said too much. She'd just barely agreed to go out on a date. He hadn't meant for things to get heavy so quickly.

But her eyes softened as a gentle smile blossomed on her face. "Well. If that isn't just about the nicest thing I've heard all day."

His muscles weakened as a heavy weight lifted from his shoulders. Dare he hope she was feeling the same as he?

"That was very honest of you." Her eyes pierced his. "You didn't have to tell me that."

"I don't want there to be any games between us, Maddy. Trust is important in a relationship—nobody knows that better than you."

She gave him a long, searching look. "I couldn't have been more wrong about you, Connor Sullivan—and that's a good thing."

He smiled at the memory of her first impression. "Are you ever going to let me live that down?"

"More to the point..." She gave him a saucy look. "Are you ever going to kiss me again?"

His breath fell from his lungs. His eyes fell to her lips, sweetly curved. He couldn't think of anything he'd like more.

"Far be it from me to keep a lady waiting," he said softly as he lowered his lips to hers. He brushed them gently. She tasted of sea air and woman. Addicting. He palmed her cheek. So soft. He could do this all night.

Her hand came to rest on his neck, her fingers toying with his hair. He deepened the kiss and pulled her closer, needing to feel her softness against him. What she did to him...He'd lost all hope of ever feeling this way again.

His heart was racing in his chest, his lungs aching for oxygen. But he needed her more than he needed his next breath.

He couldn't believe that was already true...
but it was.

God, he prayed. **I'm falling for her.
Falling hard and fast.**

He felt full to bursting inside, so many
thoughts and emotions swirling through
him, all of them good. His hand slid up
from her neck, cupping her jaw rever-
ently. She was a treasure, meant to be
adored. And he did, he realized. Could
she tell how he felt? Did he want her to
know? Did she feel the same way?

It would seem so.

He drew back, enough to nuzzle her jaw
with his nose. She smelled so good. He
couldn't get enough. If he'd thought their
first kiss had been a fluke, he'd been
proven wrong. So wrong.

The feel of her fingers threading through
his hair made every cell come to attention.

"Is it just me," he whispered, "or does it
feel like we've done this a lot more than
twice?"

"Not just you," she said on a soft breath,
drawing back to look at him beneath

hooded lids.

"Still...," he said. "We could always use more practice."

"I am a bit of a perfectionist."

"It's important we get it just right."

"Very important," she whispered.

He looked into her eyes as he lowered his lips to hers, feeling an unrelenting hope he hadn't felt in a long time. And it felt good. It felt right.

It felt as if everything he'd been waiting for—everything he never thought he'd have again—was right here in his arms.

CHAPTER 28

August 4, twenty years ago

Maddy treaded barefoot across the damp, hard-packed sand. Shells, many of them whole, were strewn across the beach as far as the eye could see, along with seagrass and driftwood. It always amazed her to see the treasures low tide turned up.

Daylight was fading fast, but if she waited till morning, all the good shells would be washed away. Besides, there was nothing else to do tonight. Everyone was busy.

Gram had gone to Bald Head Island with her friends for the weekend. Emma was in the kitchen, baking cinnamon rolls.

Mama and Daddy were in their bedroom, door closed. Jonathan was working late at the coffee shop, and Nora had gone off who-knew-where. Maddy suspected she was with Jonathan again, and her stomach knotted at the thought.

It had been over a week since she'd caught them kissing on the beach. She'd watched them when the family was together, and they seemed perfectly fine. Perfectly friendly. Sometimes Maddy thought she must've imagined what she'd seen.

But she knew in her heart she hadn't. It was true. Nora and Jonathan were betraying Emma. How could they do such a horrible thing? She had no idea love could go so very wrong.

She stooped to collect a white slipper. They were her favorite, and though she had dozens already, she couldn't resist the softly sheened perfection.

Several feet away she scooped up a spotted Scotch bonnet. They weren't the prettiest shells, ribbed and splotched with brown and amber, but this one was large and unbroken. She added it carefully to her cloth bag. She walked along, eyes scanning over the bits of driftwood, the ropes of kelp, and the broken seashells.

She walked all the way down to the inlet, then turned and walked back toward the cottage, edging closer to the water-line. On the way back she found a perfect sand dollar and a whole cockle-shell with a glossy iridescent pink underside—the largest she'd found all summer.

As she neared the beach in front of their cottage, she saw a large humped mass lying near the shoreline. A dead tarpon. Its silver-white scales glimmered in the evening light, its gills were still, and its black button eyes stared up lifelessly. A fly hovered above the dead body, and a stink rose from the carcass.

She skirted the dead fish, shaking the image of those bleak eyes from her mind. Low tide exposed the good and the bad, she supposed.

As she made her way up to the cottage she pulled the drawstring ribbons on her bag. The sand grew dry and deep near the dunes, and her feet plunged into the sugary mounds, sand sticking to her damp skin. The soles of her feet were summer-tough, numb to the jagged shells and bits of pinecone.

She spotted Emma emerging from the house and onto the deck, fingers over her mouth as she stared unseeing out over the sea.

Maddy lifted a hand, but Emma was looking off toward the inlet now, her posture stiff.

The golden hour had slipped away, but even in the waning light Maddy could see the groove between Emma's brows, a look of shock on her face. This was more than a glitch with the bridesmaid dresses or a canceled reservation.

A terrible dread rose up in Maddy. A weight pressed down on her lungs. Her heart came in heavy thumps that sped even as her footsteps slowed.

Emma caught sight of her as she neared the house. Her glassy eyes focused on Maddy as a tear slid down her cheek.

"Oh, Maddy...," Emma choked out.

"You'll never believe it."

"What—what's wrong?" Maddy made herself ask, but she didn't want to hear the answer. Wanted to go upstairs and bury herself under her covers and pretend this wasn't happening.

Another tear escaped as Emma blinked. Her blue eyes were wide with disbelief as Maddy came up the steps.

"I just—I just heard—" Emma couldn't seem to bring herself to say it.

Maddy couldn't bear it. She pulled her big sister close and folded her arms around her. How could Nora have done this? And Jonathan? He was supposed to love Emma. Is this what love looked like? If so, Maddy wanted nothing to do with it.

Emma's body shook as she wept in great sobs.

Maddy rubbed her back, her throat aching with unshed tears. "I know. I know. It's just awful. I'm so sorry, Emmie."

Emma gulped a deep breath, pulling away from Maddy. Her ravaged face tore at Maddy's heart. Her cheeks were blotched pink, and tears trembled on her lashes.

"You already know?"

"I—I saw them a week ago, on the beach," Maddy confessed, tears filling her own eyes. "I'm sorry I didn't tell you. I didn't want to believe they'd do such a thing. I hoped I was wrong somehow."

Something shifted in Emma's eyes. Her gaze sharpened on Maddy in a way that put the fear of God into her.

"I—I know I should've told you," Maddy blathered on. "But I didn't want to hurt you, and I wasn't for sure, for sure. It was dark, and her hair looked red, but I couldn't be certain."

The skin around Emma's eyes tightened, as did her grasp on Maddy's upper arms. "What—what are you talking about?"

Maddy's stomach dropped to her feet even as a new kind of tension coiled inside her. Emma didn't know about Nora and Jonathan, she realized suddenly. Something else had put those tears in her eyes. But Maddy had gone and opened her big mouth. And now it was too late to take back her words.

"I'm not sure of anything," Maddy whispered, shaking her head. "Honest, I'm not."

"Sure of what? Tell me, Maddy, tell me right now!" Emma's grip tightened painfully.

"I—I thought I saw them, Nora and Jonathan, on the beach late at night."

Emma's face hardened in a way Maddy had never seen. "Doing what?"

A tear slipped down Maddy's cheek. Regret pulsed inside with every beat of her heart. "It was dark. Really dark, Emma. I wasn't sure. I'm still not sure."

Emma's lips twisted and her nostrils flared. "Doing. What?"

Electricity thrummed in the air between them. Maddy's next words were going to send an irreversible jolt through Emma. But there was nothing else Maddy could do now.

"Kissing." The word was barely audible over the sound of surf.

Emma flinched, as if absorbing a blow.

Her breath hitched, her pupils flared, her fingers slowly loosened their grip on Maddy's arms until they fell to her sides.

Maddy couldn't look away from the hurt and anger on her sister's face. She wished she could take it all back. She was so stupid! She'd gone and ruined everything!

"Maybe I'm wrong," Maddy said. "I could be wrong."

But deep down she knew she wasn't. She hadn't imagined the flirting she'd witnessed back in June or that flicker of red hair on the beach. Hadn't imagined all the times Jonathan and Nora seemed to disappear at the same exact time—including today. If only she'd confronted Nora about it in the beginning, she could've stopped this from happening! Why, oh, why hadn't she said something?

Emma's eyes searched the horizon, and Maddy could almost see her stringing things together in her mind. As though Maddy had only exposed what Emma had already known somewhere deep inside.

Maybe it was fate, or maybe it was just

a terrible coincidence that a car rumbled
up to the cottage just then, tires crunching in the shelled driveway. Someone was
home, and it had to be either Jonathan or
Nora. Maddy didn't know which would be
worse.

Emma looked toward the side of the
house as the engine went silent. A car
door slammed shut. And then all was
quiet.

A warm breeze lifted gooseflesh on
Maddy's arms as the moment stretched
taut between them. Emma's chest
heaved, drawing in great gulps of air.

Maddy should say something—she just
didn't know what.

God...She prayed, but nothing else
came to mind.

And then Nora was coming through the
back door. Her hair flowed down around
her shoulders, and she wore a hint of
makeup. When had Nora started caring
so much about how she looked?

"Hey, you two," Nora said as she closed
the door.

Maddy's gaze swung to Emma in time

to see her eyes rake over Nora's navy top and a pair of white shorts that made her slender legs go on forever. She looked fresh and happy and sported a carefree glow Maddy had never noticed on her normally uptight sister.

"Well, look at you." Emma crossed her arms over her chest, pinning Nora with a look. "Where've you been, Nora?"

Nora's eyes shifted to Maddy, then back to Emma. "Um...I just ran a couple errands in town."

"You did, huh?" Emma said in a biting tone. "You look awfully spiffy for errands."

Nora shifted, rubbing her bare arms. They were lightly sun-burned, a fresh crop of freckles dusting her shoulders. "What's wrong?"

Maddy's feet were frozen to the deck boards. She watched the speculation on Nora's face and thought she saw a flush rising up her neck in the waning light.

Nora turned a searching look on Maddy, emitting a bleak laugh. "What's going on? Did something happen?"

Words jumbled in Maddy's throat,

locking it up tight. She looked at Emma.

Emma took three steps, coming up so close to Nora she had to look up. She gave her sister a long, scathing look. "What is going on between you and Jonathan?"

Nora averted her gaze, going unnaturally still. "What—what do you mean?"

"You know what I mean. Tell me the truth, Nora, or so help me…"

Nora took a step back, putting space between them. She finally looked at Emma, searching her face for a long, painful moment. Her chest heaved. Her eyes softened with pity as her chin trembled and her face slowly crumpled.

"I'm so sorry, Emma," she whispered. "I am so, so sorry."

Emma's lips flattened. "Sorry for what, Nora? What is it you did exactly?"

"I didn't mean for it to happen."

"**What?** You didn't mean for **what** to happen?"

Maddy tried to telegraph to Nora. **Say "the kiss." Tell her it was a mistake, and you'll never do it again. Tell her, Nora!**

"Answer me!" Emma spat.

Nora flinched. Her mouth wobbled. Her blue eyes filled with tears. "I didn't mean to fall in love with him, Emma. I swear it. It just happened. It's all my fault, and I'm so sorry!"

Emma emitted a guttural roar and bolted forward, arms reaching out.

Nora stepped back. Her foot caught on a fallen pillow, and she stumbled backward. She went down hard, her elbows smacking the wooden deck.

Maddy's hand flew to her throat. "Nora!"

"What in the world?" Mama opened the kitchen door. "What is all this ruckus about? Oh, good heavens! Nora, are you all right?"

Mama stepped outside, her gaze flying between Nora—sprawled on the deck—and Emma hovering over her, as rigid as a two-by-four.

"What on earth is going on?" She went to her fallen daughter. "Are you all right, honey?"

Nora sat up straight. "I'm fine, Mama. It was an accident."

Mama helped Nora to her feet, fussing over her scraped elbows. When she finished she looked at Emma. "Now what in heaven's name is going on here? Emma, what happened?"

"I just fell, Mama," Nora said. "That's all."

"That is very well **not** all," Emma said. "Tell her, Nora. Tell her what you just said to me!"

Daddy slid through the open door, quickly taking in the scene. "What's going on out here, girls? I can hear you from upstairs."

"That's just what I'd like to know." Mama crossed her arms, frowning at her daughters.

"Go ahead, Nora," Emma sneered. "Go ahead and tell them how you're in love with my **fiancé**!"

Mama gasped.

"How you didn't mean for it to happen, how you're so, so sorry."

"Oh no," Mama said, looking at her oldest daughter. "Nora... Tell me it's not true."

Tears slid down Nora's face, running black with eyeliner. "It is true," she whispered. "And I am so sorry…"

Daddy ran a hand over his face. "Oh, good heavens."

"You need to leave," Emma said to Nora, her face flushed with anger. "You need to get out of here right now and don't come back. I don't ever want to see you again!"

"Now, Emma…," Daddy started.

"She was kissing him, Daddy, and God knows what else she was doing with him!"

"Emma," Daddy said. "Let's just take a deep breath here. Now, Nora…What's going on between you and Jonathan? How did this happen?"

"What does it matter how it happened, Stanley?" Mama snapped. "She was kissing her sister's fiancé. She's in love with him. Does anything else matter after that?"

"I'm just trying to get to the bottom of this, **Theresa**."

Maddy'd never heard Daddy speak so

sharply to her mother.

Emma glared at Nora. "And where is Jonathan in all this, Nora? Huh? Is he in love with you too? Are the two of you just so in love now?"

Nora shifted. "I think—you should ask him that."

"Well, I'm asking **you**! Is he in love with you, Nora?" Emma's hands clenched and unclenched at her sides. Her shoulders rose and fell with her breaths.

The sound of the surf punctuated a long, painful silence.

Black smudges underlined Nora's sad, guilty eyes. "He says he is," she said softly.

A beat of silence thrummed between them. Then Emma covered her face and wept into her hands, great sobs that shook her body and left Maddy feeling hollow and helpless.

Mama put her arms around Emma and rubbed her back. "Oh, honey. Oh, honey, this is just so awful."

Nora closed her eyes as if she couldn't bear to see her sister in pain—pain she'd caused herself. More tears leaked down

Nora's face.

Maddy's throat ached, and she swallowed around the huge lump. She wished she could close her eyes and make it all go away. What had she done? What was going to happen now? The summer was ruined. The wedding—was it off? Or was Jonathan in love with both of them? Was that even possible?

Emma broke away from Mama, her eyes snapping with fire. "How long has this been going on, Nora? How long have you both been cheating behind my back?"

When Nora failed to answer quickly enough, she spun to Maddy. "How long, Maddy? When did this start?"

Heat flushed through Maddy's system as all eyes turned on her. She trembled, her legs quaking beneath her. Her mouth worked, but she had no words.

"You knew?" Mama asked, her voice full of disappointment. "Oh, Maddy..."

"I—I didn't know," Maddy squeaked. "Not for sure."

Emma stepped toward Nora, her face full of rage. "How dare you carry on with my fiancé behind my back! My own sister! Right under the same roof!"

Daddy stepped between them. "Now, Emma, you know it takes two to—"

Mama emitted a sharp laugh. "You **would** side with her! Are you kidding me, Stanley?"

"This is about our daughters, Theresa, not us! You know very well Nora didn't intend for this to happen."

"Oh, and that makes it all right, does it? As long as she intended no harm, she's off the hook!"

"Sometimes..." Daddy's tone was hard. "People keep a secret to spare other people's feelings."

Emma laughed, the maniacal sound of it drawing all eyes to her. "Secrets...Yes, you two know all about those, don't you?"

Mama's hand went to her throat. "What—what are you talking about, Emma?"

"I think we need to stick to the subject at hand," Daddy said. "We have enough on our plate here already."

"I heard you talking upstairs, Daddy,"

Emma said. "I know you're getting a divorce."

Maddy gasped. No. It couldn't be true. She searched her parents' faces, but it was getting too dark to read expressions. Nobody was denying it, however.

"They were planning to tell us after the wedding." Emma gave a blubbery snort. "But I guess that's off now, huh? Just as well we all know the truth then!" She covered her face, weeping again.

A divorce? Maddy's mind spun. Maybe Mama and Daddy had been acting a little strangely this summer. Mama harped. They fussed sometimes. But they didn't have real troubles.

"I'm so sorry, Emma," Nora said. She looked like a wilted flower, her shoulders stooped, her head hanging as if it were too heavy for her neck. "Truly, I'm sorry."

"If you're so sorry, you'll leave and let Jonathan and me work this out!"

"Now, Emma," Daddy said. "We all just need to simmer down a little and talk this through."

Emma wept louder.

"Oh, for heaven's sake, Stanley. You're only making it worse!"

Daddy ignored her. "I know you're upset, honey, but she is your sister, after all…"

"Shame she didn't remember that earlier, isn't it!" Mama threw an apologetic look Nora's way. "I'm sorry, Nora, but what you did was indefensible, and I'm not going to stand here and pretend otherwise."

"You haven't even heard her side," Daddy said. "Maybe you could just listen for once in your life. Who knows, you might learn something."

"If all you're going to do is aggravate the situation, Stanley, why don't you just leave! Can't you see our daughter is hurting?"

He gestured wildly. "**Both** our daughters are hurting, Theresa!"

"Just go on now! I'll handle this without you—like I do everything else around here!"

"Fine. Have it your way!" Daddy spun and jerked open the door. He shoved it closed so hard it bounced against the jamb. A moment later he pulled from the drive, his tires squealing on the pavement out front.

It was the last time they saw him alive.

CHAPTER 29

Present day

The next morning, news of the approaching storm was all over TV. It swirled out in the Atlantic now, and a likely path had it making landfall just south of Seahaven tomorrow night.

Maddy muted the TV and looked at her sisters. "Well, I guess we'd better start getting the house ready just in case."

"It's only a tropical storm," Nora said. "We've seen far worse."

"Does Gram have a battery-operated radio lying around?" Maddy asked.

"I think I saw one in the laundry room cabinet," Nora said.

Pippy twirled in a circle and barked, seeming to sense that something exciting was afoot.

They could wait until tomorrow to pull the shutters closed on the windows. It was always possible the storm would weaken or head off in another direction.

As the day wore on Connor texted a couple times. The marina was busy as some of his customers came to pull their boats from the water and others came to secure them there.

A smile lifted the corners of Maddy's lips as she thought of last night. They'd sat on the back deck kissing for a long time. Getting as worked up as teenagers. The man could kiss with the best of them.

By late afternoon the sisters had done as much as they could. They made sandwiches for supper and sat in front of the TV, watching images of the swirling storm on the news. It was still headed their way, and there was talk of it strengthening before it reached shore.

They'd just broken for a commercial when the front door flew open. All eyes swung toward the entryway.

Gram stood there, her bright red lips smiling broadly. "I'm home, girls!"

"Gram! You're early." Maddy jumped up from the couch and went to embrace her grandma. The woman felt slight in Maddy's arms, but Gram had always known how to give a sturdy hug.

Maddy stood back while her sisters greeted their grandmother. Louise Monroe still wore her silver-white hair short and wispy around her face. She sported a new pair of blue tortoiseshell glasses that accentuated her clear blue eyes. Her face was creased with age, her eyes hooded, but Maddy thought she was still beautiful, even at eighty-three.

"You didn't think I was going to miss all the excitement, did you? I found an earlier flight and flew standby."

"Well, how on earth did you get here?" Nora shelved her hands on her slender hips. "I was going to pick you up from the airport."

"I had an Uber come fetch me. Such a nice young man. We chatted about travel.

He's lived in Austria and Uganda and Cambodia. My, oh my, did he have some stories to tell. Can you imagine?"

"But, Gram," Maddy said, "don't you have to have a cell phone to Uber?"

Gram whipped a phone from her purse. "Ta-da! I'm in the modern age now, girls. Erma's granddaughter, Lila, hooked me up with an iPhone yesterday!"

Maddy laughed. "Hooked you up?"

"That's what the kids are saying nowadays. Lila fixed me up with the Uber app, and some nice young lady at the airport helped me figure it out. I didn't want to bother you for a ride. I knew you were busy preparing for the storm. And besides, I wanted to surprise you."

"Well, you certainly did," Emma said.

"Look at you girls, you all look so beautiful." Gram set her purse on the coffee table, glancing down at Pippy. "Well, who's this little cutie-pie?" She stooped to pet the dog, whose back end wagged gleefully. "Aren't you just the sweetest thing?"

"She's Emma's," Maddy said. "She's a

good girl; just don't let her out without a leash. She's the most curious dog I ever did meet."

Emma picked up Pippy. "And she has the sense of direction of a blind bat, I'm afraid. On top of that, she thinks she's the size of a Rottweiler. She has no fear, do you, little girl?"

Pippy yipped, and Emma gave her some love.

Maddy fetched their grandmother's suitcase, and once they assured her they had storm preparations under control, the women settled in the living room with glasses of iced tea and began catching up.

It was apparent Gram had had a fabulous time at her re union. Her face was aglow, and despite a long travel day, she exuded energy. Her girlfriends normally came out to see her in Seahaven every summer, but this year she'd headed their direction. The trip had obviously done her good.

"I had the time of my life, I tell you. That Eleanor got me on the back of her grandson's motorcycle!"

"Gram!" Nora said. "That's not safe."

Gram waved away her words. "Oh, pooh! I had a grand time. We went to a festival and ate all the wrong foods, played cards till late at night, and giggled like teenagers. I'm telling you, I haven't had so much fun in ages."

"I'm happy for you, Gram," Maddy said. "But heavens, a motorcycle? I'm afraid to ask what else you did."

"Oh, you only live once." Gram shifted in her favorite leather chair, crossing legs that were encased in a trendy pair of jeans. "Now tell me what's been going on around here. I noticed all the changes outside. The house looks marvelous. The flower beds haven't looked so nice in years, and the handrail didn't wobble as I came up the stairs!"

"Connor fixed that," Maddy said. "He's been helping out quite a bit around here."

Gram gave her a coy smile. "I imagine he has, with my three beautiful granddaughters ensconced in this old house. He's no fool, that man."

Emma laughed. "He only has eyes for

Maddy, I'm afraid."

Gram's eyes twinkled as they swung to Maddy. "Oh, this sounds juicy—do tell!"

Maddy's face grew warm under Gram's scrutiny. "Connor's a very special man. I've grown quite fond of him."

"Well, he's got good taste in women, I'll tell you that. And a finer boy you won't find." Gram clasped her age-spotted hands in her lap. "But I thought you were seeing a boy at that fancy restaurant where you work—Nick, is it?"

Maddy gave a wan smile. "That didn't exactly work out. He didn't turn out to be the man I thought he was."

"He's a turd," Emma said vehemently.

"Emma!" Maddy said as the girls laughed.

"Well, he is," Emma said. "He cheated on her, Gram. She's lucky to be rid of him."

"Oh dear. I'm so sorry, honey, but it sounds as though your sister's right." Gram aimed an eager look at Maddy, all but rubbing her hands together. "Now on to the good stuff—you and Connor. Don't you leave out a single thing."

Maddy laughed. "We've only had one date, Gram. There's not a whole lot to tell just yet."

"That's only half the story," Emma said. "He's been over here helping on the house nearly every night. And last night I happened to glance out back, and there was some serious kissing going on out there."

Maddy gasped. "Emma!"

"Well, there was. I wasn't spying, but goodness gracious!" Emma fanned her face.

"He's a good kisser, is he, Maddy?" Gram said. "You know, a man who kisses well is also good in the sack."

"Gram!" All three sisters giggled uncomfortably.

"Well, that's what I hear anyway. Best thing about getting old, girls, is you can say whatever you darn well please. I'm quite liking it." She nailed Maddy with an eager look. "Now...are you falling in love with Connor, dear? He's a widower, you know. Been sad as a puppy dog from the day I met him. But I'll bet you've put the twinkle right back in his eyes."

Maddy laughed. She'd forgotten how full of vim and vinegar her grandma was. And yes, she was definitely falling for Connor. She had all the signs: her heart beat faster when she was with him, she got a little flutter in her belly when a text came from him, and she longed to be with him. But she preferred to keep her emotions private, at least for now.

"It's too early to say," Maddy said. "But he seems like a real sweetheart."

"I'm sure he'll be over tonight," Nora said. "You can see them in action, Gram."

"Wonderful!" Gram leaned toward Maddy. "Did you notice his arms? Those muscles! I've never seen such fine arms."

"Gram!" Emma laughed. "You're not supposed to notice such things."

"And whyever not? I have eyes in my head, don't I? These days girls are always going on about six-pack abs, but I've always been an arm girl myself—and hands! Good hands are highly underrated, I think."

The girls exchanged grins. It was so

good to have Gram back home.

"Did Grandpa have nice arms, Gram?" Nora asked.

Their grandma's smile dimmed a bit. She took a sip of her tea, the ice clinking as she drained it. "Oh, he did, honey. He surely did. Now, would anyone like more tea? I'm so parched from all that dry airplane air."

CHAPTER 30

The girls showed Gram around the house, and she oohed and aahed over the newly painted walls, the freshly cleaned draperies, and the spotless attic.

"Why, I'd forgotten there was a wood floor up here. It must've taken you days to go through all that junk."

"It wasn't all junk," Nora said. "We have a couple boxes of things we thought you'd like to keep."

"We never knew you used to model bathing suits," Emma said.

Gram waved her words away. "Just for a local clothing company. Oh my, those were the days. They let me keep those suits—that's how I was paid for modeling."

"You were gorgeous," Maddy said as they made their way down from the attic. "I'll bet you had all the boys swooning."

"Your grandfather had a bit of competition, I'll admit. I only had eyes for him, however."

Maddy wondered at the hint of melancholy in her last words. A text buzzed in and she checked the screen. It was Connor—and there was that little flutter in her belly.

How's it going? Do you need help getting the house ready?

No, it's under control.
Guess what?
Gram came home early. ☺

That's terrific! Very busy here getting ready for the storm.
Chaos!

I'll bet! Don't worry about us.
We're on top of things.

**I might have to work late.
I'll try and stop over later.**

Sounds good.

See you then. XO

Maddy smiled at the X and O as she pocketed her phone. They were headed to Gram's room next, where they'd stashed the things they thought Gram might like to keep.

"There's a box of Daddy's things," Nora said. "We haven't gone through it yet."

"We wanted to wait for you." Maddy gave Gram a side hug.

"That's so sweet. Your mother sent me some things after he passed. I don't know that I ever went through the box. I was too heartbroken at the time. I just stuck it upstairs, out of sight."

They sat on the bed, and Nora set the cardboard box in the middle. A sense of eagerness filled Maddy. She'd only been a child when her dad passed away. Maybe sorting through his belongings would give her a better sense of who he was.

"How are things going with your mother?" Gram asked. "Do you see her often?"

"Not really," Maddy said. "She calls now and then, and I see her when she comes to Charlotte, once a year or so. We'll never be as close as we used to be, I guess."

"She's got her own life now in Georgia," Nora said. "We message on Facebook every now and then."

Emma pulled the box closer. "Her life seems pretty full, from what I can tell. Her husband has a couple grandkids, and she seems to dote on them."

"If you ask me," Gram said, "I think she misses her girls."

Bless Gram's heart. She was always playing peacemaker. Maddy wished the role came as naturally to her.

"How can you take up for her, Gram?" Nora said, her voice full of exasperation. "She was awful to Daddy that night. It's the reason he was so upset. If she hadn't made him leave..."

"She was going to divorce him," Emma said. "It was what she wanted—not him. She told us so herself. Daddy worked so hard so she could stay home with us girls. He was always exhausted, traveling all over the state, trying to provide for us, and she obviously didn't appreciate it. No wonder his heart gave out—and at only forty-seven!"

"Oh, girls," Gram said with a heavy sigh.

"I know you just want peace in the family, Gram," Maddy said gently. "But it's just not going to work out the way you want it to."

"I've forgiven her," Nora said. "Isn't that enough?"

"I have too." Maddy put a hand over her grandmother's. "But sometimes, with certain people, you need to set boundaries."

"Exactly," Emma said. "A little emotional distance can be healthy. We all still have a relationship with her. We're just not as close as you might like us to be."

Gram's face had fallen, and she suddenly looked every one of her eighty-three years. Maddy felt bad for bringing her down, but she wasn't going to sugarcoat the truth. Her mom was culpable for their family's demise. It was the one thing all three sisters agreed on.

Nora reached into the box and pulled out a paperback novel. Michael Crichton's **Airframe**. "Look. A page is dog-eared."

"I guess Daddy never got to finish it." For some reason that made Maddy's gut twist. There were so many things their father had never gotten to finish.

Emma pulled out a watch and clutched it to her chest. "Oh, it's his watch. Would you mind if I kept this, Gram? It's just a quartz, but I remember him wearing it."

"Of course not, honey. You girls take anything you like."

Emma pulled out a wallet, and Maddy watched as she opened it. The faded black leather creaked with age. It was empty. The sight filled Maddy with a vague sense of disappointment.

Emma set it in the growing pile on the bed.

"His fishing hat," Maddy said, pulling the beige floppy-brimmed hat from the box. It was crushed and creased, the chin cord frayed. "I can still see him in that old fishing boat of his, wearing this old thing."

"He was so happy when he was fishing," Emma said.

Nora gave a wry laugh. "Remember the fuss Mama used to put up about the fishy smell when he returned?"

"He had to undress on the deck and go straight to the shower," Emma said. "Heaven forbid he bring that smell inside."

"Girls," Gram chided.

"It's true, though," Maddy said.

"Your mother had—and has—many fine qualities. As I recall, your father **did** reek when he returned from fishing. He wasn't perfect, you know."

Properly chastised, the girls went back to the box, pulling out a few photos from happier summers and crayon-covered construction paper—pictures the girls had drawn, mostly Maddy. She'd loved drawing him pictures. He'd praised her creativity, then hung the artwork on the refrigerator for all to see.

There were a lot of meaningless things in the box too: financial papers, paycheck stubs, a few pieces of clothing. Nothing Maddy remembered him wearing. Her mother must've taken the rest of his things to Goodwill. The thought left her hollow.

A few minutes later Gram pulled out the last item in the box. It was only an old pair of readers.

Disappointment flooded through Maddy. What had she expected to find anyway? Answers? Comfort? Peace? It was just a bunch of useless mementos, most of which she didn't even recognize.

Maybe she'd only wanted to recall him afresh. Her favorite memories had faded like an old Polaroid. She could hardly even remember what he looked like some-times. And the images she called to mind always resembled the photos she had of him.

But she remembered how loved and special he made her feel. That was what she needed to hang on to.

"It's hard to believe this is all that's left

of him," Emma said, and Maddy realized the others must share her feelings.

"There had to be more than this." Nora sounded exasperated. "Just one box of things? Where are all the photos?"

"Mama probably pitched it all out," Maddy said with a heavy sigh.

Gram's lips pressed together as she began placing the items back inside the box. A strange tension hung in the air.

Maddy traded looks with Nora and Emma. They clearly felt it too. Maybe they shouldn't have stirred up all these memories for Gram. Daddy had been her only child, after all. Death had cruelly stolen both her husband and only child within five years.

Maddy caught sight of a photo in the folds of the bedding. She picked it up and turned it over. She hadn't seen this one. It must've fluttered out in the shuffle as they'd gone through the box.

It was Daddy with a woman. He had his arm around her in a very familiar—and affectionate—way. Her dad looked to be in his forties, and Maddy didn't recognize the pretty woman. A terrible foreboding settled inside.

"Gram?" She held out the photo. "Who's this with Daddy?"

Gram's eyes settled on the photo. Her face fell, her jaw going slack. The picture trembled in her age-spotted hands.

A long moment passed, the bad feeling inside Maddy swelling. "Gram?"

Gram closed her eyes, her lips moving a bit as if she were praying.

The girls exchanged worried glances.

"Gram, are you all right?" Nora asked finally.

Their grandmother lowered the photo and gave the sisters, each one of them, a pointed look. "No. I am not all right."

Emma set her hand over Gram's. "What's wrong? Who is that?"

"I'll tell you what's wrong. You girls have it all wrong about your mom and dad. I've kept it to myself for all these years, thinking I was doing right by Stanley, but I just can't do it anymore. It's not right."

Maddy felt a terrible foreboding in her gut. "What's not right?"

Gram looked from one of her grand-daughters to the other, her lips firm, her face resolute. "Your father loved you girls very much. As much as a man can love his children—I have no doubt about that, and I don't want you to either."

"Of course not, Gram," Emma said.

"We know that," Nora said.

"But he wasn't perfect." Gram's eyes went glassy as she covered her mouth with trembling fingers. "Oh, he was far from perfect."

Nora pulled the box from the bed and set it on the floor. "What are you trying to say, Gram?"

Uneasiness stirred inside Maddy. She had the childish urge to put her hands over her ears. She had a terrible feeling that whatever Gram was about to say would forever change her perspective of her father. She had wanted to know him better. But had she really wanted to know the truth? Suddenly she wasn't sure.

"You know he traveled a lot for his job. He was gone so much." Gram shook her head. "I was against his taking that job.

It's not good for a man to be away from his family so much.

"But it was good money, and it allowed your mom and dad to have the lifestyle they wanted. As the years went by, I thought I must've been wrong. Your mom and dad seemed more or less fine with the arrangement, and you girls were thriving."

Gram's eyes teared up, and she gave them a look of despair. "But things aren't always as they seem. Girls...I'm afraid your dad met somebody on one of his trips."

Maddy's breath left her body. No. He didn't.

The girls traded looks of disbelief.

"He—Are you saying Daddy had an affair?" Emma asked. "No, he wouldn't do that. He loved Mama."

"He did," Gram said. "He seemed happy with your mother. But humans are oh-so-fallible, girls. Sometimes we do things that defy logic or explanation."

"How long did it go on?" Nora asked.

Maddy's breath expanded in her lungs.

"Did Mama know?"

"I can't believe he'd do that," Emma said.

Gram's eyes pierced each of theirs. "There's more, I'm afraid. He was apparently in love with this other woman too. She didn't know about your mother or about you. Your daddy...He went ahead and married this other woman."

Maddy's lips went lax. She blinked. Married another woman? Her chest tightened painfully at the betrayal. Both on their behalf and their mother's.

"What?" Nora said on a breath.

"But he was already married to Mama," Emma whispered.

Gram nodded, her eyes leaking tears. "The marriage to this other woman wasn't legal, of course. But she had no way of knowing that. As far as she was concerned, her husband was off traveling for his job—just as your mother assumed."

Maddy swiped at her wet cheeks. "This isn't true. It can't be true."

Gram simply nodded sadly.

"Are you sure, Gram?" Nora asked.

"How do you know all this?"

"Nadine—this woman—came to see me several weeks after your dad passed. When Stanley failed to return home, she called his employer and found out what happened to him. She hunted me down. Your dad had told her he was estranged from his mother."

Gram's face crumpled and Maddy leaned in, putting her arms around her. "Oh, Gram."

"She was so distraught when I told her about your mother and you girls. She'd already missed his funeral, and now she was finding out he had another family. That her own marriage was a farce."

Gram shook her head. "He was a good man who did a terrible thing. I keep telling myself that. I didn't want to tell you girls. I knew how hurt you'd be. But I see all the blame you've put on your poor mother, and she just doesn't deserve that."

Their mother...Maddy drew back. "That's why they were divorcing."

Gram nodded. "After Nadine left, I causally asked your mom if she knew a

Nadine. That's how she knew I'd found out. She'd found out about Nadine shortly before that last summer. I'm sure she was quite devastated. They'd agreed to one last summer here in Seahaven."

"Why didn't she just tell us the truth after he died? We've held her at arm's length all these years."

"Same as me, honey. She didn't want to hurt you."

"Did Daddy have children with this... other woman?" Nora asked.

Gram shook her head. "You were his only kids. And he loved you girls so much. Despite his terrible choices, he was a good father to you. Your mom knew it would break your hearts to find out what he'd done.

"And once he was gone...she didn't want to sully your memory of him. And truth be told, I didn't either. But it just isn't right, the way your mother has taken the blame all these years."

Gram wore a pained look. A distant expression came over her face, her eyes looking off to some faraway place. "I

should've known. I should've done something. But I never dreamed Stanley would
turn out just like his—"

Her eyes refocused on the present, and
she snapped her mouth shut.

Gram straightened, sniffling, and
knuckled her tears away. "Well. Never
mind. We should get this box stowed away
somewhere. Did you girls take whatever
you wanted to keep? Nora, did you get
the fishing hat? Oh yes, there it is."

The sisters stared at each other. An
odd silence had fallen over the room.
Gram had eased off the bed and began
pushing the light box into the closet. As
she disappeared into the closet Nora
finally spoke.

"Gram? What were you going to say?"

A moment later their grandmother
appeared at the closet door. Her face
was crestfallen, her shoulders stooped.
Her eyes looked so sad Maddy could
hardly bear it.

"That Daddy would turn out just like
who?" Maddy asked.

The air-conditioning kicked on, filling the

house with its quiet hum. Maddy couldn't move. Could hardly breathe.

Gram was quiet so long Maddy wasn't sure she was going to answer. But finally she did. "Your grandfather. Stanley turned out just like his daddy."

Maddy felt a shock down to her core. She had only vague memories of her grandfather. He'd passed when she was eight. But everyone talked about him as if he were a paragon of virtue—including Gram.

Maddy shook her head. She was so confused.

"What are you saying, Gram?" Nora asked. "Was Gramps…?"

Their grandmother's sigh seemed to come from her toes. Emma made room for her on the bed, and she sat down again.

"He was a good father to your dad. And I know he loved me… but yes, your grandpa was unfaithful. It was nothing like what your dad did. He had long periods of faithfulness. Then I'd hear something or find something in his pants pocket and…" She shook her head. "He'd always break it off once I found out, because I'd threaten to leave him. But I was never going to leave. I think he knew that. Otherwise, why would he betray me so many times?"

Maddy grabbed her grandmother's hand. "Oh, Gram. I'm so sorry. I always thought…"

"I know," Gram said. "You thought exactly what I wanted you to think. The truth of the matter is I was too big a coward to draw a line in the sand with him."

Maddy sat there, letting the shock of revelations roll over her like waves crashing the shore.

"Once I found out what your dad had done to your mother, I tried to be there for her. We've kept in contact over the years. We have a lot in common, and I feel so guilty for what your father did to her. I allowed your grandfather to cheat on me, and your dad had a front seat to it all."

"He knew Gramps cheated on you?" Emma asked.

Gram shook her head. "If he did, he never brought it up. I've been over and over this in my mind since I found out about Nadine. Did your dad learn the behavior from his father, or was it generational sin, passed on genetically? The Bible talks about that, you know, generational sin. I just never believed Stanley would—" She shook her head. "Well. I have regrets, I'll tell you that."

Maddy squeezed Gram's hand, reeling from the news. "I always thought you'd never remarried because no one else could live up to Gramps."

"But you probably just wanted nothing more to do with men after all that," Emma said.

"Oh, I don't want you to think we had forty miserable years, girls. We had good times." She gave them a wobbly smile. "More like thirty-two happy years and eight miserable ones."

Maddy's breath escaped on a laugh.

But the levity evaporated like a morning mist over the harbor. Her wonderful father had had a secret wife. Her honorable grandpa had been unfaithful. And even as her head spun with the revelations, a vague fear rose inside her, old and familiar, its darkness nearly swallowing her whole.

CHAPTER 31

The sisters quietly went about supper preparations and sat down to sandwiches and soup. A strained silence hung over the table. Each of them seemed lost in her own thoughts. After supper Gram retired, exhausted, no doubt from her travel and the emotional conversation.

The sisters rehashed everything until Nora went to bed. Emma took a call from Ethan out on the deck, and Maddy found herself at loose ends. She retreated to her room but couldn't seem to settle. She paced the floor, wishing she could shake the feelings that welled up inside.

She could hardly absorb it all. Everything she'd believed about her dad was a lie. If he loved her mother, how could he have done something so hurtful to her? To all of them? Is that what love was? She didn't understand at all.

She grabbed the back of her neck. Her poor mama. She couldn't imagine how it must've felt to find her husband had betrayed her in such a terrible way. To find out he'd had a second wife tucked away.

Her whole marriage must've seemed like a lie. She must've been so heartsore. She must've felt like a fool. Maddy felt a little like a fool herself even though she'd only been a child.

Daddy, how could you?

Her eyes burned and her throat ached. She dropped to the edge of her bed and wept quietly.

She wasn't sure how long she'd sat there when a text buzzed in. She wiped her eyes and checked the screen. Connor.

Finishing up now. Be there in a half hour or so.

Maddy's stomach clenched hard at the

thought of seeing him. Her heart felt bruised and achy. She was in a terrible frame of mind. Furthermore, the thought of surrendering to the love she was beginning to feel for him felt like taking a step off a cliff.

She thought of Nick and the way he'd betrayed her so blatantly. Maybe she was attracted to men like her father and grandfather. Was there something inside her that made her fall under the spell of unfaithful men?

She thought of Nora and how she'd fallen for Jonathan—a man who'd betrayed Emma to be with her.

Her thoughts went back to that night that last summer. To the way her father had sided with Nora when he'd found out what had been going on. No wonder. He'd no doubt related to her because of the way he'd been carrying on behind their mother's back.

And her mother…Maddy's skin tingled with sudden realization. No wonder Mama had been so cross with Daddy that night. He'd all but excused what Nora and

Jonathan were doing. And she had sided with Emma because she knew all too well what betrayal felt like.

The pieces clicked together as understanding washed over her. Even so it was all so disheartening. Maddy raked her fingers through the hair at her neck. So overwhelming.

She looked back at her phone, scanning Connor's text. She couldn't see him tonight. She just couldn't. The thought of a relationship with him now felt like a terrible idea. She'd been stupid to pursue it. What was she, a glutton for punishment or something? Shouldn't her cluelessness with Nick have been enough to warn her off relationships?

In her heart she believed Connor would never cheat on anyone. But hadn't she once thought the same thing about Nick? About her father? About her grandfather?

She'd been right all along. Love was too big a risk.

She lifted her phone. **If you wouldn't mind, maybe we could take tonight off. There's a lot going on over here with**

Gram's return.

Her thumb poised over the Send button for a long moment while she read her words. Then she touched the button. Her heart stuttered in her chest as she waited. As she watched the screen, three dots appeared in the text box.

Then his text came in. **Everything okay?**

Maddy gave a rueful laugh. Nothing was okay. Not by a long shot. She felt as if her entire world had been turned on end.

But that wasn't what Connor meant.

We're fine. Get some rest. You've got another busy day tomorrow.

His text came in within seconds. **All right. Take care. XO**

This time, at the sight of that **X** and **O**, a vise tightened around her heart.

CHAPTER 32

Maddy woke to the first rays of morning and the sound of someone retching in the bathroom.

Poor Nora, she thought, pushing back the sheet. Was the morning sickness new, or was this only the first time Maddy had noticed? Maybe she should go to her sister.

The pregnancy must not be good news if Nora was still hiding it from them. She'd had plenty of time to tell Jonathan. Maybe he'd been unhappy about the news. He loved Chloe, of course, but most men in their forties wouldn't relish the idea of starting over with a baby just when they'd finally reached the empty nest.

Before Maddy could decide whether or not to go to Nora, the toilet flushed. A minute later the steps creaked as her sister went down them.

Oh well. She obviously wasn't ready to fess up. Besides, Maddy didn't want to think about Nora's problems this morning. She had enough to digest with all Gram had divulged last night. Truthfully, she didn't want to think about that either. Better to focus on the tasks ahead today.

She checked her phone for the time. The room was a little dark for this time of morning, a hint at the coming weather. She crawled from the bed, threw on a light robe, and went downstairs.

Nora was at the kitchen table, reading the newspaper. She looked pale, though she hadn't applied her makeup yet.

"Good morning," Maddy said as she made her way to the coffeepot.

"Morning."

The steamy brew smelled like heaven. She poured herself a mug and filled up the carafe. "Would you like another cup?"

"No, thanks. I've already had two."

Maddy spied Emma through the windows, knitting on the deck. Dark clouds rolled on the horizon. Gram must still be in bed.

Maddy's stomach tightened as their conversation from the night before played back in her head. The disclosures had left them all in shock. It was going to take some time for it to settle in.

"The storm's turning this way," Nora said. "We have a tropical storm warning and a hurricane watch."

"Are they saying when it'll make landfall?"

"This evening around nine."

Maddy took a sip of coffee and looked toward Connor's house. He'd be at the marina already, preparing for the storm. She couldn't imagine the work entailed in securing so many boats.

Her heart bucked at the brick wall she'd erected around it last night. It was for the best. Her initial instincts had been right. She never should've started a relationship with him. Now their hearts were involved, and ending it was going to hurt them both.

"We have a lot to do today," Nora said. "I sure hope all our hard work on the house doesn't go to ruin."

"This place has been through worse. I don't think it'll be that bad."

"Let's hope."

Connor spent the busy morning with customers who were removing their boats to a haul-out facility. Some had no choice, however, but to let their craft weather the storm at the marina.

They helped owners reroute lines to stronger anchor points, reinforced cleats with secondary lines to back up anchor points, or spread the load to multiple anchor points. They removed canvasses, sails, and furling jibs and made sure the decks of all the remaining boats were clear. Even a dense object could become a missile during a hurricane.

Connor shook a customer's hand after they stepped from the sailboat. "That should do it. Let's hope for the best."

The customer gave him a wave and hurried away, probably to ready his home.

Connor checked his phone for the time. He still had his own home to secure, but there was a lot more to do here.

He checked his texts and saw Maddy had responded only briefly to his earlier text. He glanced back through the last few texts from her. She'd been short and to the point. He sensed something was going on, had that uneasy feeling in his gut.

He didn't really have the time, but he punched in her number anyway. He walked up the pier, away from the noise of a radio someone had blaring on his boat. The phone rang several times, then her voicemail kicked on.

Strange. She always answered her phone. That uneasy feeling grew. But he couldn't see a reason to leave a voicemail when she'd texted him only an hour before that preparations were going smoothly.

"Hey, boss!" one of his dockhands called. "Can I get your help over here?"

Connor pocketed his phone as he headed down the pier. But the disquiet persisted all afternoon.

CHAPTER 33

Maddy and her sisters had spent the morning closing the hurricane shutters that had been installed long ago and recently painted by Connor. Maddy did the second story, insisting she didn't mind the heights. She had to keep Nora safely on the ground.

The newly dried paint on the shutter hardware made the job more tedious than it should've been. Maddy peered nervously at Connor's cottage. He didn't have hurricane shutters, but she'd seen plywood in his garage. He was so busy taking care of everyone's boats at the marina that he wasn't going to have time to protect his own home.

They'd been texting off and on, and each time a text came from him her heart gave a hard squeeze. She kept her answers brief. He must've sensed something was wrong, because around two o'clock he called and didn't leave a message. She couldn't talk to him right now. He'd hear it in her voice, and this was terrible timing for a breakup.

There isn't going to be a good time, her heart cried.

When the storm was upgraded to a category one hurricane, Maddy took one last look at Connor's house and enlisted her sisters' help. The wind had already picked up, and it buffeted them as they boarded up Connor's windows. Sand pelted Maddy's skin, and she squinted to keep it out of her eyes as they hammered the boards in place.

He'd already brought in his lawn furniture and his one potted plant, so when they were finished with the windows they headed back to the cottage. Darkness had fallen even though sunset was at least a half hour away. Maddy shot Connor a brief text, letting him know his windows were boarded.

He replied with gratitude and confirmed the marina was still flocked with customers. He was staying there until everything was under control. She didn't text him back.

Maddy pulled open the kitchen door, and the sisters ducked inside. She was relieved to be out of the wind. Gritty sand coated her skin and had worked its way into her scalp. She was desperate for a shower.

Pippy was trembling, clearly unhappy to have been left at the house with Gram during all the excitement.

Nora picked up the dog. "There, there, sweetie. It's all right. We're home now."

"Here's some nice cold tea for you girls," Gram said, pouring them glasses. "The wind's already blowing up out there, isn't it?"

"My mouth tastes like sand," Emma said.

It was unnaturally dark in the kitchen with the shutters closed. Maddy hoped the power wouldn't go out, but they were prepared. Gram had set out flashlights and candles on the kitchen counter, along with a battery-operated radio.

The phone rang, and since Maddy was closest she grabbed it.

"Hello?"

"This call will be recorded," a stilted male voice said. "I have a collect call from inmate...Jonathan Winters...at the Pondville Correctional Center. If you would like to accept the call, press one. If you would like to deny the call, press two. If you would like to block the call, press three."

Maddy turned to Nora, who'd set Pippy down and was drinking her tea. Jonathan's name had been said in his own voice. He was in prison?

Emma saw the look on Maddy's face first and froze. "Who is it?"

"It's...it's for Nora." The recording had begun repeating itself.

Nora approached, her look turning wary as she took the phone from Maddy. "Hello?" Her face went slack, and her eyes swung to Maddy, holding her gaze for a long moment before she pulled the phone from her ear and hit the Power button. She set the phone on the counter and went back to her iced tea as though the call had never happened.

Maddy's thoughts scattered. Nora obviously wasn't surprised her husband was in prison. And apparently she wasn't taking his calls.

"Nora?" Maddy shook her head. "What in the world is going on?"

Gram closed the refrigerator door and looked between them.

Nora reached for her tea, holding the glass like a barrier between them.

"What happened?" Maddy asked softly.

Nora's hand shook with the glass of tea. Her spine seemed to shrivel. "Jonathan's in prison."

Emma gaped. "Prison!"

Nora's chin thrust forward. The refrigerator hummed in the silence. Pippy barked at the back door.

Suddenly Maddy remembered the credit card issue Nora'd had at the restaurant.

She remembered her sister's new frugal habits, her lack of calls home, and her reluctance to leave Seahaven. What exactly was going on here?

"Honey..." Maddy gave Nora a compassionate look. "Just tell us, whatever it is. Is Jonathan in trouble? Does he need help?"

Nora pressed her lips together.

Maddy came around the counter and took her sister's hand. Nora's fingers trembled. They were cold in spite of the sultry day and their recent physical exertion.

"Come on, come sit down," Maddy said.

"No, I—I look a fright. I need a shower... We all do."

"Never mind that. What's going on? Why is Jonathan in prison?"

Nora pulled her hand away, but she didn't go anywhere. She set her iced tea down on the counter. Her shoulders slumped, as if finally giving up the pretense that everything was peachy.

Nora's gaze moved to Emma and Gram, then back to Maddy. "He's been in prison for weeks. He was convicted of fraud."

Gram's breath whooshed out. "Oh, good heavens."

Nora closed her eyes, as if the weight of the burden was just too much. "He's robbed people—friends, even—of their hard-earned money. And he's not even remorseful. Just mad he got caught. We've lost everything, including the house."

"Oh, honey." Maddy pulled her into her arms, and Nora collapsed against her. It all made sense now. Of course Nora wouldn't have wanted to admit something so horrible, especially with Emma here to potentially rub her nose in it. No, Emma would never be that cruel.

"How long has all this been going on?" Gram asked.

"Months," Nora said. "He said he was innocent, and I believed him at first. Then he was convicted. They had so much evidence."

Maddy drew back. "You should've said something. You shouldn't be carrying around this load all by yourself. It's not healthy—especially for the baby." Maddy's fingers covered her mouth. She had not meant for that to slip. She gave Nora a pained look.

The wind howled outside and whistled through the shutters. Over by the fridge, Emma and Gram had gone still.

Nora only looked confused. "Baby? What baby?"

Maddy tilted her head sympathetically. She regretted bringing it up, with all Nora's other worries and everything that had come out last night. But maybe it was time to get everything on the table. How else could they properly help her? With Jonathan gone away, she needed their support more than ever.

"I'm sorry. It just slipped out," Maddy said. "But I know you're pregnant. I found the test in the trash. And I heard you throwing up this morning."

Nora huffed a soft laugh. "Maddy, I don't know what you're going on about, but I am not pregnant. For heaven's sake, I'm forty-three years old."

Maddy frowned at her sister. Was Nora

losing it, with all the strife she had going on? Who could blame her? Maybe she was simply not ready to admit the truth.

Maddy shook her head. Unless…

"It's not Nora," Emma blurted, drawing everyone's attention. "It's me." With eyes wide and windblown hair, Emma looked wild and distraught. "The test was mine. I'm pregnant."

"What?" Maddy said. "But I thought you and Ethan…"

"Right." Emma nodded. "We are separated, but—"

"Separated?" Nora said. "Since when?"

"Oh, honey," Gram said. "Why didn't you say anything?"

Emma's eyes swung to Nora, looking at her bleakly. "Since just after Christmas."

"But…" Maddy's gaze slid down to Emma's still-flat belly. She obviously wasn't very far along. And even Maddy knew morning sickness was a first trimester thing.

"Right," Emma said, a wan smile curling her lips. "There was an…unexpected night a couple months ago. He came over to talk, and one thing led to another. When he first left I was so angry with him that I trashed my birth control pills.

"That night he came over...I was so used to being protected, I didn't give birth control a single thought. But the next morning we had words, and he left again. Things were just awful after that. I never told him I'd stopped my pills. I just hoped and prayed I didn't get pregnant." Emma gave a wry laugh. "But of course that's exactly what happened."

"You haven't told him about the baby yet?" Maddy asked.

Emma shook her head. "I'm scared to death to tell him. We've been trying to work things out since I got here. We're making real progress, and I'm afraid this'll push him away for good."

"Maybe it'll draw you closer together," Maddy said.

Emma shook her head. "You know he never wanted kids. We agreed to that before we ever married. When he finds out what I did...he's going to hate me."

"Oh, honey." Maddy pushed Emma's

hair over her shoulder. "First of all, you both did this. And second of all...that's just not possible."

"I never wanted children, not really. But ever since I found out about this baby, I just..." She placed a hand on her flat tummy. "I want him, you know? I really, really want him."

"Of course you do," Gram said. "You'll be a wonderful mother, Emma."

A long silence hung in the room as they digested everything that had just been revealed. Between last night and today, Maddy's mind was spinning.

Outside the wind howled. Pippy barked again, now sitting at the door and looking at them beseechingly.

Maddy looked at her sisters. They hadn't been close in so many years, it was only natural that they hadn't opened up to one another. But maybe that could change. Maybe this was a chance for a new beginning.

"Sounds like we've all been keeping a secret or two," Maddy said.

"Except you," Nora said.

Maddy gave a wan smile. She'd hardly been forthcoming. "Not so fast, sister."

Three sets of eyes searched hers.

Maddy felt hollow inside at having to admit her failure. But if her grandma and sisters could be vulnerable enough to bare their secrets, so could she. "You know that great career I had? That fabulous new promotion I was set to get?"

"Oh no," Emma said.

"Yep. Lost it all. The job…the promotion …the boyfriend. All in one fell swoop. It must be some kind of record."

Maddy told them about that last day at Pirouette, taking comfort in their indignant expressions when they found out Nick had betrayed her with their boss and all but stolen her job.

"Losing him was a blessing." Emma said. "But why didn't you tell us about the rest of it?"

Maddy gave her a look. "Same reason you didn't tell us you were pregnant. Same reason Nora didn't tell us her husband was in prison. My career was the one thing I had going for me. The one area of my life where I was a success. I just...It's demoralizing to lose it so suddenly and have nothing left."

"Oh, phooey," Gram said. "You're so much more than your work, honey."

"Maddy, you're a wonderful human being," Emma said. "You have a lot going for you."

Nora snorted.

Emma shot her a scathing look. "What's your problem, Nora?"

"Look who's talking," Nora said. "You've always taken such great pride in your wonderful marriage. And when it crumbled, what did you do? You hid it."

Emma's nostrils flared. "You're a fine one to talk. Your husband's been sitting in prison all this time and not a peep out of you."

"Emma," Gram chided.

"Did you think I'd relish the idea of telling you what a sham our marriage had become, Emma? After I threw away our relationship to have him? You think I wanted to sit here and spill my guts while you gloated over my misery?"

"I never would've done such—"

"Or how you would've enjoyed hearing that I'm now destitute and homeless, and my own daughter will barely speak to me. And, oh yes, let's not forget how I was investigated for culpability in my husband's crimes and how my name was dragged through the mud. I was humiliated. All those women who professed to be my friends—where are they now? They won't even return my phone calls."

"Oh, Nora," Gram said on a breath.

"That sounds just awful," Maddy said.

"I was never more happy to receive Connor's call that day. Of course I prayed you were safe, Gram, but there's nothing more I wanted than to escape my so-called life. I was days away from sleeping in my car. At least here I have a roof over my head and people who aren't staring straight through me."

Nora brushed her tears away and straightened, as if trying to regain her dignity.

"I'm so sorry, Nora." Maddy's heart

ached for her sister. "I should've been there for you. I will be, from here on out. You have my word."

Emma turned away, knuckled her own tears. She put her glass in the sink. "If y'all will just excuse me...I think I'll go shower off all this sand and lie down for a bit."

Gram's brows scrunched together. "Are you feeling all right, dear?"

"I'm fine, I just—feel a little worn out right now."

It seemed Emma took all the oxygen in the room with her. Maddy turned to Nora and Gram, and they stared at each other for a long, poignant moment. So much had been disclosed in the past twenty-four hours.

The wind howled, pushing the door open with a quiet squawk. Pippy slipped out through the crack.

"Oh no," Nora said.

"Pippy!" Maddy called.

She and Gram followed Nora onto the deck and scanned the area for the little dog. The sea oats bent to the wind's demands, and a plastic grocery bag tumbled across the dunes. But Pippy was nowhere in sight.

"Pippy!" they called again and again.

Where had the dog gone off to? Of all the times for her to get out. Emma would be frantic with worry. That little dog meant the world to her. And Pippy wasn't very big. If they didn't find her soon she could literally be blown away by the storm.

The sky was a gray abyss, and the sea churned with foam. The heavens chose that moment to open up, and raindrops pelted them. The wind kicked up. The storm was making landfall.

Nora shielded her eyes with her hands. "I'll go after her. You take Gram back inside."

"No," Maddy said. "It's getting worse out here. It's too dangerous."

"I have to—it's my fault! I didn't shut the door all the way, and if anything happens to Pippy, Emma will hate me even more."

"I'll go too."

"No...I think I know right where she is. I'll be back soon." Nora took off down the deck stairs.

Maddy ushered Gram inside, wiping the grit from her own wet face and still thinking she should've gone after the dog too.

She decided to take a quick shower in case they lost power. They'd already filled the tub with water, but she drained it, showered, and refilled the tub. She emerged from the bathroom and went downstairs. Gram said there'd been no sign of Nora or the dog. She had tried to call Nora's cell phone, only to realize it was sitting on the kitchen counter.

Outside, the wind buffeted the shore, and the gray sky seemed to have dropped down to earth, making visibility poor. Debris swept by, tumbling through space. A sudden thought made Maddy's chest tighten. What if something had hit Nora and knocked her out? She could be lying unconscious all alone out there.

CHAPTER 34

"I'm getting worried," Gram said from the other end of the couch. It had been twenty minutes since Nora had gone after Pippy. "I called 911, but they made no promises. They're swamped with calls."

"That was a good idea."

On the TV images of the storm played out as it made landfall thirty minutes south of them. Maddy couldn't hear the TV for the sound of rain pelting the roof.

Oh, Lord, where are they? Keep them safe. Bring them back.

Finally she set down the remote. "We have to tell Emma."

Gram nodded, and Maddy went up-stairs. She hated to dump more on her sister's plate, but it couldn't be helped. Outside Emma's door she could hear her sister moving around.

She tapped lightly. "Emma? Can I come in?"

"Just a minute."

A long moment later Emma pulled open the door, dressed in one of Gram's thick robes. Her damp hair hung in wet ropes around her pale face, and her eyes were bloodshot. She looked as if she'd spent every minute of her shower crying.

"I hate to tell you this," Maddy said, "but Pippy slipped outside a while ago. Nora went after her, and they're not back yet."

Emma's face fell. "When? When did this happen?" She rushed back inside her room and began flinging open drawers and grabbing clothes.

"Right after you came upstairs. Nora insisted on going after her, and I'm getting worried. Gram called 911, and they said they'd keep their eyes out for her, but they're pretty swamped."

"I'll go after them myself."

"No, Emma. It's not safe. The storm's

picked up since they left, and there's debris flying around everywhere."

"Which is exactly why I'm going after them." Holding an armload of clothes, Emma came to the door and began closing it on Maddy. "I need to get dressed."

"No, Emma. You need to stay put. I'll go find them."

"She's my dog," Emma said with a stubborn tilt to her chin. "It's my fault Nora went out in this. I need to find them."

"I know you're worried. We all are, but you have to think of the baby."

Emma blinked, then the fight seemed to drain right out of her. "You're right."

Maddy backed into the hall and let her shut the door. She needed her shoes and a raincoat. She headed down the stairs, and as she reached the bottom the door burst open.

Someone pushed inside as the wind swept into the room.

Oh, thank God!

But it wasn't Nora at the door.

Connor stepped onto the rug, shoving the door closed behind him. His pants were rain-soaked, and his hair was plastered to his head despite the black slicker he wore.

His gaze cut to Maddy. "It's getting pretty bad out there."

"I know. Nora's out in it. Pippy slipped outside, and she went after her."

"What? Which way did she go?"

"I'm going after her." Maddy grabbed her tennis shoes from the closet and sank onto the stairs to put them on.

"Let me go."

"She's my sister. I have to do something."

"There's no need for both of us to go. And I know the area better than you."

Gram entered from the kitchen, giving Connor a warm hug. "Thank God you're here."

"Maddy told me. Got the house buttoned up tight?" he asked when Gram stepped back.

"We're all set," Gram said. "Just worried about Nora. I'll go put on some tea; it's going to be a long night."

"Is everything secure at the marina?" Maddy asked after Gram was gone.

"As much as it can be. I checked on my house. Thanks for getting the windows covered." There was a tense pause. "I tried to call you earlier."

Maddy finished tying her shoes and stood. "I was, uh, in the middle of something. A lot's happened in the last twenty-four hours. My head's still spinning."

Connor had cocked his head and was searching Maddy's face. "Sounds like a long conversation. But we can catch up later."

Maddy looked into his eyes. There was a gray storm brewing there. His brows were creased with worry. She was going to do much worse to him before everything was said and done.

"It'll keep." She dredged up a smile. "If you're going after Nora, I'll see to Gram—"

"Maddy..." Connor took her arm. "Wait."

He let the word hang out there as the pause lengthened between them. She took the moment to relish the warmth of his hand. Would it be the last time he touched her? Her heart twisted at the thought.

His thumb moved against her skin, his touch so tender. His expression so earnest. "Are we all right? You seem distant today. Even now…something seems off. More than just Nora."

A fist tightened in her gut. She should've known she couldn't get anything past Connor. But this was terrible timing. She didn't want to end things with a storm underway and Nora out there somewhere.

"Listen, we really don't have time for this."

"Maddy, come on. Just tell me what's wrong."

How could she deny him anything when he looked at her that way? She didn't want to string him along or make him suffer longer than necessary. She owed him the truth, and sooner was kinder than later.

"Connor…I just can't do this anymore, all right?"

Something flickered in his eyes. "Do what?"

Maddy had trouble getting her tongue to function. "Us," she said finally.

He blinked. Reared back. A long,

uncomfortable silence hummed between them, his eyes locked on hers. She saw all the emotions flitter across his face. The shock was bad enough. The confusion made her ache. But the hurt in his eyes was just about her undoing.

She'd put that there. After all he'd been through, causing him pain just about hollowed her out. Her eyes burned, and she could hardly swallow past the rock lodged in her throat.

"What's going on?" His voice sounded as if it grated across a gravelly throat. He shook his head. "What happened? Two nights ago we were fine."

Two nights ago they'd been making out on the deck. Two nights ago they'd been happy and hopeful. Two nights ago they'd had a lifetime of possibilities ahead of them.

How had she let herself forget how much love hurt?

She reminded herself of what she'd learned over the past day. She just couldn't go there again. Not even with Connor. Her eyes stung, but she forbade the tears to form.

"Maddy?" He gave her arm a squeeze. "Come on, talk to me."

She shook her head, hardly able to speak. If she said anything the tears were going to come. She could feel them now, burning behind her eyes. Could feel the emotions bubbling up inside.

The sound of feet on the stairs pulled Connor's eyes from her.

Emma was coming down the steps, her footsteps quick. "You haven't left yet?"

"I'm going after her," Connor said, his gaze never leaving Maddy. Finally he sighed. "Which way did she go?"

"North, along the shore," Maddy said. "She said she thought she knew where Pippy might be, but I have no idea what she meant."

They looked to Emma, who only shook her head.

His face still looking dazed, he gave a final nod and left. As soon as the door shut behind him the electricity went out.

CHAPTER 35

Connor ducked his head against the wind as he made his way across the dunes along the shore. Despite the slicker, he was wet to the skin. It was impossible to protect himself against the driving wind and rain, even with his hood up.

"Nora!" he called.

He wavered a moment as a gust of wind hit him so hard it moved him bodily. He thought of the dog and prayed she'd found a safe spot to hole up. This wind could literally blow the tiny thing away.

A piece of driftwood scuttled across the beach, nailing him in the ankle. He limped a couple steps, working it out. He was glad he'd come by the house when he had. Hoped Maddy had the good sense to stay inside.

Maddy.

His chest squeezed tight at the thought of her. At the guarded look she'd given him at the house. He'd known something was wrong earlier today. Those texts had felt too distant. What had happened to put that guarded look back in her eyes?

She was back to the old Maddy. The cautious Maddy. She'd said last night that a lot had happened since Gram's return. He wondered if it had anything to do with Nick. Had her old boyfriend contacted her again? Convinced her to go back to him?

Connor gave his head a hard shake. Why would she go back to the man who'd hurt her so badly? No, he'd seen the fear in her eyes. It was as if her distrust had been reawakened somehow. Her fears of heartbreak resurrected.

And that was a fear he understood all too well. A man didn't suddenly lose his young wife and not battle these feelings. And now there was that familiar hollow spot inside him again. The one he'd carried with him for years after Annie died. His chest ached with loss, and the muscles around his lungs felt like an iron cage. It was just how he'd felt after he'd lost Annie. Connor stopped in his tracks, his body wavering under the assault of wind.

I'm in love with Maddy.

He gave a wry laugh. How ironic that he hadn't realized it until he'd lost her.

The wind pushed him, making him stagger sideways a couple steps. He used the momentum to start walking again.

It had been a crappy day all the way around. In the middle of all the chaos at the marina, Cheryl had called. Her dad had had another stroke—a bad one, it seemed—and she had gone home again. She didn't know when she'd be back, but she needed to leave before the storm made landfall.

Connor had no idea how he was going to cover her position. He sure couldn't ask Maddy now. But he shouldn't be thinking about any of this.

He blinked against the rain and sand,

scanning the area. Visibility was so poor he couldn't see beyond the nearest house. A lawn chair went airborne and crashed into the deck railing. Twigs and small branches took flight.

"Nora!" Connor called for the hundredth time, waited for a response. But the only answer was the storm's fury.

He began to move again. His eyes scanned the landscape for movement, especially up near the beach houses.

Pippy was a curious thing, always wanting to snoop around the neighboring houses. How far could she have gotten in this? Where would Nora have gone to look for her?

He looked up at a darkened two-story with a fenced-in yard. A golden retriever named Charlie lived at the house. The one time Connor had taken a walk on the beach with the sisters, Charlie had been in the yard. And Pippy, completely oblivious to her small size, wanted at him.

Connor made his way slowly over the dunes toward the yard. The fence was made of wooden slats with plenty of room for Pippy to wiggle through.

"Pippy!" he called when the wind died down for a brief moment. The sound of the surf rose up in its place.

He heard a cracking sound and ducked automatically. A large section of siding flew by.

Connor looked over the fence into the house's empty yard. He shielded his eyes against the rain, blinking away the water dripping from his forehead. It was hard to see anything with the house lights off and the heavy bank of clouds shielding the moon and stars.

"Pippy!" he called, listening for a long moment, scanning the yard for signs of movement. "Nora!" The storm all but swallowed his bellow.

After waiting for a long beat, he decided to move on. How long had he been looking? Fifteen, twenty minutes? How far would Pippy have gone? Nora may have stopped at one of these houses and taken refuge. Folks around here would gladly offer a stranger shelter.

The wind pushed at him, making him

feel as if he were moving through thick molasses. If he didn't find them out here, oceanside, he'd circle up to the street and make his way back toward home. But had he gone far enough to turn back now?

It made sense that the dog would head inland out of the storm's direct path. Would Nora have thought the same thing?

Yes, he decided as a gust of wind blew him that direction. He turned and began cutting a path between two tiny cottages. The wind was at his back now, pushing him. He leaned back to keep from being propelled forward. The strength of the wind worried him. Not only for Nora and Pippy, but also for himself.

He heard a loud crack but kept his head ducked against the driving force of the wind and rain. It wasn't safe to be out here.

It was his last thought before a blow to the head knocked him sideways. He staggered, slumping to the ground. And then everything went dark.

CHAPTER 36

Maddy checked her phone for the dozenth time. She had to stop doing that. She was already down to 20 percent power with no way to recharge. Her car charger was locked in Nora's car, and she'd taken her keys with her.

The home phone was useless, of course. Emma's cell battery was already dead, and neither Connor nor Nora had Gram's new number. Maddy was the only one they'd be able to reach. She was encouraged that they still had cell reception.

Something crashed against the side of the house, making Maddy jump.

"That can't be good." Emma's attempt at levity fell flat.

"Where could they be?" Maddy said. "It's been over an hour since Connor left."

"Why don't you try calling him again, dear?" Gram, her face aglow in candlelight, looked at Maddy.

Maddy opened her contacts and tapped on Connor's number. The wind howled through the shutters, an eerie sound she was coming to hate.

The phone rang once. Twice. After the fourth ring, his voicemail kicked in. She'd already left one message, so she wouldn't leave another. But she listened to his message, just the same. Just to hear his voice. Her heart rate doubled at the sweet sound of it.

God, please keep him safe. Keep Nora safe. Bring them home.

She ended the call. "No answer."

"There'd be no way to hear it out there." Gram looked toward the window.

"Or even feel it vibrate," Emma said. "I'm sure he's fine. They all are." The quaver in her voice made the declaration sound more like a wish.

Maddy should've convinced Nora to

stay home. As much as Maddy loved Pippy, she loved her sister even more. And Connor…Now he was in danger too.

"I can't believe Nora went out in this," Emma said.

Maddy took comfort in Emma's tone. There was a softness not usually present when she spoke of Nora. "She knows how much Pippy means to you."

Emma blinked rapidly. "What if something happens to her? After we argued, after…after everything that's happened?"

"Have faith," Gram said with a confidence Maddy envied. "It's all in God's hands."

"Maybe they've taken shelter somewhere," Emma said. "Surely they have."

Maybe Nora had. But if Connor thought she was out there in this, he wouldn't give up until he'd turned over every stone. But if Nora had taken shelter somewhere, wouldn't she have called on a borrowed phone? She didn't say the words aloud.

Gram stretched her hands out on the table, palms up. "Come on, girls, we need to pray."

The sisters joined hands with their grandmother and bowed their heads.

"Lord, we're grateful for Your many blessings. For Your comfort and Your peace and Your gracious mercy. Father, we pray for our dear ones: Nora and Connor and little Pippy. They're lost in the storm and in need of Your loving care. God, we pray You'll protect them and bring them home safely. Even in the midst of the storm give them peace and—"

A loud crash sounded. Maddy's eyes snapped open. What now? It had come from the living room. She jumped from her chair and dashed toward the sound, the others on her heels.

Maddy stopped on the living room threshold, her flashlight's beam focusing on a stilled figure. Nora stood dripping on the entry rug, the door wide open. Pippy was wet and shivering in the cradle of her arms.

"They're back!" Emma said.

"Thank You, Jesus," Gram breathed.

Maddy rushed forward.

"Pippy!" Emma took the dog from Nora's

arms, and Pippy began licking her owner's face.

"Oh dear!" Gram grabbed a throw from the recliner and began dabbing at a gash on Nora's temple. "Just look at you."

"Just a little scrape," Nora said. "I'm all right."

As Gram daubed at the wound, Maddy saw that Nora was right. It was just a little scrape, but the rain had made a bloody mess of her sister's face.

"I must look like a drowned rat." Nora was breathless. Her auburn hair was plastered to her scalp, and her clothes pressed to her body like a second skin.

"It's awful out there," she said. "And getting worse by the second."

"Oh, heavens," Gram said. "Your elbow's bleeding too."

In all the commotion, Maddy only now noticed Nora had come in alone.

Her blood froze in her veins. "Where's Connor?"

"Connor?" Nora asked. "What do you mean?"

"He went after you." Maddy's voice

sounded frenzied even to her own ears. "You didn't see him out there? He didn't find you?"

"No. I finally found Pippy at that house where the golden retriever lives. She was hiding under the deck. I grabbed her and ran back along the street, but we about got blown away." Nora's gaze toggled between the others. "How long has he been gone?"

Maddy's chest felt weighted, making it difficult to draw a breath. "Over an hour."

A long silence hung between them. An hour was a long time out there.

God, where is he?

What if something had happened to him? What if she never saw him again? What if her last words to him were **I can't do this anymore?**

She had to go after him. She reached for an umbrella in the base of the coat tree, though it would provide little protection.

"What are you doing, Maddy?" Emma said.

"I'm going after him."

Gram took the umbrella with surprising force. "No, you are not."

"I have to find him. What if something happened to him?"

With stealth beyond her years, Gram pivoted in front of the door. "Do you think any of this is a surprise to God? He's in control. He has Connor in His own hands, and we can't forget that."

"Then He'll take care of me too, Gram."

Gram pursed her lips and tilted her chin at a stubborn angle. "Well, He also expects us to use our noggins, young lady."

"Honey, it's dark as pitch out there," Nora said. "And the rain…You can hardly see two feet in front of your face."

"Connor knows what he's doing," Gram said. "And he'd have my head on a platter if I let you go running after him. I have to live right beside the boy, so you're staying here."

Maddy stared into her grandmother's set face. She'd never seen the woman so adamant.

Her heart thrashed against her rib cage

as realization sank in. Gram was right. She didn't want to admit it, but she knew it was true. Helplessness closed around her lungs like a cage, making it hard to draw breath.

Gram squeezed her arm. "I'm sure he's just fine, honey. The Lord will take care of him."

Maddy wanted to believe that. He'd brought Nora home safely, after all. But He didn't always keep everyone safe. People died in the prime of their lives. Daddy had died, hadn't he?

Maddy's shoulders slumped. "All right."

Gram put the umbrella back and wrapped a spare throw around Nora's shivering shoulders. "You need a warm shower, honey. But first, let's go get you patched up."

"I'll do it," Emma blurted. All eyes turned to her. "It's the least I can do after you brought Pippy back safe and sound."

Something passed between Nora and Emma as Maddy looked on. Something soft and sweet. Something long overdue.

"You risked your life for her," Emma

choked out. "I'll never be able to thank you for that."

Nora's eyes flooded with tears. "I'm so sorry for everything, Emma. I'm sorry I hurt you back then. I'm sorry I betrayed you. And I'm sorry I've been so stubborn all these years. I was just drowning in guilt. I handled it all wrong. Please forgive me."

"I do." Emma gave Nora a sad smile. "I haven't exactly handled it well either, and I'm sorry for that."

A quiet moment passed, as though the air was sighing in relief.

"Well, it's about time," Gram said, all smiles. "Nora, you're bleeding all over the place. The first aid kit is in my bathroom under the sink. Wait a second, take a flashlight." She scurried to the kitchen and returned with a heavy-duty flashlight and a jar candle with three flickering wicks.

The sisters headed upstairs, Pippy still tucked like a football into Emma's side.

Maddy's legs quivered under her. She looked at the door feeling more helpless than she'd felt in years. Heart in her throat, she pulled out her phone and dialed Connor again. She could hardly hear the ringing over the sound of her blood rushing in her ears. When his voicemail kicked on, she disconnected the call, fighting the tide of despair.

Gram took her arm, leading her to the sofa. "Sit down, honey, you're shaking. Give me your phone. I'll call 911 and give them an update."

After Gram made the call she sank down beside Maddy. "They said they'd keep an eye out for Connor."

"Thanks, Gram." Her words sounded mechanical. She clasped her phone, willing it to ring.

"My, my," Gram said. "You really are smitten with that boy, aren't you?"

Someone had set the flashlight upright on the coffee table. Its cone of light spread onto the ceiling above them, giving the room an eerie glow.

"He's a man's man, dear. He knows how to take care of himself. Don't you worry."

The rain pummeled the roof, and the faint sound of radio warnings drifted in from the kitchen.

Maddy stared into the darkened room, her chest aching with regret. "You don't understand, Gram."

"Sure I do. You're in love with him, anyone can see that. But you have to have faith."

Maddy's eyes stung until her vision blurred. All she could think of was the look of hurt on Connor's face. The pain in his eyes. The raw scrape of his voice.

"You don't understand." Maddy bit her quivering lip.

"Aw, honey. Come here." Gram wrapped her arms around Maddy. "What is it?"

Maddy buried her face in her grandma's soft shoulder, letting the tears come. Connor was a good man. He deserved so much better than her. He deserved to fall for someone whole. Someone unbroken. She was an awful person.

"I broke up with him," Maddy said, sniffling. "Right before he left."

Gram rubbed her back. "Now, what did

you go and do that for?"

"I don't know."

Gram drew back, giving her a direct look. "Well, that's just nonsense. Of course you know."

She was right. Maddy knuckled her tears, trying to form words to explain the deep well of emotion that roiled inside.

"I'm afraid, I guess," Maddy said. "Afraid of getting hurt again."

"Well, that's natural enough. Sometimes love does hurt. And you've just been through a betrayal. You're a little gun-shy is all. But Connor would never treat you that way."

Maddy shook her head. "It's not Connor. I know he's a good man. It's **me**. I'm broken, Gram. I don't think I'll ever believe in love. Look at Mama and Daddy. Look at Jonathan and Nora. Look at Gramps! How can you even believe in love after what he did to you? It's not worth it. It's just not."

"Oh, Maddy. Is that what you've learned from all this?"

She could hardly bear to look into her

grandma's sad blue eyes.

"Honey, that ol' Nick failed you, no doubt. Your father failed your mother too—in a huge way. And yes, your grandfather failed me repeatedly. But it was they who were broken, honey." She huffed. "Well, I could've stood up for myself, to be sure. I guess we're all a little broken when it comes right down to it."

"I'm not strong enough to go through something like that."

"Hogwash. That's a lie straight from the pit of hell. You've got more mettle than you know. But you watched the demise of your parents' marriage and lost your father, all in the same day. It happened so suddenly, jerked the rug right out from under your feet. I saw it shake your world. Why, of course it did. It's no wonder you avoided love for so many years."

She blinked at Gram's insight. She'd never even talked to her grandmother about her fear. Maddy should've known better. The woman missed nothing.

"What if I'm too scared to try, Gram? Every time I think it's worth the risk, something happens, and I find myself right back where I started."

"Then what you need is faith, dear. Faith in God, that He'll get you through no matter what happens. Trust the Lord with your future, honey. He won't let you down."

Maddy reflected on her grandma's words. Did she believe God would get her through? That He had a plan for her life?

"What else can you do?" Gram asked. "Live without love? Keep a houseful of cats? Pah! What kind of life is that? How lonely an existence. Love's not always easy, but it's worth it. You'll never find happiness if you let fear stand in the way of what you truly desire."

Gram gripped Maddy's arm with surprising strength. "You're a strong woman, Maddy. Stronger than I was at your age. Strong enough to handle any heartache that might come your way. Until you believe that, you're going to struggle to give your heart away."

And that was it in a nutshell, wasn't it?

She didn't trust herself, and ultimately, she didn't trust God to get her through the heartache.

Lord, help my unbelief.

She blinked away the tears that clouded her eyes.

Gram rubbed her arm. "I know it can be hard to trust again, honey. But when you find someone worthy of your trust…it'll be worth the risk. I promise you that."

Maddy thought of Connor and felt a new resolve building inside. A strength that defied all explanation.

"And, sugar, trust me on this," Gram said, confidence shining from her eyes. "Connor Sullivan is worth that risk."

CHAPTER 37

A noise startled Maddy awake. A branch or something had hit the house. Rain pounded the roof and wind rattled the shutters. The hurricane was still wreaking havoc outside.

Gram had drifted off around midnight, and Emma and Nora had followed soon after. Maddy hadn't meant to fall asleep at all. She checked her phone, hoping she'd somehow missed a text or call from Connor. But the screen was void of notifications.

Her heart sank as she caught sight of the time on the screen. She'd been asleep for two hours, and it was past four in the morning. Her battery power was almost gone, but she tapped on his phone number.

It rang through to voicemail. She closed her eyes, listening to his voice.

Where is he, God? Please keep him safe. I want to tell him I love him. Even if he doesn't want me anymore, I need him to know how I feel.

How many times had she breathed those words over the past several hours? She disconnected the call and clutched the phone to her chest like a lifeline.

The room had grown chilly. A jar candle still flickered from the coffee table, making shadows dance around the room. Across the room Gram slept in her recliner, an afghan tucked around her. Nora and Emma slept beside Maddy on the sofa, Emma leaning on her sister.

Earlier the two of them had stayed upstairs together for over an hour. When they'd come down it was obvious something had happened between them. Something good. There was a lightness between them that had been missing since they'd arrived in late May. Actually, since that last summer in Seahaven. Forgiveness had taken place. The healing could finally begin.

The four of them had talked late into the night, catching up. Now that everything was out on the table they could be real with each other. Maybe it was painful when people unburdened their secrets. But transparency was necessary for honest relationships, for real intimacy. And Maddy longed for that with her sisters.

She heard their heavy hearts as they shared. Nora grieved over her relationship with her daughter and struggled to know how to start over with nothing. Emma worried that Ethan would end things for good when he found out about the pregnancy—and just when they were finally on the same page.

And Maddy...She was just worried about Connor. Everything else took a back seat.

She lay listening to the storm rage around them. Her stomach was all twisted up inside, just knowing Connor was out there somewhere. Gram had talked to her about having faith in God. Trusting Him with her future. If that applied to her love life, it certainly applied to the storm and Connor's safety.

Give me faith, God. I want to believe. I want to trust. Maddy kept praying. It was all she could do. It would be enough. It had to be.

A while later Nora stirred on the other end of the couch. Her eyes fluttered open, and she found Maddy in the shadows. "What time is it?"

Maddy could barely hear her over the pounding rain. "After five."

"You haven't heard anything yet?"

Maddy shook her head. "How much longer till the storm passes, do you think?"

"Earlier they were saying about twelve hours."

It had started around nine. They still had about four hours left, but Maddy had already made up her mind. The sun would rise about six, and she was going to drive around looking for Connor, hurricane or no.

She glanced at her watch. Less than an

hour to go.

She needed something else to think about or she was going to drive herself crazy. "So you and Emma cleared the air last night?"

A smile tipped Nora's lips as she glanced down at her sleeping sister. "Yeah. I think we're going to be okay."

"I think you're right."

They talked quietly for a while, and when they ran out of things to say, Nora drifted off to sleep again.

At six it was still awfully dark, the sunrise shielded by a thick cover of clouds. But Maddy got up and quietly slipped on her shoes. She'd have to let someone know what she was doing. She headed toward Nora, stretched out on the sofa.

A melody suddenly filled the room. Her phone! She pulled it from her pocket. The screen showed a number she didn't recognize.

She punched the green button. "Hello."

"Hi, is this Maddy Monroe?"

Her heart was in her throat. "Yes, who's this?"

"I'm a nurse at Dosher Memorial. A Connor Sullivan was brought in by ambulance a little while ago, and we found your contact information in his phone."

"Is he okay?"

"Are you a relative of Mr. Sullivan's?"

"No, I'm his…friend."

"I'm trying to locate next of kin. Can you point me in the right direction?"

Cold fingers of dread raked down Maddy's throat. "Is he all right?"

"He's had an accident and we need to reach his next of kin. Your calls and texts were on his screen, so I started with you."

"His parents and his sisters…Is he all right? Please tell me."

"He's alive, but I really can't share any more information than that. But we'll be asking his next of kin to come to the hospital as soon as possible."

Oh God, she prayed. Maddy's eyes closed in a long blink. Her breath felt stuffed in her lungs. She couldn't breathe.

"What?" Nora asked. "Is he all right?"

Gram and Emma had awakened and all eyes were on her.

Shrugging at them, she forced herself to get on with it. "His parents live in Florida, but his sisters, Tara and Lexie, live in Whiteville. They're in his phone."

The nurse thanked her and disconnected the call.

"What did she say?" Gram asked.

"Only that he's alive, and they're asking the family to come as soon as possible. I have to go."

She was already grabbing her purse, half expecting the others to put up a fight. But that's not what happened.

"I'll go with you," Nora said.

"Me too," Emma said.

Gram began slipping on her shoes. "We'll all go."

CHAPTER 38

Driving a car during a hurricane was definitely not advisable, Maddy thought as she watched Nora navigate the Mercedes. Rain pounded the windshield, making it almost impossible to see the road. Debris flew by, barely missing the car, and the gusts of wind threatened to blow them off the road.

Connor had been out in this, Maddy thought. Unprotected. She fought against the rising tide of panic.

"The hospital probably gave his sister more information," Emma said from the back seat. "You could call her and find out what's going on."

"I don't have her number," Maddy said.

"Slow down," Gram said to Nora from the back seat. "There are wires down up ahead. See?"

Gram was right. Maddy peered through the rain-splattered passenger window into the predawn landscape. A telephone pole was down by the side of the road. But there were no wires on the pavement that she could see.

"I think we're clear," Emma said.

"I don't see anything either." Nora crept past the downed pole, then increased her speed as much as she could with the bad visibility.

Maddy clutched her phone in one hand and her shoulder strap in the other. A moment later they slowed again to maneuver around a large puddle, and the wind rocked the car. Maddy just wanted to be there, at the hospital. She wanted to be looking into those soulful gray eyes and know Connor was all right.

She wondered if they'd even let her see him or tell her anything once she got there. His sisters lived farther from the hospital so it would take them longer to get there. If they could even find a clear path with the flooding and such.

Maddy prayed continually. She repeated the same lame phrases over and over, hoping God wouldn't hold that against her. She just couldn't think straight with fear bathing her brain.

Faith, she prayed. **Give me faith, God.**

It seemed hours later when Nora finally turned into the hospital. She dropped Maddy, Emma, and Gram off at the ER door and went to park. Maddy rushed into the building, then across the waiting room, where she got in line at the desk behind a middle-aged man.

Maddy tapped her foot impatiently, but the man in front of her was cradling a bloodied hand and seemed to be in a lot of pain.

When it was finally her turn, she stepped forward. "Excuse me."

The grandmotherly woman behind the desk closed a folder and put it in a stack.

"I'm looking for Connor Sullivan. He was brought in a while ago. Someone called me."

The woman began typing. "Are you a relative, dear?" she asked without looking up.

Maddy's heart dropped. "No, but I'm his girlfriend." The statement wasn't entirely true, but close enough.

More typing. "Is a relative on the way, do you know?"

"Yes, his sisters, but can you just tell me—"

"I'm sorry." The woman gave her a compassionate smile. "I know you must be terribly worried, but it's hospital policy to only divulge—"

"Phyllis," Gram exclaimed as she rushed up with Emma. "Thank heavens. Maybe you can help us."

The woman behind the desk beamed. "Louise. How lovely to see you."

Gram set her hand on Maddy's back. "This is my granddaughter, Maddy. She's awfully worried about her boyfriend who was just brought in. Can you tell us anything? Anything at all?"

A conflicted look washed over Phyllis's face. She glanced covertly around the desk, then lowered her voice. "Well...I suppose I can tell you that he's in stable condition. I'm afraid that's all I can say until his family arrives."

"Can I see him?" Maddy asked.

"Let me check, dear. Why don't you have a seat in the waiting room?" The woman disappeared through swinging doors.

Maddy and the others made their way to the far corner. Nora had come in, and they updated her.

On the other side of the room a mother paced with a wailing baby. Nearby a little boy lay sleeping in his dad's lap, his face flushed. Everyone seemed to be waiting on news of a friend or loved one, like they were.

Maddy checked the time on her phone. It seemed to be taking Phyllis forever, though probably only a couple minutes had passed.

The exterior doors whooshed open, and Tara rushed into the room. She was wearing a pale blue slicker over yoga pants, no makeup, her short brown hair flat on one side.

Maddy met her at the desk. "Tara."

"Maddy!" The woman embraced her. "Have you heard anything?"

"They won't tell me much. Only that he's alive and stable. What did they tell you on the phone?"

"Only that he was unconscious and undergoing tests. He was out in the storm and got hit in the head, apparently."

Maddy drew back, giving Tara a pained look. "I'm so sorry. He went out looking for my sister. Nora came back, but he never did. We called 911, but they never got back to us, and I didn't have any way of reaching you."

Tara squeezed her arm. "He's in good hands now."

The others had joined them, and Maddy made quick introductions. She was just finishing when Phyllis returned.

"This is Tara," Maddy said. "Connor's sister. Can we go back and see him now?"

"The doctor's in his room right now and would like to speak to a relative. I can walk you back," she said to Tara. Then she addressed Maddy. "You'll need to wait a bit, dear."

Tara squeezed Maddy's hand. "I'll be back with an update. Hang in there and please pray!"

And then she was gone. Maddy wanted to cry. Her eyes burned and her throat ached. But at least Tara was going to him now. He wouldn't be alone anymore, and they'd tell her what was going on.

"Come on, honey." Gram took her arm. "Let's go sit down. It shouldn't be long now."

It seemed an eternity later when Tara came back through the doors. Her face was splotchy and her eyes were blood-shot.

Maddy found herself beside the woman without any memory of getting up or walking over. She set her hand on Tara's arm. "What's going on? Is he awake?"

Tara shook her head, swiping a finger under her eye. "He's still unconscious. He definitely has a concussion, and they're concerned, since he hasn't woken up yet."

Maddy's lungs wouldn't fill. Her heart felt as though it might explode from her chest. "Is he—is he in a coma then?"

"The doctor didn't use that word. He's had an x-ray and an MRI, but the results haven't come back yet." Tara covered her trembling lips as her eyes watered. "He just looks so pale and lifeless, lying there."

"Did the doctor say anything else?" Gram asked. The others had followed her over.

"There's not much they can say until the test results come back. But the sooner he wakes up, the better. Some guy found him when he took his dog outside early this morning. Otherwise he'd still be lying there."

Maddy hated to think of it. He must've lain out there unconscious and bleeding for hours.

"Maddy..." Tara gave Maddy a tortured look.

Maddy's blood seemed to freeze at the look on Tara's face. "What? There's more, isn't there? What is it?"

"The doctor said we're dealing with a traumatic brain injury. He doesn't know the extent of it, but he said it's at least what they call a 'moderate TBI.' If someone's unconscious more than six hours, it's considered to be severe. But, of course, we don't know how long he's been unconscious."

"Oh no." Maddy's chest tightened until it ached. Her eyes burned.

"He did say you can go back and see him. Only one of us at a time, though. I'm going to call my family and update them. Lexie had to stay with the kids—my husband's out of town. Connor's in room 114, but they're planning to move him upstairs soon."

Gram squeezed Maddy's arm. "We'll be right here storming the gates of heaven, sugar. Don't lose hope now, you hear? God's got this."

"All right." Numbly Maddy pushed through the door and strode down the long corridor. Her shoes squeaked on the sterile white tile. She breathed in the smell of disinfectant and the faint odor of burnt popcorn—from the break room, she supposed.

The florescent lights flickered, and she realized the hospital must've been using an emergency generator. Thank heavens for that.

Room 114 seemed to be at the other end of the hall. Her heart was beating double time, and her lungs couldn't seem to keep up.

She knew only a little about traumatic brain injuries. The mother of a server at Pirouette had suffered one following a car accident. She had trouble processing and spoke very slowly. She also had seizures, Maddy recalled. She tried to remember what else Lauren had mentioned, but she came up blank. That was bad enough, though. The accident had changed the woman's quality of life. She was on disability now, unable to even hold down a job.

Please, God. Please. Not Connor. He's so kind and selfless. He doesn't deserve this. He's already lost his wife,

so young. And he went looking for Nora in a hurricane. And he went in my place, God.

Maddy's steps faltered. She should be the one lying in that bed right now.

She blinked back tears, reading the room numbers as she got closer. She passed 112. Then 114. There it was.

She pushed through the door, so eager to see him. Her breath caught when her eyes fell on him.

There was a white bandage around his head. He looked as if he were merely sleeping, though the harsh lights gave him a ghostly pallor. An IV was stuck in the back of his hand, which lay curled on top of the crisp white sheet. His chest rose and fell reassuringly. His hair was disheveled and still damp from the rain.

Dear God, how long did he lie out there in the storm?

Her heart squeezed. "Oh, Connor."

She moved forward, letting the door fall shut behind her. A monitor beeped quietly. He was still alive. There was still hope.

When she reached the bed she took his

hand, finding it wonderfully warm. His golden lashes swept downward, hiding his lovely gray eyes.

"Oh, Connor," she whispered, running her thumb over the back of his hand. "I'm so sorry. Please wake up. Please be all right."

Her gaze drifted over the familiar planes of his face, over the golden scruff on his jaw and the subtle cleft that she loved so much.

"You have to fight hard, hear me? You have to be all right. There are so many people who love you." She swallowed against the achy lump in her throat. Tears leaked out. "Including me, Connor."

She gave a feeble laugh. "Yeah, yeah, I know. I was just trying to break up with you only hours ago. But I was wrong. I was just afraid, honey. I didn't mean what I said. You just make me feel so much, and I was afraid you'd break my heart. So I went ahead and broke it myself."

She breathed another laugh. "I know, that sounds so stupid. It **was** stupid. You're the best thing that's ever happened to me, and I was willing to throw it all away out of fear. And now I'm scared silly I'll never get to tell you how I feel."

She looked at his still face, at the features that had become so familiar so quickly. A love for him welled up so strongly it nearly overwhelmed her. Along with the strength she needed to carry her through. Even if, God forbid, he never got better, she'd be here for him. She knew it with everything in her.

She squeezed his hand, tears now coursing down her face. But her voice carried all the strength she felt inside. "I'm not going anywhere, no matter what, you hear me, Connor Sullivan? You can't get rid of me, so don't even try."

She thought she must've imagined the movement under her hand. She stilled, staring at his hand. She stopped breathing. Had she only imagined it? Wishful thinking?

There it was again! She not only felt it, she saw it too. Her eyes darted to his face. She found him staring at her from beneath his sleepy lashes.

"Connor! You're awake."

His lips moved but no sounds escaped.

"You had an accident, but you're going to be all right."

His tongue darted out to wet his lips. "Must be dreaming."

She barely made out the low scrape of his voice. She frowned at his words. Dreaming? He was looking at her almost blankly. What if he didn't even know who she was? Her heart gave a stutter.

"What—what do you mean?"

He gave a long, tired blink. "Thought I heard…you say you love me."

Oh, thank God! Her breath tumbled out. She squeezed his hand, smiling at him. "I did, honey. I do love you. And as much as I want to sit here and discuss that, we need to get a doctor in here pronto."

She pressed the call button, requesting help, then turned her attention back to him.

His eyes were closed again. A frown puckered his brows. "Headache. What happened?"

"You were out looking for Nora in the

hurricane. You don't remember?"

He started to nod, then winced.

"You got hit in the head with something, and a neighbor found you lying in his yard this morning."

His eyes opened. "Nora?"

"She's fine. She and Pippy both. They came home late last night. It's almost seven in the morning now. You must've lain out there all night. Tara's in the waiting room, and the rest of your family will be here as soon as they can."

His eyes closed again.

The door opened, and a man entered. He looked to be thirty-ish and wore a lab coat. "Well, good morning. Good to see you're awake, Mr. Sullivan. I'm Dr. Kadambi. How are you feeling?"

Maddy moved to the side as the doctor stepped up to the rails.

"Head hurts."

"I'd be surprised if it didn't. That was quite a hit you took."

He asked Connor to recite some basic information about himself, which he did successfully, much to Maddy's relief. He seemed just fine cognitively.

"Do you remember what happened last night?" Dr. Kadambi asked as he continued his exam.

"I was out looking for a friend."

"Must be a good friend to go searching during the middle of a hurricane. What's her name?"

"Nora."

The doctor checked his pupils, nodding toward Maddy. "And who's this young lady?"

"Maddy." Connor's gaze flickered over to her, his lips twitching ever so slightly. "My girlfriend."

Her heart expanded in her chest. Did that ever sound nice. Her lips curled upward.

"Are you having any symptoms other than a raging headache? Any nausea or vomiting? Ringing in the ears?"

"No."

"How's your vision?"

Connor stared toward the muted TV for a long moment. "A little blurry."

"One eye or both?"

Connor closed one eye at a time. "Just the left one, I think."

"That's not unusual after a concussion. It usually clears up with plenty of rest. If it doesn't, you'll need to see an optometrist."

The doctor straightened, dropping his hands into his lab coat pockets. "Well, your vitals look good—and your tests came back normal. We did an x-ray and an MRI while you were out. We'd like to keep you for observation, though, since you were unconscious so long. They'll probably do more assessments upstairs. I'm optimistic, though. Everything looks really good. You're a lucky man."

"Blessed," Connor corrected, his eye-lids drooping. "Thanks."

Dr. Kadambi looked at Maddy as he went to the door. "He's going to be pretty tired and need a lot of rest over the next several days. We'll move him to a room as soon as we can."

"Thank you so much."

The doctor nodded with a smile and left the room.

Maddy needed to go tell Tara the good news. His whole family must be so anxious for him. She grabbed the door.

Hating to leave him, she paused on the threshold, giving him a lingering look. Long enough to memorize his precious features. Long enough to feel over-whelmed again by the power of her love. Long enough to breathe a prayer of gratitude. He was going to be all right. They all were.

CHAPTER 39

Tara extended a hand to Connor through the passenger-side door. "Easy does it now."

He scowled at Tara but took her hand anyway. "I'm not an invalid, for pity's sake."

Lexie was already clearing a pathway to the front door—there was a lot of debris from the storm. After helping him from the vehicle Tara began unloading what seemed to be a month's worth of casseroles from the back of her crossover.

When had Tara even had time to cook anything? What, did she have ready-made meals just waiting in her freezer for

such an opportunity? Probably. Good
grief, they were going to drive him crazy.
They'd already been hovering around his
hospital bed for the past two days.

He'd somehow managed to convince
his parents to stay put in Florida. They
hadn't been able to get a flight anyway on
account of the storm, and he sure hadn't
wanted them driving with all the flooding.
He FaceTimed them yesterday from his
hospital bed just to assure them he was
all right.

"Straight to the couch," Tara said as
they entered the house.

He gritted his teeth, both against his
raging headache and his bossy sister. Too
bad it was too soon to take something
for the pain. His left eye was still blurry,
which made it hard to see. But all in all he
felt like a blessed man. It could've been so
much worse. He understood that now—
his sisters had made sure of it.

Once inside Tara disappeared into the
kitchen, picking up a pair of stray socks
as she went. She started making a racket
with pots and pans. Lexie had run upstairs,

probably getting a pile of quilts and a bedpan or something equally ridiculous.

He picked up the remote and turned it to ESPN. At least a Braves game was on. Sunlight streamed in, making his head throb. It seemed someone had already taken the boards off his windows.

Tara returned a few minutes later, handing him an ice pack. "On your head for twenty minutes." She covered him with an afghan he'd never even seen, then snatched the remote from his hand and pointed it at the television. "No TV, doctor's orders. You heard what I promised Mama. And bear in mind, if not for me, she'd be here hovering over you too."

He scowled. He felt like an old lady. "I see how this is going to go."

Tara turned a dark look on him. "You bet your sweet bippy you do. The doctor said plenty of rest, and we're here to make sure that happens. I know you, Connor Sullivan. We leave you alone, and you'll be out in that yard picking up debris the second we walk out the door. You need time to recover—you don't want blurry eyes the rest of your life, do you, or some other awful affliction? Do you even know how blessed you are that it isn't so much worse?"

Tears. Oh, good grief, not again.

"You could be permanently impaired or even dead right now. Your brain has had an awful trauma and needs time and rest to recover properly, and if that means we have to stand here over your stubborn self and keep watch, that's just what's going to happen. You hear me?"

"All right, all right. I'll stay put." Women. Sheesh.

He'd heard the doctor clearly enough. Someone was supposed to be here at all times, monitoring him for new symptoms, for at least forty-eight interminable hours. No challenging activities, physical or mental, including watching TV, reading, or messing around on the computer.

They'd already confiscated his phone—but not before he'd called the marina. The place had fared pretty well through the storm, and he felt comfortable leaving Brandon in charge—at least there was that. And though the restaurant was closed today for cleanup, Lexie had volunteered to step into Cheryl's place temporarily.

Meanwhile, here he was. Connor looked around the quiet room. "What am I supposed to do if I can't watch TV or even think too hard, for crying out loud?"

"Sleep," Tara said firmly. "You're supposed to sleep. You can just lie on the cold pack."

"I'm not even tired." He'd slept in the hospital, as much as he could with everyone coming and going. "I can't just order myself to sleep, you know."

Tara turned out the living room light and drew the shades until the room was awash in gray shadows.

"Nighty-night." She disappeared into the kitchen.

Connor sighed. The next two days were going to be very long ones. His sisters had made a schedule that assured him of a babysitter every single hour. And while they were here they'd no doubt give his house a top-to-bottom cleaning that would assure he'd never find anything again.

The only person he really wished were here was currently at the drugstore, picking up more ibuprofen and a softer ice pack and anything else she might decide he needed. Maddy had been hovering too—but he didn't mind that so much. In fact, he found himself craving her company.

He was a man in love, there was no denying it.

Waking to the concern in her voice the previous morning had been such a relief. The last he'd spoken with her, she'd been breaking it off. Concern seemed like a very good sign.

And though his memory was a little fuzzy now, he remembered enough of her sweet words to feel like ten kinds of fool for his response. The girl of his dreams had proclaimed her undying love for him, and he'd just lain there like a lump.

Sure, sure, he'd had a brain injury. But come on! It wasn't like him to miss an opportunity like that. Ever since, he'd been looking for a chance to redeem himself. But between his sisters and her sisters and the hospital staff, there'd always been someone around. Was he ever going to get her alone?

He shifted the cold pack under his head. Then he spent a while thinking about what he might say to Maddy when he finally got the chance. But soon his thoughts grew distant and fuzzy. His breathing slowed and evened out.

And then he wasn't thinking of anything at all.

CHAPTER 40

Maddy picked up an asphalt shingle and threw it into the trash barrel. She and her sisters were making pretty quick work of the cleanup. The tide was pushing back out to sea. The storm surge had left more than the usual treasures: driftwood, a cracked sand pail, a lawn chair armrest.

The sun rode low in the sky, the storm clouds long gone. The ocean was calm today, not a whitecap to be found. One would never have believed there'd been a storm less than forty-eight hours ago.

Sweat beaded on the back of her neck, but there was a gentle breeze coming in off the water.

The house itself had weathered the

storm pretty well. There were a few missing roof shingles, and her landscaping had taken a hit. The mulch had washed away, and the flowers had taken a beating. Not too bad.

Maddy meandered toward the dunes where her sisters were picking up bits of limbs and branches. Her gaze drifted toward Connor's place. Earlier when she'd dropped by with his pain meds he'd been sleeping soundly. He was covered with an afghan, and his sisters were just sitting down to eat.

They invited her to stay, but she'd grabbed a bite at the hospital. She'd longed to stay with Conner, but Tara and Lexie had things well in hand, and there was a lot of cleanup to do around their properties.

It had been an exciting and exhausting few days. Maddy was ready for things to settle down a bit. She had a lot to digest. They all did.

"Hey, look." Emma was holding up a sodden sandal. "It's a nice one too. Birkenstock. Oh well."

She tossed it into the trash barrel, then finger-waved at Gram, who stood by the back door cradling Pippy in her arms. Emma put a hand on her lower back, stretching.

"Take it easy, little mama," Nora said. "We don't need you straining your back and ending up on bed rest or something."

"I'm fine. It feels good to be out in the sunshine."

"I didn't hear you tossing your cookies this morning," Nora said. "Maybe the morning sickness is passing?"

"I hope so. My appetite has kicked in, that's for sure. I want to eat everything in sight."

Maddy smiled. "The baby's hungry. You have to feed him."

"Or her. Girls do seem to run in the family." Nora tossed a chunk of driftwood into the woodpile and cast a sideways look at Emma. "When do you think you'll tell Ethan?"

Emma bit her lip as she bent for another small branch. "I, uh, I already did."

Maddy straightened. "What? When?

How'd it go?"

"Why didn't you say anything?"

"There's really nothing to say," Emma said. "I—I didn't exactly tell him outright. I just couldn't. I tried to, but..." She covered her forehead. "I left it on his voicemail."

"You what?" Nora said.

"I know, it was such a chicken thing to do. I wish I hadn't. I was calling to tell him, but his voicemail kicked in, and it suddenly seemed like such an easy way to do it—Ugh! Terrible idea. That was this morning, and he hasn't called me back. He probably hates me. He's probably filing for divorce as we speak." Her eyes filled with tears.

"He doesn't hate you," Nora said.

"I just...After worrying about Nora and almost losing Connor...I got to thinking about Ethan, and I had to tell him right away. None of us really knows how long we have, you know?"

Maddy winced. "But a voicemail..."

"I know, I know." Emma knuckled the corner of her eye.

Next door, Tara carried a rug out onto the deck. She gave them a little wave, then started shaking out the rug. Dust mushroomed around her.

"Poor Connor." Nora laughed. "Those sisters of his are a force."

Maddy smiled. "He's met his match, that's for sure. I'm glad he has them, though. They're taking good care of him."

They'd been at the hospital nearly every moment. Maddy had also met Connor's best friend, Lamont, who'd stopped by twice.

"He's looking some better today," Emma said. "And the two of you seem to be faring well."

Maddy's smile rose naturally. Even though she'd had no time alone with him in the hospital, the furtive glances they exchanged were encouraging. For the first time in a long time, she felt optimistic about her future. Hopeful. Which was funny, since she didn't even have a job.

Though everything she'd learned about her dad and grandpa had been unsettling, it also made sense of things, like the last piece of a puzzle clicking into place.

"What do you think you'll do next?" Emma asked her. "I mean, the house is finished, and apart from a little cleanup, our work here is done. Are you going to follow up on that job Nick told you about?"

Maddy shook her head. "He called last night on my way home from the hospital. I told him he could cross my name off the list."

Nora snorted. "I hope you told him he could do more than that."

Maddy hitched her shoulder. "I kind of feel sorry for him. He's putting all his eggs in the wrong basket."

"I feel something for him too," Nora said. "But it's not pity."

Nick had tried to change her mind, but Maddy was firm. He didn't even mention missing her this time. Must've heard the resolve in her tone and known he'd only be wasting his time.

"What are you going to do then?" Emma asked. "Have you heard back from any of the restaurants you've applied to?"

"I've gotten two emails requesting interviews. Both are great restaurants. Good opportunities. I'll call them back this week and schedule them." She thought of Connor and wondered how they were going to negotiate a long-distance relationship.

"What about you and Connor?" Nora asked. "You're going to date long distance?"

"I don't know. We haven't had a chance to talk about it."

"Maybe you should put in some applications around here just in case," Emma said.

"It seems so quick, though," Maddy said. "We haven't even known each other two months. We've only had one date!"

Emma shrugged. "When you know, you know. I knew Ethan was the one for me on our third date."

"You're obviously in love with each other," Nora said.

Well, Maddy thought, **I'm in love with him. He has yet to return the words.**

Nora walked to the top of a dune and

stared out to sea. "What are you going home to, other than an empty apartment?"

"Nothing really, except my friend Holly. I do have an apartment lease, but that's up in another month anyway."

"It sure would be nice to have another sister here in Seahaven."

Maddy and Emma stopped what they were doing and gaped at Nora.

"You're staying?" Maddy asked, joining her sister on the dune.

Nora blew her hair out of her face. "I've been talking to Gram about it. I've also been checking out the job opportunities in the area. There's an opening for a librarian in the next town over, and I've got that master's degree just going to waste."

Maddy smiled. "You've always wanted to be a librarian."

"The current one is retiring next month, and Gram knows the manager. I have an interview scheduled for later this week."

"That's just wonderful, Nora," Emma said. "I'll be praying you get the job."

"I might have to live with Gram awhile,

but she's all right with that. I have to get back on my feet. It won't be easy, but I'm determined to make a life for myself here."

"What about Chloe?" Emma asked.

"She's my top priority. I'm going to go see her at college this weekend. We have a lot of catching up to do."

"She's a bright girl," Maddy said. "She'll come around."

"She's mad at the world right now," Nora said. "And that includes me. I can't blame her. I hope she makes more out of her life than I have."

"Thank God for fresh starts," Maddy said.

"Hear, hear," Emma said, climbing the sand dune, her bare feet sinking into the damp sand. "Speaking of fresh starts—and mothers and daughters—has anyone talked to Mama yet?"

"We need to call her," Maddy said. "I feel horrible about the way I've misjudged her."

"Me too," Nora said. "When I think about how I talked Daddy up in front of her I just want to smack myself."

"I can't believe she never told us the truth," Emma said.

"I can," Nora said. "You'll do anything to protect your kids. I'd give anything if Chloe didn't have to know about her dad. It's torn her in two. But even if there were a way we could have kept it from her, I think I've learned the damage of keeping secrets."

"We should invite Mama here for a weekend," Emma said suddenly. "We have a lot of catching up to do."

"A lot of making up to do also," Maddy said.

"Can I invite Chloe too?" Nora said.

"Of course," Emma said. "She's family. I can't wait to tell Mama about the baby. She'll be so happy."

The faint sound of a car engine carried over the sound of surf, and Maddy looked back toward the street. A blue Mazda was pulling into their drive. Her sisters hadn't noticed and continued talking as Maddy shielded her eyes from the sun.

The man caught sight of them and,

lifting a hand to Maddy, walked around his car and along the side of the house toward them.

Maddy almost didn't recognize him. Hadn't seen him in a couple years. He was wearing his brown hair longer now, and he'd lost the little paunch around his middle. But he still had a teddy bear build and wore that full beard.

"Um, Emma...," Maddy said, getting her sister's attention. "I think there's someone here to see you."

Emma turned. Her lips parted as she caught sight of her husband. She froze in place, a look coming over her face that carried so many emotions Maddy couldn't distinguish one from the other.

Then Emma took a step forward. She took another and another, her feet seeming to move of their own volition. As she and Ethan grew closer, her steps quickened.

And so did Ethan's—a smile blooming on his face.

They came together, wrapping their arms around each other.

Goose bumps washed over Maddy's skin. Tears stung her eyes as she watched the happy reunion. She put her hand to her heart. **Oh, thank You, Jesus.**

The couple held each other for a long, poignant moment. Then Ethan drew away. He cradled Emma's face in his big hands and said something, the wind carrying away his words. Then he kissed her.

Silently Nora took Maddy's hand.

Maddy squeezed it, speechless in the face of love's enduring beauty.

CHAPTER 41

Connor became aware of his throbbing head before he was even fully conscious. His neck ached as he stretched, and he realized he was still on the couch. The lights were out, the house quiet. He spotted a lump on the sofa across from him. Tara.

He sat up and found a glass of water and his pain meds on the end table. Thank God. He took them, wishing the pain away. He closed his blurry left eye and read the clock on the DVR. It was after eleven. He'd been asleep since suppertime. His stomach gave a hefty growl at the reminder that he'd missed a meal.

Taking his water, he padded into the kitchen and found a plate of croissant rolls on the stove. He took down three of them, standing over the counter. By the time he was done his headache was measurably better.

Outside, a full moon rose in the black sky, and its ethereal light glistened off the darkened water. The distant sound of the surf beckoned him. He slipped quietly outside, not wanting to alert Tara that her patient had escaped.

The mild breeze was a welcome reprieve from the stuffy air in the house. He drew in a breath of sea air, letting it stretch his lungs. His gaze drifted next door, to Maddy's house. All the windows were dark.

He felt a stab of disappointment. Much as he loved his sisters, it was Maddy's company he craved. As his eyes swept back toward the sea, a movement caught his attention. Between the dips of the dunes, a silhouetted figure huddled on the beach, hair blowing on the breeze. The sight of her familiar form drew a smile.

He was off the deck before he could even think twice.

Maddy stretched out her legs, resting her weight on her arms. Her palms dug into the gritty sand. She couldn't sleep. She had too much on her mind.

Earlier Emma and Ethan had taken a long walk on the beach before joining the rest of them in the house. When they'd returned it had warmed Maddy's heart to see the love shining in Ethan's eyes. It was clear the man was tickled pink about the baby. The two of them hadn't been out of arm's reach all night, and they'd disappeared upstairs hours ago.

Maddy was so happy for them.

And for Nora too. Her oldest sister still had a long road ahead of her, but she was in a good place mentally and spiritually. She was making plans and seemed optimistic about her future. She was going to be just fine.

But what was next for Maddy? She was jobless and running low on funds. And long-distance relationships presented their own challenges. Would she be just fine too?

Will I, God?

A measure of faith rolled over her like a wave, bathing her in peace. She would be all right, one way or another. God had her back.

"Save me a spot?"

She turned to see Connor lowering himself slowly onto the sand beside her. He was wearing the basketball shorts and T-shirt he'd worn home from the hospital. Even in the dark she could see his hair poking up at odd angles.

"What are you doing out here?" she asked. "You should be in bed."

"I've been sleeping for hours. Now I'm wide-awake." He had a familiar pinched look on his face.

She smoothed down his hair. "You still have a headache, don't you?"

"I just took a pain med. Thanks for picking that up at the store, by the way. It sure is a lifesaver."

"I checked in on you earlier, but you were asleep. How are you feeling otherwise?"

He wrapped an arm around her, tucking her into his side. "Better every minute."

She dropped her cheek to his shoulder. She reveled in his warmth, in the masculine smell of him, in the solid feel of him against her.

Love could be scary, that was for sure. But with a little faith it could be wonderful too. She'd focus on that part and trust God with the rest.

"What's going on in that head of yours?" he asked.

She gave a wry smile. "It's reeling, that's what. So much has happened over the last forty-eight hours, Connor. I haven't even had time to process it all."

"Tell me," he said in that deep, rich voice she loved so much.

And so she did. She filled him in on everything she'd learned from her grandmother. Everything she'd found out about her father and her grandfather. Everything she'd learned about her sisters' lives. She finished with the latest news —Emma's pregnancy and the reunion between her and Ethan.

Connor listened intently and patiently.

"I'm sorry," she said at last. "I shouldn't have thrown all this at you tonight." She looked up at him, finding his face closer than she expected. "You're supposed to be resting your brain, and I'm dumping our family's dirty secrets on you."

"I want to know what's happening in your life." His finger whispered along her cheek, and his eyes smoldered with heat. "I want to be part of your life, Maddy. All of it. The good and the bad."

"I want that too," she said softly.

"You really scared me the other night when you said—"

She put a finger over his lips. "I didn't mean it. I didn't mean any of it. I was just running scared."

He took her hand. "After everything you just told me it's no wonder. It's a lot to digest."

"I may need therapy," she said on a laugh. Though it was no joke.

Finding out her dad had had another life had been a hard blow. She was angry with him for doing that to her mother, to them. And he was no longer here to untangle the mess he'd made. Still, she'd have to find it in her heart to forgive him. They all would.

Connor looked deeply into her eyes, seeming to see beneath the brave surface. "It's a good idea, actually. And you're a strong woman, Maddy. You'll get through this."

Hard to believe that only two months ago she'd been working at Pirouette, dating Nick, and—if she were honest— lacking in joy. Lacking in peace. So much had changed in such a short time.

She shook her head in wonder. "Weeks ago when you called and I rushed to Seahaven, I never could've dreamed everything that would happen. The family history coming out, my sisters coming back together, Emma's pregnancy and reunited marriage—it's downright crazy."

"It's a straight-up miracle," he said, wonder in his voice.

"You're right about that. So many secrets have come out. But I'm learning that once secrets are exposed…they lose their power."

"The truth will set you free."

"Exactly."

She'd been held in fear's grip and hadn't fully understood why. She was beginning to see what she'd come from and how it had affected her. She'd only just scratched the surface, she knew, but it was a start. And now that the secrets were out in the light…they didn't seem so scary anymore.

"Maddy…," he said. "Have you thought about what's next? For you? For us?"

She straightened a bit so she could see his face. "Actually, that's just what I was thinking about when you came out here."

His lips slanted in a grin. "Good thing I got out here in time to weigh in."

"Oh, you want a vote, do you?" she asked saucily.

"If you'll let me have one." He gave her a lingering look, then brushed his thumb across her cheek. "I love you, Maddy Monroe. With all my heart."

His words filled her to overflowing. Her

lips pulled upward. It seemed she'd been waiting a lifetime to hear those words. "I love you too, Connor."

His eyes pierced hers as his breath fell on her mouth.

Her lips tingled, and her insides hummed with energy. This man. He spoke to her, soul deep, with just a look. Just a touch.

"Stay," he said softly.

She fell headlong into his gaze as a shiver rippled over her. "Yes."

The corners of his lips notched upward. He came closer, and his lips brushed hers. He pulled her into his chest, deepening the kiss.

Maddy forgot everything but the feel of his lips, the scent of his skin, the warmth of his touch. She could happily stay in his arms for the rest of her life.

When they parted she was breathless. So was he. Their breaths intertwined, mingling with the sea air.

His nuzzled her nose. "I don't suppose you'd consider a position at a glorified crab shack."

She drew back a bit. "The Landing?

What about Cheryl?"

"Her dad had another stroke. She's moving back home for good to take care of him."

"Oh no. I didn't know that."

"New information. Listen, honey...I know you're way overqualified for the position. If you'd be bored silly working there full-time, then—"

"Would I get complete control?" she asked with a cheeky thrust of her chin.

His face relaxed as his lips twitched. "Back to that, are we?"

"By your own admission you know nothing about managing a restaurant."

"True enough." He held up his right hand. "No micromanaging. No undermining your authority. Promise."

Maddy thought over his offer, hope rising like the tide. She could definitely see a future in Seahaven, at Sullivan's Landing —and right here in Connor's arms. She could see it all working, so beautifully.

A slow, confident smile broke out on her face. "You have yourself a deal, mister."

"We haven't even talked salary yet."

She nuzzled his nose and whispered, "I'm sure we can work something out." And then they went back to the real negotiations.

EPILOGUE

Maddy set the bowl of mashed potatoes on one of the picnic tables they'd set up on Gram's deck. The red-and-white checkered tablecloth fluttered in the breeze, and the delicious aroma of grilled burgers wafted by.

It had taken two and a half months to make this picnic happen. But they'd ended up with a perfect day, the temperatures hovering at eighty and fluffy clouds rolling in off the tranquil sea.

She looked over to the deck's corner where Connor and Ethan manned the grill. Emma hovered nearby, dropping slices of cheese onto the thick, sizzling patties. Her tummy was now slightly rounded under her gauzy summer top.

They'd found out last week that she was carrying a boy. Everyone had opinions on names, but they already seemed set on Grant William, after Ethan's father. Emma's cheeks were flushed, her skin glowing. She was wearing this pregnancy like a second skin.

Connor's eyes met Maddy's over the open grill. He winked at her, and she shared a private smile with him before heading back inside.

She scanned the kitchen for more food to carry out. Gram was giving the green beans one last stir and telling Mama's husband, Russell, some outrageous story from her trip to Boise. He listened intently, laughing in all the right spots. He was a genuinely nice guy. Maddy was sorry she hadn't given him half a chance before now.

Across the room Nora and Chloe were filling glasses with iced tea. It was obvious the two of them had come a long way in recent weeks. Nora had gone up north to see her at college, and Chloe had come to Seahaven for two weekends. At the moment they were talking quietly, relaxed expressions on their faces.

Nora had gotten that librarian job, a position she was loving. She and Maddy had rented a house together, a two-bedroom in a quiet neighborhood not far from the beach. The property featured a lovely live oak that spread its shade across the entire yard. The living situation was working well for both of them.

As for Maddy, she was loving her job at Sullivan's Landing. She had a great rapport with the chef—and the owner—and they were working on some new dishes to liven up the menu. The staff was thriving under her instruction, and as promised, Connor had taken a hands-off position—with the restaurant, that was.

Maddy pulled the potato salad from the fridge and headed toward the door. Her mother stopped her on the way.

"Take these on out, would you, sugar?" She handed Maddy two bags of hamburger buns.

"Sure thing, Mama."

Last night the family had played cards late into the night, then spread around the house, some of them taking couches and sleeping bags on the floor. It was wonderful to have everyone together again. It would never be the same as it had been—or as wonderful as she'd **thought** it was as a child. But it could be a new kind of wonderful. A real kind of wonderful.

Maddy was starting to appreciate the concept of new beginnings. She and her mom had grown closer since that first teary phone conversation back in July, when Maddy confessed to knowing about her father's double life. She'd asked her mother's forgiveness for holding her at arm's length all these years. They talked at least once a week now.

Things were still a bit awkward between them, but time would mend that. She longed for the closer relationship they'd once shared, and she knew Mama wanted the same. Nora and Emma were on similar paths.

Outside, Ethan was setting a platter of

burgers on the table. "Come and get it!"

The family descended on the table like a flock of hungry sea gulls. After they settled, Gram said a brief but heartfelt prayer and they dug in. The food was delicious, but nothing could beat the company. The feeling that her family was together again.

They were mostly finished eating when Connor took her hand under the table. She met his questioning gaze and gave his hand a squeeze. Then she reached into her pocket.

When she was finished with her quick task, Connor lifted his glass and clinked it with his fork.

The chatter quieted as every gaze turned his way. He gave her a tender look before letting his eyes drift around the table.

"Maddy and I have an announcement to make," he said. His gaze fell on her again, softening as they lingered on her features. "Last night she agreed to make me the happiest man in the world."

"We're engaged!" Maddy blurted, lifting her hand. She waggled her fingers, showing off the ring he'd placed on her finger out on the beach after everyone else had gone to bed.

Gasps and well wishes and hugs followed, the happy chaos ringing in Maddy's heart. Pippy, sensing the excitement, barked from her spot at Emma's feet.

She and Connor told the story of the proposal, the women swooning as the story progressed. Questions followed, and the couple was happy to appease their curiosity. The wedding would take place next June, a small one, right on the beach.

Maddy kept grinning down at her finger, then up at Connor's beaming smile. Every now and then she remembered her first impression of him and couldn't help chuckling.

She didn't know if he really was the happiest man in the world—but she definitely felt like the most blessed woman.

After the excitement at the table dissipated, everyone went their separate ways. Gram and Maddy's sisters began setting the kitchen to rights, Pippy underfoot. Chloe went down to the beach with Mama, where they were tossing a Frisbee. The men had settled in the living room, watching a Braves game.

Maddy brought the last of the dishes inside, and then, craving a quiet moment, she wandered over to the deck railing. The breeze tossed her hair and tugged at her shirt. She breathed in the familiar scent of briny air—it smelled like home now.

She watched as Chloe tried to teach Mama how to throw the Frisbee straight, but the girl wasn't having much luck. Laughter rang out as her mother's throw ended up in the foamy waves.

Maddy smiled at the pair, her thumb finding the unfamiliar feel of the band on her ring finger. She looked down to admire the sparkling solitaire, twisting it this way and that, letting the sunlight glint off it.

As happy as she felt right now...one thing was missing.

Connor appeared behind her, wrapping his arms around her. He dropped his chin to the top of her head. "What are you doing out here all by yourself?"

She snuggled into the strength of his chest and wrapped her arms around his. "Just thinking, I guess."

"About what? "

She smiled. "Mostly about how happy I am right now."

"You were looking kind of...somber."

"I guess I was. I was just thinking about Daddy. I can't help but miss him today. I wish he were here to see how happy I am. How happy we all are."

"He knows." Connor gave her a squeeze, his breath tickling the hair near her ears. "He loved you, you know. Don't lose sight of that."

Maddy nodded. In spite of her dad's foolish choices, she knew Connor was right. She was working through the past with a good therapist. It was helping. Life wasn't perfect. If it were, would she adequately appreciate all the good things? She didn't think so.

She turned in Connor's arms. And there were a lot of good things, she was beginning to see. She couldn't help smiling up at her fiancé's handsome face.

"It's a perfect day," she said. "But it's a little sad that this might be our last family gathering here."

He tipped her chin up. "What if I told you that didn't have to be the case?"

She searched his eyes. "What do you mean?"

"I've been in negotiations with your grandma. What would you think if I sold my cottage, and we bought this one?"

She gasped. "Really?"

"Really."

She grabbed him, giving him a hard hug. "Can we afford it? Are you sure you want to do that?"

He drew back. "She cut me a good deal. I can see us living here, Maddy. Filling up all these rooms with little Sullivans. Can't you?"

"Yes!" She could see them coming home to eat supper on the deck. Could see them taking long walks on the beach. And yes, she could definitely see their little family growing larger right here on the beach.

Her mouth stretched into a grin.

He placed his hands on the railing, trapping her there, then tilted his head, an inquisitive look in his eyes. "And what are you thinking about now, my soon-to-be bride?"

She gave him a slow, flirty smile. "You. Me. Us."

The look in his eyes shifted, going to smoldering. "Hmm. I'm liking the direction of this conversation. Talk to me."

She cupped his face, bringing his mouth to hers in a slow, lingering kiss that sent a shiver through her. Made her knees go wobbly. He deepened the kiss, dragging her closer, making her heart thump, her head spin.

"Mmm," he murmured against her lips a moment later. "Tell me more."

She smiled and did just as he suggested.

ACKNOWLEDGMENTS

Writing a book is a team effort, and I'm so grateful for the fabulous fiction team at HarperCollins, led by publisher Amanda Bostic: Matt Bray, Kim Carlton, Allison Carter, Paul Fisher, Jodi Hughes, Becky Monds, Jocelyn Bailey, and Kristen Ingebretson.

Thanks especially to my editor, Kim Carlton, for her insight and inspiration. I'm infinitely grateful to editor L. B. Norton, who saves me from countless errors and always makes me look so much better than I am.

Author Colleen Coble is my first reader. Thank you, friend! Writing wouldn't be nearly as much fun without you!

I'm grateful to my agent, Karen Solem, who's able to somehow make sense of the legal garble of contracts and, even more amazing, help me understand it.

Kevin, my husband of thirty years, has been a wonderful support. I'm so blessed to be doing life with you, honey! To my kiddos, Justin and Hannah, Chad, and Trevor: You make life an adventure! Love you all!

Finally, thank you, friend, for letting me share this story with you. I wouldn't be doing this without you! I enjoy connecting with friends on my Facebook page, facebook.com/authordenisehunter. Please pop over and say hello. Visit my website at the link DeniseHunterBooks.com or just drop me a note at Deniseahunter@comcast.net. I'd love to hear from you!

ABOUT THE AUTHOR

Photo by Neal Bruns

DENISE HUNTER is the internationally published bestselling author of more than thirty books, including **A December Bride** and **The Convenient Groom**, which have been adapted into original Hallmark Channel movies. She has won the Holt Medallion Award, the Reader's Choice Award, the Carol Award, and the Foreword Book of the Year Award and is a RITA finalist. When Denise isn't orchestrating love lives on the written page, she enjoys traveling with her family, drinking green tea, and playing drums. Denise makes her home in Indiana, where she and her husband are currently enjoying an empty nest.

DeniseHunterBooks.com
Facebook: Denise Hunter
Twitter: @DeniseAHunter